Death of a Squire

A Templar Knight Mystery

Maureen Ash

BERKLEY PRIME CRIME, NEW YORK

THE BERKLEY PUBLISHING GROUP
Published by the Penguin Group
Penguin Group (USA) Inc.
375 Hudson Street, New York, New York 10014, USA
Penguin Group (Canada), 90 Eglinton Avenue East, Suite 700, Toronto, Ontario M4P 2Y3, Canada
(a division of Pearson Penguin Canada Inc.)
Penguin Books Ltd., 80 Strand, London WC2R 0RL, England
Penguin Group Ireland, 25 St. Stephen's Green, Dublin 2, Ireland (a division of Penguin Books Ltd.)
Penguin Group (Australia), 250 Camberwell Road, Camberwell, Victoria 3124, Australia
(a division of Pearson Australia Group Pty. Ltd.)
Penguin Books India Pvt. Ltd., 11 Community Centre, Panchsheel Park, New Delhi—110 017, India
Penguin Group (NZ), 67 Apollo Drive, Rosedale, North Shore 0632, New Zealand
(a division of Pearson New Zealand Ltd.)
Penguin Books (South Africa) (Pty.) Ltd., 24 Sturdee Avenue, Rosebank, Johannesburg 2196,
South Africa

Penguin Books Ltd., Registered Offices: 80 Strand, London WC2R 0RL, England

DEATH OF A SQUIRE

A Berkley Prime Crime Book / published by arrangement with the author

PRINTING HISTORY
Berkley Prime Crime mass-market edition / January 2008

Copyright © 2008 by Maureen Ash.
Cover art by Griesbach & Martucci.
Cover design by Judith Lagerman.
Interior text design by Kristin del Rosario.

ISBN: 978-0-425-21959-1

BERKLEY® PRIME CRIME
Berkley Prime Crime Books are published by The Berkley Publishing Group,
a division of Penguin Group (USA) Inc.,
375 Hudson Street, New York, New York 10014.
The name BERKLEY PRIME CRIME and the BERKLEY PRIME CRIME design are trademarks belonging to Penguin Group (USA) Inc.

PRINTED IN THE UNITED STATES OF AMERICA

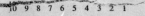

10 9 8 7 6 5 4 3 2 1

In loving memory of Garnet

Historical Note

Since much of the following story takes place outside the confines of a town, it might be helpful to explain that the words "forest" and "chase" had different connotations in the medieval era than they do in our modern one. Aside from the standard definition, "forest" was often used to describe an unenclosed area of countryside that was reserved for the sole use of the ruling monarch and could, and usually did, include not only woodland but marshes, heathland and villages.

Within these areas, forest law prevailed over common law, and was enforced by a complex hierarchy of forestry officials who were permitted to hold their own courts and possessed the authority to mete out punishments to any who committed offences against the harsh edicts they administered.

A monarch would often grant to one of his subjects a section of land for use as his own "forest." It then became known as a "chase." Although there was, in a juridical sense, a distinction between the two terms, in common usage they were often interchanged with almost no discrimination.

Another term that might be confusing is "wolf's head." At the beginning of the thirteenth century, the wolf population in England was declining, but enough remained for a bounty granted in earlier times still to be paid as an incentive for their extermination. The proof needed to claim this reward was the head of the dead animal. Since any man who had committed a crime and fled to escape punishment was considered just as dangerous as a wolf, Anglo-Norman law stated that any such fugitive was to be proclaimed a "wolf's head."

One

◆┼◆

Lincolnshire
Late Autumn 1200 A.D.

THE TREES IN THE FOREST WERE NEARLY DENUDED OF leaves. Those that remained were brown and curled, rattling with dry whispers when the wind blew. On the forest floor bracken still struggled with life, but dark and musty, full of dead insects and the remains of spiders' webs. It was quiet, only the distant irritating call of a lone crow marring the silence. The pale sun pushed tentative fingers through the remaining foliage, glistening on the dew that lay thick upon the ground.

High in the branches of an oak tree a man crouched. Dressed all in brown, and with a dark beard covering most of his face, he could hardly be seen as he kept close to the trunk of the tree. Slung from his waist was a quiver of arrows and he held his bow loosely in his left hand, ready for use when his prey appeared. Below him, secreted in the thickness of the undergrowth, were two of his comrades, one on each side of a trail marked with the delicate hoofprints of deer and liberally scattered with droppings. They, too, had arrows and bows at the ready.

The trio had been in their places nearly two hours, since

before dawn, for the track was one used by deer to water at a small stream some few hundred yards distant. Their muscles were cramped, and eyes and ears sore from straining to catch some sign of the quarry they were after, but the desperate hunger in their bellies kept them in place.

Finally a movement could be heard, just a gentle thud as a hoof touched bare earth. The deer was a large one and male—perhaps a *soar*, in his fourth year. Sensing possible danger, the stag paused in mid-stride and lifted a quivering nose to investigate the air for any scent that would tell of an enemy nearby. As he did so, his dappled shape glinted amongst the trunks of the trees, and his antlers could be seen. They were a broken mass of spikes, torn during battle in the recent rutting season. When he finally took a hesitant step forward, there was a meaty ripple of the flesh on his haunches that brought a gush of saliva into the mouths of the waiting men.

Slowly, and with the greatest of care and held breath, the men nocked arrows to their bows. Though they made hardly a sound, the deer became aware of their presence and started to bolt. With a great leap he sprang forward, but his alarm had been triggered a split second too late. The hunter in the tree loosed an arrow that sped like a popping flame true to its mark and buried itself deep in the side of the stag's neck. The deer faltered but kept to its feet, hooves scrabbling on the ground as it tried to gain purchase to run. Two more arrows flew through the air, one taking the stag in the side, the other lodging in the vulnerable flesh of its underbelly as it crashed to the ground, throwing up a cloud of leaves and rotting vegetation as the heavy body began its death spasms.

"Heigh-ho, we've got him!" The yells of the two jubilant hunters on the ground echoed through the quiet wood before being hastily hushed by the man in the tree as he clambered down.

"Quiet, you fools. Do you want every forester from here to Lincoln to know we have made a kill? With the noise you're making even the sheriff in his keep will be able to hear you."

Both of his companions immediately fell silent and when

one of them spoke, it was in low tones. "Aye, you're right, Fulcher. Sorry. But it is a rare beast, is it not? And will make good feasting for many a meal. Talli and I just got carried away, that's all. It won't happen again."

"See that it doesn't, Berdo. There might still be some villagers around collecting hazelnuts or cutting bracken. At best they'll want a share of meat; at worst they'll raise an alarm. Quick now, let's get done and away before we're seen."

The men set to work, slicing meat from the carcass without regard for the niceties of their butchering and stowing the bloody chunks in rough sacks they had brought rolled up and thrust in their belts. When they had hacked off as much as they could carry, they prepared to depart, wiping their knives by thrusting them point first into the earth. Talli, still exuberant with the excitement of their good fortune, pushed aside from the track to relieve his bladder, while Fulcher and Berdo did their best to cover the remains of the kill with handfuls of dead leaves. As they finished, Fulcher quietly called to Talli to hurry.

"You can piss as much as you need once we're away from here," he remonstrated. "It won't be long before Camville's forester is on his round."

There was no answer from Talli and both of his comrades looked at him questioningly when he reappeared on the track, white-faced and silent.

Fulcher was the first to react. "What is it, Talli? Are we discovered?" He looked around fearfully, peering down the path the deer had taken, seeking any movement that would indicate the dreaded presence of authority, but there was only stillness and again the raucous call of the crow, this time answered by another of its kind.

Talli came slowly forward. "No, there's no one about. No one living, that is." He motioned with his arm towards the ceiling of tree limbs above them. "Look up, over there."

His companions gazed skyward, in the direction that he was pointing. "Sweet Jesu," murmured Fulcher. Berdo gripped Talli hard by the arm as he, too, saw what his friend had found.

"I was looking to see what that crow was fussing about," Talli explained. "Thought it might be they had seen someone we couldn't. So I looked up.... God's Blood, I wish I hadn't."

The trio moved to where Talli had gone to relieve himself, still with upturned faces, their eyes rooted to a spot on the limb of a huge oak tree. There, motionless among the almost bare branches, hung a body, secured to the tree by a rope around the neck. Another rope was tied tightly around the wrists, so that the hands hung together at the corpse's waist. The face was mottled, tongue extended, eyes popping almost from their sockets. On a nearby tree, the two crows were now perched in silence, watching the men with bright black eyes. In the sky above them more crows were making an appearance, gliding on silent wings in ever-decreasing circles before landing beside their brethren, until the upper branches of the tree were filled with their dark forbidding shapes.

"That's a fine meal those scavengers will have today," murmured Talli.

"And fine in more ways than one," observed Fulcher. "Look at those clothes. Good velvet tunic and woollen hose. Those don't belong to the likes of us. He's from a lord's household, maybe even a lord himself. When he's found, there'll be a hue and cry all over Lincoln."

With long steps he returned to where the sacks of meat waited, the blood already seeping through the rough cloth and forming pools on the ground. "Let's be away from here, lads. This is nowt to do with us and we best try and keep it that way."

Berdo remained where he was, then said slowly, "If I stood on your shoulders, Fulcher, we could cut him down. His clothes would make fine pickings, and I think I see a dagger in his belt. We could use that."

"No," said Fulcher vehemently. "Like I said, we'd best be away from here. If we're caught in the act of robbing him, we'll be blamed for his death as well. I want no part of this."

"If they catch us, we'll be hanged for the deer anyway. A man can only die once," Berdo replied.

"Then you do it on your own, Berdo, without my connivance. If Talli is of a mind to help you with the plunder, then so be it. But I will not."

At the reluctant look on Talli's face, Berdo gave in and they joined Fulcher in hefting the sacks of meat onto their shoulders.

"He's nowt but a lad," said Talli. "Looks to be no more than fifteen or sixteen. And from the way he's been trussed, he didn't string himself up there. Why would anyone bring a youngster like that out here and hang him?"

"I don't know and I don't care," Fulcher replied. "I'm going to forget I ever saw him and if you two have any sense in your addled pates you'll do the same."

Laden with their booty, the three men made haste down the track towards the stream that had been the destination of the deer they had killed. In its water the poachers would place their steps until they were well away from the scene of their crime so that any dogs used to track them would lose their telltale scent and the smell of the deer's blood. Above them a slight breeze rattled the dry branches of the oak and the body swayed slightly, then moved a little more as the first of the crows landed on the bright thatch of hair that topped the corpse's head. Twisted under the noose, caught by the violence of the tightening rope, was the boy's cap, the colourful peacock's feather that had once jauntily adorned it now hanging crushed and bedraggled. As the crows began their feast, it was loosened and fluttered slowly to the ground.

Two

❧✝❧

LINCOLN CASTLE STANDS HIGH UPON A HILL, OVER-
looking the surrounding countryside. Sharing the summit is
the cathedral and below the castle and church, on the southern slope of the hill, the town of Lincoln spills like dregs
from an ale cup until it reaches the banks of the Witham river.

The bail of Lincoln castle is large and, on this late autumn morning, was busier than usual. King John, recently
crowned monarch of England in May of the year before, had
sent warning of his intention to visit Lincoln and meet there
with the king of Scotland in mid-November. Feverish preparations were being carried out for his visit. Not only the king
and his retinue would need to be catered for, but also the
large number of guests that would flock to show loyalty to
their new monarch. Provisions needed to be readied, sleeping accommodations prepared and entertainments arranged.
Every servant, from lowest kitchen scullion to high steward,
was engaged in the task.

Amidst the scene of this ordered confusion the soldiers in
the garrison of Lincoln castle kept to their usual routine. Inside the barracks, a long timbered building set hard against

the inner wall of the fortress, the men-at-arms went methodically about their duties. Some recently come off night shift were sleeping, others sat on pallets rubbing goose grease into leather boots or wrist guards, and one was plying a heavy bone needle threaded with gut in an attempt to repair a rip in a leather tunic. There was a low hum of desultory conversation.

In front of a brazier of burning coals set in the farthest corner away from the barracks door, Bascot de Marins, a Templar knight, sat warming himself. Beside him, huddled on the floor, was his young servant, Gianni. Both were cold. They had been in Lincoln only eleven months, having arrived at the onset of the previous year's winter. Although at that time they had both been in ill health, a year of good food and plentiful exercise had seen them well on the way to recovery. Except for this curse of feeling the icy fingers of winter deep in their bones.

Bascot looked pityingly at Gianni. The boy was a mute and even though he could not voice his discomfort, it was readily apparent for, despite the thick undershirt of lambskin he wore beneath his jerkin and the old cloak of Bascot's that was wrapped around his shoulders, he was visibly shivering. The Templar scooped more charcoal into the brazier and urged Gianni to move closer to the fire.

A broad stocky figure entered the building and walked towards them. "*Hola*, de Marins. Does the weather already chill your bones?" Ernulf, serjeant of the garrison, was clad only in a jerkin of leather and summer hose. "It is mild yet," he admonished, "not even a touch of frost. What will you do if snow comes?"

He had been grinning as he walked up to them but, noting Gianni's distress, his tone changed from derision to concern. "Still not used to our English weather, are you, lad?" he asked, remembering the boy came from the warm climes of Italy. "It will take a little while for the humours in your body to adjust, but they will, never fear. Wait here a moment. I will get something to ease your discomfort."

Moving to the back of the barracks, Ernulf went to a small room partitioned off from the rest of the communal space shared by the garrison. As he rummaged in a large chest he cursed himself for not recalling the plight the Templar and the boy had been in when the pair had arrived the year before. Bascot, an eye lost and an ankle smashed during eight years of captivity by the Saracens in the Holy Land; and the boy, a waif picked up by the Templar during his long journey home, thin as an arrow shaft and recovering from malnutrition. They were much improved, but still—he grunted with satisfaction as he found what he had been looking for and went back to the brazier.

"Here's what you need, lad," Ernulf proclaimed, waving in the direction of the Templar's servant an object that looked like one of the stuffed pig's bladders children use to play foot-the-ball. Unwrapping the bundle, he jammed the outer portion on the boy's head. It turned out to be a large cap, two pieces of leather sewn together and coming down over the ears, the inside lined with the soft fleece of a lamb. He then produced two strips of thin calfskin, each sewn on one side with patches of rabbit fur.

"Wrap these bindings around your feet and wear them under your boots," he said to Gianni. "Take it from an old campaigner, keep the head and feet warm and the rest of the body will be content. Those have served me well during many a long night's shift of duty."

Bascot laughed. Ernulf was as crusty as most old soldiers but he was, for all that, a man who cared for his fellow human beings, especially children and women. Gianni looked at the serjeant in silent surprise, his lips curving in a smile of thanks as he pushed the cap farther over his mop of dark brown curls until the brim came down almost to his nose. With caressing fingers he rubbed the rabbit's fur on the bindings, then promptly sat down on the ground, removed his boots and began to wrap his feet and ankles in the warm covering. Every few moments he would look up at Ernulf and mime his pleasure by loudly clapping his hands.

The serjeant pulled up a stool and sat down beside Bascot. Against the wall a couple of grooms from the stables were munching on sour winter apples and drinking small mugs of ale. Ernulf called to one of them and told him to fetch a wineskin from his quarters. When it came, he offered it to Bascot. As the Templar took the proffered flask, Ernulf studied the countenance of the man seated on the other side of the brazier. The dark leather of the patch that covered the socket of his missing eye and the permanently sun-browned hue of his skin made, by contrast, the colour of his remaining sighted eye shine like a shard of blue ice. His dark hair and beard were prematurely threaded with strands of grey. Captivity in the hot lands of Outremer had taken its toll, and even though Bascot had regained lost flesh and muscle during the time he had been in Lincoln, he still seemed weary. And still felt the cold. The serjeant knew only the bare bones of the Templar's history, but he knew enough to surmise what the man had suffered. Even though Bascot never spoke of his time as a prisoner of the infidel, or of the grief he must have felt when he returned to England and found that all his immediate family had died in his absence, there was pain written large on the Templar's lined face. The only time his expression softened was when his glance rested on the lad he had rescued from starvation. The relationship between them was more that of father and son than master and servant.

The wine was thin stuff, but warming, and both men felt better for having taken a long pull from the depths of the skin.

"Bit of a ruckus up at the hall this morning," Ernulf remarked conversationally, but with a slight frown furrowing the space between his grizzled eyebrows. "Seems one of the squires from William Camville's retinue got himself hanged out in the woods. A forester found him in the sheriff's chase, right next to a deer that had been unlawfully slain and butchered."

William Camville was brother to Gerard Camville, sheriff of Lincoln and husband to Nicolaa de la Haye, the hereditary castellan of Lincoln's fortress. Bascot had met William only a couple of times before the baron's recent arrival a few days earlier, but he had been acquainted with another Camville brother who had accompanied King Richard on his crusade to the Holy Land in 1190. William had come to Lincoln with a small retinue, an early arrival of the large number of guests expected to pay attendance at King John's visit.

"What was the boy doing out in the woods?" Bascot asked.

Ernulf shrugged. "Nobody knows. He's been missing since last night but no one took much notice. Thought he was out on the prowl for women or mischief of some kind or another, like most boys his age. Whatever he was up to out there, it's most likely he came upon the poachers and got killed to prevent his witness to the deed. That's what the sheriff thinks, anyway."

"And Lady Nicolaa?" Bascot asked the question with a touch of amusement. Ernulf was devoted to his mistress, and had been in service to the Hayes since she was a small child. Anything that distressed her, in turn, discomfited Ernulf.

"'Tis her husband's business. His and his brother's. My lady has no call to be involved, not unless it reflects on the security of the castle." Although the serjeant had spoken firmly, his next words betrayed his lack of confidence in his statement as he added, "But, for all that, we both know she'll be troubled by the matter. And scarce has need of it. She's been up before dawn every day this last sennight seeing that all is prepared for the king's visit. Since William of Scotland is coming here to pledge homage to King John, all must be in order and reflect well not only on our king, but on Lincoln. She has no want of any of this trouble."

Bascot agreed with the serjeant, then leaned closer into the warmth of the brazier, smiling at Gianni's look of contentment beneath the brim of Ernulf's hat. He was just beginning to feel some benefit from the charcoal's warm glow when a young page came to the door of the barracks and ran over to where they were sitting.

"Lady Nicolaa bids me greet you, Sir Bascot, and asks that you attend her in her private chamber," the youngster said.

Bascot stepped out of the barracks and began to thread his way across the ward. Lincoln castle possessed two keeps, one newly built, which the sheriff and his wife used as a principal residence, and another older one that was used as an armoury and had a few sleeping chambers above. There was a host of other buildings inside the protection of the castle walls—storehouses, stables, dairy, kitchens, mews, smithy, as well as sheds for coopers and fletchers. In and out of all these buildings people moved as they carried out their duties. A line of carts ran right across the bail from the main gate, each heaped with baskets of nuts, root vegetables or dried apples, all of which were to be added to sacks of grain already stored in the lower section of the keep. A bevy of household servants was clambering over the carts, inspecting the contents as they checked to see that all were in good condition and had been tallied. Cattle lowed in makeshift pens and chickens and geese registered protest at their incarceration from the inside of cages piled haphazardly nearby. In a far corner, out of the main swirl of dust, a washerwoman was hard at her task, draping bedclothes and napery on poles after extracting them from the huge tub of water mixed with wood ash and caustic soda in which she had washed them. The fabric flapped and swirled in the breeze created by the people milling about. Over all this cacophony the clang of the smith's hammer rang out and smoke from fires used for drying fish lent a tang to the air that caught in the throat and brought tears to the eyes.

The forebuilding of the new keep was reached by a steep flight of wooden stairs and, as Bascot approached them, his attention was caught by a group of men gathered in front of the stables. Gerard Camville—booted, spurred, and wearing a hooded shirt of mail—stood watching as one of the grooms led a huge destrier from the stable. Beside Camville was his brother William, similarly clad in mail. Both men were armed, swords in serviceable leather sheaths hanging from belts slung on their hips. In physical appearance they were as unalike as two brothers could be. Gerard was a man of immense girth, with muscle swelling at shoulders and thighs, his black straight hair cut high at the nape. His brother was taller and slimmer, with sandy-coloured locks that fell in roughly cut curls onto his shoulders. Their hair now covered by hoods of mail, the one similarity between them was apparent. This was in their expression, a forward thrust of the jaw that warned of an unruly temper and an irascible nature. Accompanying them were half a dozen knights, mostly from the castle's household. Horses had been brought for all, and it was only moments before the contingent was mounted and sweeping across the bail towards the gate in the western wall of the castle. As the horses passed they threw up a wake of dust and feathers, carving a path through the press of servants and carts, heedless of anyone or anything in their way. A horn sounded as the huge iron-bound gate was flung open and, without pause, the sheriff and his party rode through.

Bascot climbed the steps up to the forebuilding and went into the keep, cursing the ache in his ankle. The injury was better than it had been a few months ago, mainly due to the acquisition of a new pair of boots made by a cobbler in the town. The shoemaker's skilful fingers had inserted pads that protected and strengthened the ill-knit bones, but stairs still caused Bascot pain. Once inside the hall, he took a moment to ease his leg before tackling the winding flight of stone steps that led to Nicolaa de la Haye's chamber at the top of a tower built into a corner wall of the keep.

Inside the hall was almost as much turmoil as outside in the bailey. The steward of the Haye household was overseeing the placing of kegs of ale and tuns of wine into the buttery, while several minions ran at his direction with supplies of candles, wooden platters, and containers of salt and spices. Bascot was relieved to reach the relative quiet of the stairwell, even though he faced another climb.

When Bascot reached the top of the stairs, he knocked lightly on the door in front of him. Nicolaa's voice bidding him to enter came swiftly and when he went into the room, he found her seated behind a large wooden table with a sheaf of parchment in front of her. She was a small plump woman with delicate hands and a face relatively unlined by time. Only the few grey strands that threaded the margin of copper-coloured hair showing at the edge of her coif gave a clue to the fact that she was mature enough to be mother to a son almost as old as Bascot. Now she looked unusually weary, her skin tinged with the pallor of fatigue.

"You are well come, de Marins. Be seated. I know the stairs are a trial to your leg." Her voice was calm but Bascot had come to know her well enough to recognize the edge of worry in it.

"You have heard of the death of the squire?" she asked without preamble. When Bascot nodded, she rose from behind the table and went to where a small flagon of wine sat on a side table and poured them both a measure. As she handed the cup to the Templar, she said, "There is no doubt it was murder, but even apart from that it is a most distressing death, not only for the manner of it but because of the boy's connections and the impending visit of the king. That he was in my brother-by-marriage's retinue also causes an added difficulty."

Bascot remained silent as she continued, "The boy, whose name was Hubert de Tournay, had just passed his seventeenth birthday. He was put in William's household to train as page and squire some years ago and has remained there ever since. But he is, or was, a distant relation of Eustace de Vescy who, as you will probably know, is married to Margaret, illegitimate daughter of William, the king of Scotland. Since the Scottish king is coming here to meet our own king, and hopefully settle the differences between them, it would be disastrous if de Vescy decides to make an issue of this boy's death at a time when relationships are already strained between our two countries."

"Is de Vescy liable to do so?" Bascot asked.

Nicolaa had remained standing while she had been speaking. Now she returned to the chair behind the table and sat down with an audible sigh. "I do not know, de Marins, but I do not like de Vescy, nor do I trust him. He seems to be complaisant towards King John, but these northern barons are often fickle and prone to make trouble. I have no grounds for doubting de Vescy, but the feeling is there and I cannot rid myself of it."

Nicolaa and her family were noted for their loyalty to the reigning monarch. Her husband did not possess such a reputation, for he had rebelled against the chancellor left by King Richard to govern the country while he was on crusade. His partner in that defiance had been John, then prince. Now that Richard was dead and John on the throne, their former liaison had not endeared the king to his one-time coconspirator but had rather made the new monarch distrustful of him. If trouble arose during John's visit to Lincoln, it would not take long for his overly suspicious mind to include Gerard Camville in the blame. Hence Nicolaa's concern.

"I would like the mystery of this death cleared up, de Marins. My husband believes the boy was up to some prank or other and got himself caught by outlaws in the wood. He has gone now to scour the area where the boy was found, but if the outlaws were indeed the culprits they will be long gone, most likely into Sherwood Forest. The eastern edge of the forest spreads down to the Trent river not far from where the boy was found. Gerard will not find them if that is the case. Sherwood is thick and dense. It provides ample cover for any outside the law to evade a pursuer."

"Do you not agree with your husband's opinion, lady?" Bascot asked. He had heard the doubt in her voice.

"I would wish it so, for it would provide an easy solution to what could become a difficult situation. But unless my husband can find the outlaws who killed the boy, and provide proof that they are guilty, it might well be said that he has merely taken the most expedient way of explaining the murder. Especially since the body had not been stripped of clothes or dagger, which outlaws most assuredly would have done. And why was he killed by hanging? Again, outlaws would have carried out the deed as quickly as possible, most probably with a knife or cudgel, and left the body on the track, not taken the time and trouble to string him up from a tree. No, I do not think it likely that the murderer is to be found amongst the wretches in Sherwood."

Nicolaa took a sip of wine before she continued, "The manner of death suggests a punishment, a reprisal for a serious misdeed on Hubert's part. The boy had a reputation as a troublemaker. He was not well liked by the others of his rank in William's household, and even William himself says he found the lad disagreeable. Hubert was, apparently, prone to boast of his connection with de Vescy and that he was therefore privy to information denied to the rest of the squires in William's household. He also made no secret of his opinion that Arthur of Brittany, Richard's nephew, should be king, not John, and hinted that there are more supporters for Arthur's claim to the throne than are publicly known. And, of course, he intimated that he knew their identities."

"It sounds as though he was an impudent, and imprudent, young man," Bascot replied.

"He was. William says he did not pay the boy's claims much heed when a member of his household staff mentioned it to him. He thought it likely to be more of the lad's vain boasting. But it may not have been. It is true there are many in Normandy and Brittany who favour young Arthur as king—and they have supporters here in England—but John has been crowned. He is our monarch and only war can come of gainsaying him." She paused a moment, then said, "There is an old legend, de Marins, telling of a curse that will befall any king who enters Lincoln. I do not wish that myth to become reality. If Hubert's words had any truth in them, it could be that he was killed to stop up his prattle and perhaps warn others to keep their lips sealed tight. If that is so, I must know of it. It is my duty, not only to John, but to the safety of my lands."

The Hayes had been hereditary castellans of Lincoln castle for the past eighty-five years when an ancestor, Robert de la Haye, had married a daughter of the Saxon family that had held the post since the days of the Conquest. Nicolaa's father had died without male issue, either legitimate or bastard, and she, as the eldest daughter, had inherited the office as well as much of the Haye demesne. Although Gerard Camville, as Nicolaa's husband, was nominally lord over her estates and governorship of the castle, the sheriff was a lazy and discontented man, more suited to the battlefield or the excitement of the hunt than to managing the various mundane details of running the large fief. Nicolaa undertook these tasks herself and carried them out efficiently and well.

"What is it you require of me, lady?" Bascot asked.

Nicolaa leaned forward, her hands clasped together as they rested on the table in front of her. "If it is at all possible, it is imperative that the truth be found out. To do that, the matter must be delved into. I am asking you to undertake that task, de Marins."

Bascot gazed at her, his one sighted eye locked into the two of hers. They had played this game before when there had been murder done in an alehouse in Lincoln town during the summer. She had asked him for assistance then and, since both he and Gianni were accepting the shelter of Lincoln castle and the largesse of its mistress at the time, he had complied. More through good fortune than his suitability for the venture, the murderer had been caught. And Bascot, to his surprise, had felt a great satisfaction for the part he had played in the apprehension of the culprit—and she knew it.

With a wry smile, he nodded his acceptance. Nicolaa, in turn, quietly thanked him.

"Is it known why the boy was out in the forest?" Bascot asked.

"No, not yet. That is my concern. Why was he there? Did he go willingly or not? The track nearby where he was found is one frequently used by those who have reason to travel in the chase—villagers, my husband's forester, our bailiff and the like. If he was not killed by the brigands that poached the deer, it may be that he was abducted and taken there to be killed, or perhaps lured there for a false appointment with the murderer. It may even be simply that he was followed as he went about some purpose of his own. These are the questions for which answers need to be found, de Marins."

Bascot nodded as she went on. "My husband's forester is in the hall below. I asked him to wait there so that you can speak to him. There is probably little he can tell you, but it is a place to start."

She stood up and so did Bascot. "The other pages and squires in William Camville's retinue—how many are there?" he asked.

Nicolaa frowned in thought. "Seven altogether, I believe. Three pages and four squires. Two of the older boys are almost at the end of their training and hopeful of soon attaining the rank of knight. William tells me that all of them deny any knowledge of the reason for Hubert's absence from the castle last night."

"Still, it might be worthwhile for me to speak to them. They may know some fact that is pertinent and not realise its import."

Nicolaa nodded. "I will have my steward summon them to one of the chambers below. And also instruct the forester to wait upon your pleasure." With a decisive movement, she picked up the papers that lay on her desk and began to walk towards the door. "If there is nothing else, de Marins, I shall await your report after the evening meal."

Dismissed, Bascot left the chamber. Once again he was embroiled in secret murder and he sent up a silent prayer that the outcome of this investigation would be as successful as the last one.

Three

✦✦

"Hubert was worse than a pain in the gut! I'm not sorry he's dead. And I'm not afraid to say so."

The pages and squires of William Camville's retinue had, on instructions conveyed by the Haye steward, gathered in a small chamber to await the arrival of Bascot. The room was small and dusty, used as a repository for records of the revenues of Haye tenants, and was piled high with rolls of parchment and tally sticks. There was barely enough room for all to sit or stand in comfort.

The boy who had spoken was one of the younger ones, Osbert, who sat cross-legged on the floor and stared defiantly up at the two eldest, Alain and Renault, who were standing and leaning against the embrasure of the one small window in the room.

"Your honesty does you credit, Osbert," Alain said to him with a small smile, "but I do not think it would be wise to be quite so forthright with Sir Bascot."

"Perhaps not, but it is the truth," Osbert maintained. He was nine years old, with hair the colour and shape of a wheat sheaf, and his green eyes glowed with outrage as he continued, "He was always sneering at us younger ones, saying we didn't know one end of a lance from the other and that no amount of training would ever make us into knights. He was a bully and a braggart and you know it well, Alain, for you yourself changed angry words with him more than once."

Alain, tall and slim at eighteen years old, with a sober face and rigidly erect posture, flushed slightly at the youngster's words. "It was my duty to correct him. I was his senior in age and rank," he said quietly.

"You weren't correcting him when you told him you'd break his head if he dared approach your sister again," Osbert retorted angrily. "And I'd have done the same if I had been you. He deserved what he got and I give praise to his murderer, whoever he may be." His voice dropped a little lower, but was still defiant, as he added, "Even if that murderer was someone from our own household."

Renault, a few months younger than Alain, straightened up from his relaxed position. He was a Poitevin, the only one of the group whose family did not possess a fief in England. He was wirily built, with black hair, sallow skin and dark eyes. Always moving with a slow unhurried grace, he had nevertheless proved his skill at the quintain and on the practice field, and gave promise of one day being a redoubtable knight. He now looked down at the feisty little Osbert, smiled and said languidly, "You have an impertinent tongue, little one. Be careful it doesn't get you into trouble."

The words, spoken so carelessly, nevertheless held a hint of warning and Osbert reluctantly clamped his mouth shut, contenting himself with clenching his small fists and bunching them on his knees.

One of the other boys spoke up, a lad whose name was Harold but who was always called Rufus for the redness of his complexion. At fourteen, and having just obtained the rank of squire, he was not quite as fearful of Renault as the younger Osbert. "You hated Hubert as much as any of us, Renault. I remember when you found out that he had taken your new belt and worn it. You were very angry."

Renault turned his gaze on Rufus. "No angrier than you when he dropped one of his boots in the midden and made you clean it."

Rufus lowered his head and made no reply. Pushing himself upright, Renault heaved a sigh. "But you are right, Rufus, and so is Osbert. All of us have reason to rejoice that pig's turd is dead." He glanced around at them all and, with a lazy grin, added, "My only regret is that I promised Hubert a good thrashing if he continued with his pilfering ways. I should have given it to him then. Now he is dead, I will not get the chance."

This remark brought titters from all the rest of the boys except one, a lad about Rufus's age named Hugo. He was sitting on the floor, fiddling with a piece of straw, and had not raised his head once since they had all gathered in the room.

"What ails you, Hugo?" Alain asked. "Are you ill?"

Hugo finally looked up. Alain was his cousin and it was no secret that the youngster had a great admiration for his elder kinsman. "No, Alain, I am not ill," he replied with a tremble in his voice. "I just wish that Hubert was not dead. I did not like him any more than the rest of you, but still I wish that he was not dead."

The two youngest of the group, seven-year-old pages sent by their families, like the rest, to William Camville to spend the long years of training for knighthood, looked fearful at the anguish in Hugo's voice. One of them rubbed at his eye with a knuckle, trying to stem the tears that were threatening to trickle down his cheeks.

Osbert, who was sitting near the lad, gave him a sidelong glance and then a push on the shoulder along with a command to stop snivelling. The boy smothered his sobs with an effort and wiped his running nose on his sleeve.

Alain moved forward into the midst of the group. "These speculations are not profitable, nor are they just. It is clear that none of us had any love for Hubert or are sorry he is dead. And if we feel this way, there must be many others not of our household who feel the same. But we must be wary of what we tell the Templar. Suspicion is easily cast on an innocent person. To be circumspect is the only honourable course."

"And the most advisable," Renault commented wryly. "The less that is made of this matter, the better for all of us. Even the little ones know that it would hardly help the reputation of any of us here, or that of our families, to be suspected of secret murder. I do not intend to risk losing the chance of winning my spurs for such a one as Hubert, whether he be alive or dead."

Although Alain gave his friend an angry glance for the baldness of his words, the rest of the boys nodded to each other in agreement; Osbert and Rufus enthusiastically. All, that is, except Hugo. He only gave his cousin Alain a surreptitious glance filled with fear, then bowed his head before it should be noticed, and resumed his mournful contemplation of the musty trampled rushes beneath his feet.

Four

Bascot's talk with William Camville's pages and squires left him feeling both amused and confused.

All of the young men and boys had denied any knowledge of the reason Hubert had been out in the forest on the night he had been murdered. When Bascot had suggested that the person or persons who had killed the squire might not have been outlaws, but someone known to the dead boy, they had all easily accepted that as a possibility.

Their general dislike of the dead squire had been evident in the way they had spoken of him, but none had admitted to having a particular grudge against him, nor of knowing anyone who had. This seemed an unlikely proposition in view of how disagreeable they had made Hubert sound. Only Osbert had offered any information that might be of interest. Hubert had, the page proclaimed, often boasted of his prowess with women, bragging that once he had bedded a wench she could not wait for more of the same.

"I don't know if what he said was true, Sir Bascot," Osbert had added, his small face quite serious. "Especially since his bollocks and shaft weren't much bigger than mine.

But it could be that he was meeting a lover in the woods, and was perhaps discovered by an outraged husband who took his revenge." Osbert had glanced, almost defiantly, at the two eldest squires, Alain and Renault, as he said this, but their faces had remained impassive.

Bascot had been hard put to hide a smile at the boy's words, but they had made him pause for thought. It was possible that Hubert had strayed into a relationship that had led to his death, but it was hard to believe that it would have been with anyone he had met in the few days he had been in Lincoln. Did he know someone from previous visits? Perhaps Hubert had already been acquainted with a woman from the town or in the retinues of nobles come to attend the king's visit. It was a suggestion worth pursuing.

Making his way down to the hall to talk to the forester who had found the squire's body, Bascot cast his mind back to the days when he had been the same age as Hubert. He had been spared the necessity of going to the household of one of his father's peers to train for knighthood since he had spent much of his younger days within the walls of a monastery, having been placed there as an oblate—an offering for Christ—to prepare for the day when he would take his vows as a monk. It had not been until he was well past Osbert's age that his father had removed him, one of Bascot's older brothers having died, leaving a gap, which his sire had been anxious to fill. But still Bascot could remember how he had felt when he had returned home and begun to practice with sword and lance. Despite his reluctance to leave the monks, he had been excited, full of the joy of young manhood and anxious to indulge in all the pleasures he had so far been denied in his life behind the monastery walls. Wine had tasted sweet, as had platters full of roasted venison and boar, and the most delicious of all had been sampling the charms of the many willing women servants on his father's demesne. There had not been many ready to deny a son of their lord his pleasure, or their own. It was not until he had taken his vow of chastity as a Templar that he had eschewed the charms of women and, although he had never broken his pledge, the temptation at times had been hard to resist. But as a young man he had not viewed it as a transgression, and had indulged the hot blood that rose at the sight of a softly curved breast or a slim ankle as readily as Hubert had apparently done. None had been wife to another man, however, but still, Osbert's opinion might bear merit.

In the hall he found the forester, Tostig, in the company of Ernulf, drinking ale. When Bascot approached, the serjeant introduced them. The forester was a tall man, clad in a leather jerkin over a green tunic and hose, with stout boots on his feet and a handsome strongly boned face that had been weathered by the elements. His hands, although calloused, were large and well shaped. On his left forearm he wore a leather bracer, used by archers to strengthen the aim of an arrow shot. At his feet lay a dog, a lymer hound, its keen eyes surveying Bascot dolefully as he approached. Ernulf told Bascot that Tostig had been employed as a mounted forester by Gerard Camville for the last fifteen years and that his bailiwick—the area in which he carried out his duties—was the chase granted by the king to the sheriff for his own use.

"It was the birds that told me something was amiss," Tostig said in answer to Bascot's question as to how he had come to discover the body. "Gathered and circling like the carrion eaters they are. I thought it could be a dead animal and went to investigate. I found the deer first, the carcass half-buried under leaves. But then I noticed that the birds hadn't disturbed it much and looked around, thinking there might be another one slaughtered nearby."

He took a swig from the ale in his mug, swallowed, then spat among the rushes on the floor. "Made my gorge rise when I looked up and saw what those damned crows had been feasting on," he told Bascot. "The lad's face was almost gone, and they'd been at his body, too, pecking through his clothes."

He shook his head sadly and crossed himself before continuing. "They still kept watch even after I cut him down, landing near me and croaking like imps from hell, though my dog was doing his best to forestall them. So I wrapped the boy in his cloak, which was still pinned to his shoulders, slung him over my horse and carried him out of the woods. If I had left him there to get help, they would have been at him again."

"What about the boy's own mount?" Bascot asked. "Surely he wouldn't have gone into the forest on foot."

"Found it not too far from where the lad was strung up," Tostig replied. "It was loose and came to follow me on my way back to the castle. The reins were knotted at the end, and trailing, as though the lad had left the horse loosely tethered somewhere."

Ernulf reached over and filled the man's flagon again. Bascot waited until he had taken a deep drink, then asked, "Did you notice if there were any other marks on the boy's body besides that made by the rope and the birds?"

"You mean, had he been killed first, and then strung up?" Tostig asked. When Bascot nodded, the forester shook his head. "Apart from the damage done by the crows there was nothing else. Sir William and Sir Gerard stripped him themselves when I brought him in, looking for an answer to the same question, but there was no wound from a blade or arrow on his person or any mark on what was left of his head. Even allowing for the bird's feasting, there would have been trace of damage if his skull had been caved in."

"Nothing at all?" Bascot persisted.

The forester shook his head again. "As far as could be told it looks as though the boy just stood peaceful-like and let that noose be dropped over his head."

"Or else he didn't struggle because he was faced with a greater threat," Bascot said.

The forester looked straight at him, "Like a sword or a bow, you mean?"

Bascot nodded. "Either that or else he was taken by surprise before he had the opportunity to defend himself."

In a private upper chamber Gerard Camville and his brother sat sharing a cup of wine. They had just returned from the tract in the forest where Hubert had been found and, as they had expected, could locate nothing to indicate how the boy had come to be there or who had killed him. After a circuit of the perimeter of the chase they had called a halt for if outlaws had been the cause of the boy's death, they had long since disappeared into the depths of Sherwood. Gerard was in a foul temper, which even the rough questioning of the inhabitants of a nearby village had done nothing to assuage. All had claimed not to have seen or heard anything, or to have known the identity of the dead boy. Threats to take some of the young men of the village into Lincoln castle for questioning had elicited no further information. Finally, Gerard, at his brother's urging, had left them in peace and they had returned to Lincoln.

"Bloody peasants, always the same. You'd think they were deaf and blind to all that goes on around them. Until you ask for a reckoning of their livestock or the grain yield from harvest. Then they know down to the last dead lamb and stray kernel of wheat just how much they owe to their lord, and all the while they're stealing their masters blind." Gerard poured himself another cup of wine and began to pace the chamber from one end to the other.

"For the love of Christ, Gerard, sit down," William expostulated. "I cannot talk to you while you roam about so. And talk we must. This death could become a serious problem."

William refilled his own wine cup, looking intently at his brother. Gerard had ceased his pacing and was standing by a small fireplace built into a corner of the wall, staring into the flames. The fireplace had a hood, in the latest fashion, and the applewood logs that burned in the open grate gave off a pleasant aroma. Gerard, however, gave no indication that he had heard his brother. He drank deep from his cup, then threw the lees of the wine into the fire before resuming his contemplation of the burning logs.

"Gerard, this death—it has nothing to do with you, has it?" William asked softly.

The sheriff turned and gave his brother a tight-lipped smile that held no humour. "You, too, Will? I thought my own brother would have more faith in me. Do you really believe I could be so base as to secretly murder a young stripling to advance my own ends?"

William ignored his brother's accusation and asked instead, "Has someone else spoken to you in this regard?"

Gerard strode over to the table and poured more wine. "De Humez. Thinks because he is married to my wife's sister he has the right to question me as though he were my liege lord."

William leaned back in his chair and spoke quietly, "You cannot blame us, Gerard. It is well known that you and the king are not complaisant with each other, and that it is only due to John's regard for Nicolaa that he allows you to retain the offices and lands you hold."

"He was *complaisant* enough with me when he needed an ally against Longchamps, wasn't he? Then I could do no wrong, even if I was defying the very chancellor his own brother had left to govern the realm while he was on crusade. And I lost my office when Richard returned while John, forgiven and indulged, did nothing to help me. That I got the shrievalty back eventually was not due to assistance from him, but because of the silver I paid for the privilege. And now I am expected to curry his favour in order to keep it, regardless of how much money it has cost me."

The sheriff crashed his fist down onto the table, setting the thick oak shivering. "John is devil's spawn. And so was Richard. They killed their father between them. I was a fool ever to put my trust in either."

William knew how much his brother had loved King Henry and how much he missed him. He tried to placate the anger he could see rising in his sibling. "Perhaps you were foolish not to realise that neither prince has the integrity of their father, Gerard, but you had little choice as matters turned out. And Henry has been dead a long time. You cannot mourn his loss for ever. He was a good king and held you in high esteem, but now it is his son that is on the throne. You must be circumspect in your dealings with John."

"I will leave that to Nicolaa. She has a fondness for him, although only the Good Lord above knows why. And he returns her affection. I will leave his entertainment—and goodwill—to her."

"You still have not answered my question, Gerard,"

William said, now standing to face his brother. "Did you have anything to do with this boy's death? It is rumoured that he spoke of being in the confidence of men who favoured Arthur to be king of England. He could have been killed to dam his overflowing mouth. Were you one such as those of whom he spoke?"

Gerard glowered at his brother. "I have as little use for John's nephew filling his grandfather's place as I had for Richard, or for John himself. Is that what you wanted to hear?"

William sat down again, glancing doubtfully up at his brother. "Yes, it is, Gerard. But if the king should ask you the same question, try to be more politic in how you frame your answer."

Five

✦✦✦

BASCOT DECIDED TO VISIT THE PLACE WHERE THE BOY had been found and asked Tostig to take him there. They left the castle in late afternoon, Bascot riding an easy-gaited grey gelding from the stables with Gianni on the pillion behind and the forester astride his own mount.

Tostig took a path that led slightly southwest, towards the stretch of forest where Gerard Camville's chase was located. As they rode, he told Bascot the hunting ground that had been granted to the sheriff began some two miles from Lincoln town and was bordered on the west by the Trent river and on the south by the slant of the old Roman road called the Fosse Way.

"The royal chase, within which the sheriff's own lies, is much larger, of course," Tostig explained. "It extends a good way farther to the north and, in the south, down to the greenwood at Kesteven. There is a lot of good marshland for hawking and hunting smaller game within both, though, as well as a fair bit of timberland."

"Are there any villages in the sheriff's chase?" Bascot asked.

"Yes," replied Tostig. "At the northern tip is a small one, just before the beginning of an open stretch of heath land. And there's another, larger, hamlet adjacent to the southern boundary."

"Are either of these villages near where Hubert's body was found?" Bascot asked.

"The one in the north is," Tostig replied. "It's on the edge of Sir Gerard's chase and the boy was not far into the forest from there."

"Is that where your quarters are located?" Bascot asked, knowing that in his position as a mounted forester Tostig would receive, as part payment for his services, shelter for himself, his horse and his dog.

"No. 'Tis my right if I wished to do so, but Sir Gerard lets me stay in his hunting lodge. It's more comfortable and I don't have the villagers taking resentment at my presence amongst them. Since the royal chase is so close and they must have licence for any activities they would pursue there, they would always be wary that I might report them to the king's agister or woodward if I should see them taking liberties." The forester shrugged. "I pretend ignorance most times when they set loose a few more pigs to forage for acorns than are allowed, or perhaps take a coney for the pot, for I know what it is like to be hungry. But it would be more than my life is worth if I were to be too lax and they know it. So, to save their temper, and mine, I stay in the lodge."

"This lodge, is it near where Hubert was slain?"

"Not the new one, the one where I keep my gear. There is an old lodge a little closer, but it's ramshackle now and deserted."

"Were you abroad in the forest last night?" Bascot asked.

The forester shook his head. "No, unfortunately, I was not. Yesterday I went to the southern part of the chase. One of Sir Gerard's woodwards looks to that area mostly, as he has kin in the village nearby and stays with them so he is handy for the work. But I like to take a circuit there every few days to check and see that he's doing his job as he should. My mare threw a shoe while I was down there and I had to seek a blacksmith to replace it. By the time I got back to my lodgings it was well past the middle of the night. I wanted only to get my mare bedded down and find my own pallet. I did not leave the lodge until the morning was well on. That was when I saw the crows and found the boy."

When they reached the chase, Tostig took a path that was almost imperceptible to Bascot. It wound through the trees in no particular manner that the Templar could see, but before long they came to a track that was more defined, with plentiful piles of deer dung and hoofprints, mingled with the deeper marks of the shod feet of horses. The sheriff and his brother must have taken the same route. This track appeared to be well used by both man and beast. In the distance the ring of an axe sounded and there was the smell of smoke in the air.

"It's just a little way on from here," Tostig flung back at Bascot over his shoulder. The narrow path had forced them to ride in single file and, as they neared the spot where the poached deer and Hubert's body had been found, Bascot took care to look about him, telling Gianni to do the same. The boy may be mute, but his other senses were sharp, especially his eyes. With Bascot being blind on one side, he would have to depend on Gianni to notice anything he missed.

Before long Tostig led them to a spot on the path where the slain deer still lay, half-buried under a hump of leaves. "I shall have to get help to remove the carcass. Looks like scavengers have already been at it."

Tostig dismounted and Bascot did the same, Gianni dropping lightly to the ground with the resilience of youth. The light was beginning to fade, but the scuffs of the poachers' feet could still be seen amongst the multitude of tracks and the blood of the dead deer was splattered in dark patches onto the moss beside the path.

"Where was Hubert?" Bascot asked, and Tostig led them a few feet off the trail, pointing to the branches of a large oak tree.

"Up there," he said.

From a solid bough about halfway up, a remnant of rope

still hung, cut at one end. It dangled a few feet above the ground and swayed slightly as a cold breeze shook the tree, sending down a shower of dead brown leaves. Through the denuded branches could be seen the other end of the rope, fastened to one of the lower limbs.

"I cut the lad down. Could just reach him while I was mounted," Tostig said. "Didn't wait to see where the other end was fastened."

The forester strode towards the trunk of the oak, moving with the familiarity of one who has spent his life in the forest, and loosened the knot that held the rope in place. He pulled it down and coiled it over his shoulder and brought it for Bascot to look at. It seemed fairly new, with little fraying and no other marks except where Tostig's knife had sliced it. The forester scuffed among the leaves and held up the noose, still knotted into place.

"Here's the bit I took off his neck," he said unnecessarily. "I'll put it and the rest away at the lodge. Shame to waste a good bit of rope."

Bascot made no comment as he and Gianni searched the ground. It was fairly untouched except for a faint disturbance of dead leaves that must have been made by whoever had hanged the boy and, later, by Tostig. Gianni went a little way into the trees. Bascot could hear the soft swish of his steps as he moved through the dying bracken.

The Templar gazed around him. They were completely encircled by trees, most of the branches bare. In full summer it would be a dense forest of green, but now it was damp and smelled musty, with a tang of sharpness to the air that heralded winter.

"How far is the nearest village?" he asked Tostig.

"A little over a half of a mile north."

"And the sheriff's hunting lodge?"

Tostig swung about, gesturing with his hand in the opposite direction. "About twice the distance that way. The old hunting lodge is a little nearer but, like I said, it's not used anymore."

Due south a thin trail of smoke was rising. The scent of

burning wood came again in faint wisps. "That smoke, where is it coming from?"

The forester shaded his eyes and looked up. "Oh, that's just old Chard burning his charcoal. He's within the chase, but he has permission. The castle needs a good supply with all the guests coming. Usually Chard does his burning outside of the chase, but there's a good stand of birch over there and it's one of the best for his trade, so the sheriff gave him licence to use it."

The sky was beginning to darken as they stood talking, not only for the lateness of the day but also from the shadow of rain clouds that were beginning to gather, blowing in from the east.

"I shall need to go to the village, Tostig, to see if anyone there heard or saw anything untoward last night. I will also want to talk to the charcoal burner, but it's too late today. It will be full dark before long. Tomorrow morning, as soon as it gets light, I would like you to meet me here and take me to the village."

Tostig nodded his agreement and suggested he also bring the agister for the area. He was the forest official that collected payments from the inhabitants of the villages for the exercising of their rights as agreed with Gerard Camville and the king. "He knows more of the people in the village than I do," Tostig said. "As I told you, I stays away from 'em if I can, except to watch they don't trespass on the chase. His name is Copley."

Tostig began to walk back to the path where they had left their horses. "Besides, he often acts as deputy for the chief forester of the king's chase. He'll know who had licence to be out here gathering nuts or bracken, maybe chopping wood or letting their pigs loose to forage."

He gave a satisfied grin. "Time he did a little work for a change; he likes his wine cup too much. I've had to cover for him more than once. He's lucky he gets his stipend from the crown and not the sheriff. My master is meticulous about his hunting ground and its keeping. If any of us who were in his pay shirked our duties like Copley does, we'd soon be sorry."

This last was said with a kind of affectionate pride. Bascot was surprised. It was not an emotion that he would have expected Gerard Camville to foster in his servants. Perhaps the choleric sheriff had a side to him that was seldom seen outside the greenwood.

Six

❖—❖

"WELL, ALYS, ARE YOU GOING TO TELL ME WHAT HU-bert said or not?" Alinor demanded. She stood over her companion, face set in determination, hands clenched into fists and set on her hips.

The other girl looked up at her, soft blue eyes awash with tears. "Yes, I will. But you must promise me that you will not tell Alain, or your father."

It was the next morning. Outside the weather was gloomy from a light rain that had fallen overnight and the temperature had dropped. The two young women were in a small chamber at the top of the new keep, both wearing gowns of heavy wool as protection against the chill. For the moment, they were the only two occupants of the room, but soon, with the arrival of more guests for the king's visit, others would invade their privacy. The floor was spread with pallets and covers in anticipation.

Alinor was daughter to Richard de Humez, who was married to Petronille, one of Nicolaa de la Haye's two younger sisters. Although both her parents were dark haired, Alinor had inherited the Haye glints of copper in her tawny-coloured locks, which now streamed down her back in two long plaits. She was a forceful girl, fifteen years of age, gently rounded and passingly pretty, but with an intractability that she had inherited from her Haye forbears.

The girl she was berating was Alys de Carston, sister to Alain. Alys had lived in the de Humez household for the past three years, since she had been betrothed to Alinor's younger brother, Baldwin, a boy who was four years her junior. As the two girls were of an age they had been thrown much into each other's company and had become fast friends. Alys resembled her brother only in her upright posture. She was a gentle girl, with long fair hair that stubbornly curled in tendrils around a heart-shaped face, and with an air of innocence about her that was genuine.

Now she mopped her eyes with the edge of her sleeve and said, "It was the time Sir William came to your father's manor house, in the summer, and brought Hubert with him."

"I remember," said Alinor. "When we had that new minstrel from Anjou."

"Yes, that's right," Alys confirmed. "I was in the chapel—Baldwin had just had a bad attack of his illness and I had gone there to offer up a prayer for him—and Hubert came up behind me. I was all alone, and . . ." She began to sob softly again, but Alinor interrupted her, impatient.

"Get on with it, Alys. What did he say?"

"He . . . he put his hand on my breast and said that he wanted to bed me." Now Alys looked up at her companion and her words came in a rush. "I pushed him away, Nora, but he just laughed and said that if I did not he would tell everyone that I had anyway. I told him to go away and leave me alone, that no one would believe him. But . . . but he sneered at me, said whether they did or not it would still cast doubts on my chastity and your father would look for another bride for Baldwin. He left then, and said he would give me time to think about it, but if I did not, I would be sorry."

"Why did you not tell me then, Alys? Or at least tell my mother? She is fond of you, and kind. She would have seen to it that Hubert did not trouble you again." Alinor's tone had softened at the real distress in her friend's voice, and she sat down beside Alys and put an arm around her shoulders.

"I did not know what to do, and then Sir William left the next morning and Hubert was gone with him. I thought that perhaps he had taken too much wine and had been foolish only, did not mean what he had said. I tried to forget it. I did not want to think about it." She raised her tear-stained face to her friend. "Can you understand, Alinor?"

The other girl nodded. "But you still should have told someone. Did he threaten you again when we came to Lincoln?"

"Yes. Almost as soon as we arrived. It was the day before he disappeared. Alain saw him talking to me. In the hall, by the entrance to the kitchen. He—Hubert—had taken hold of my wrist. He wouldn't let go and then he saw Alain coming towards us."

"And your brother, did he challenge Hubert?"

"He did not get the chance. Hubert released me and left, hurriedly. Alain asked me what cause Hubert had for being so familiar with me. I . . . lied. I told Alain that I had tripped and Hubert had merely been helping me to my feet." She took a deep breath, then let it out in a sigh. "I don't know if Alain believed me or not, but I saw him talking to Hubert later, in the bail. It looked as though they were arguing." She buried her head in Alinor's shoulder. "Oh, Nora, what if it was Alain who killed him? It would be my fault. All my fault."

Alinor patted her friend's shoulder. "No, Alys, not your fault, but Hubert's own. You have done nothing for which to reproach yourself."

Alys lifted her head, tears now flowing fast and free. "What shall I do, Nora? Shall I talk to Alain . . . ask him . . . ?"

"You shall do nothing, little poppet," Alinor said firmly. "You will leave Alain and this whole coil to me."

IN A CORNER OF THE BAIL A GROUP OF SQUIRES WERE AT practice with the quintain, a swinging crossbar set with a circle of metal on one side and a heavy bag of sand on the other. The young men were taking turns riding at it, lances poised to strike the metal and, when their aim was successful, trying to avoid the buffet of the sandbag that swung towards their heads in response. A group of pages watched, cheering those who were successful and deriding those who tumbled to the ground.

From a vantage point set at a distance across the bail, by the door of the armoury, William Camville and Richard de Humez watched the young men. Across their line of vision the work of the castle staff went on, carts still arriving with stores of root vegetables, maids milking cows and goats, and the blacksmith busy at his forge.

"Your young men show well, William," de Humez said. "Mine could learn a thing or two from Renault, or even Alain. Did you take a hand yourself in their training?"

William Camville shook his head. "No, one of my household knights is their mentor. I leave it to him."

"He has done well in his instruction."

The conversation petered out, then de Humez gave William a sidelong glance and said, "Has Gerard told you of his intentions in the matter of Hubert's death?"

"Why not be explicit, de Humez?" William replied with a lazy smile. "You want to know if Gerard had a hand in the boy's murder."

De Humez bristled. He was a melancholic man, of middle years and smaller stature than his companion. The Camvilles always engendered a mood of discontent in him, their bold brash manner an affront to what he considered his dignity and, although he did not realise it, a tinge of jealousy for their confidence.

"If he had, I would not expect him to bruit it abroad," de Humez replied sharply. "Although I would not be surprised if he had done the deed, or ordered it. Your brother is a rash and hasty man, as ill judgement in his past actions has shown."

William threw back his head and laughed loudly. "I wager you would not accuse Gerard of that to his face."

De Humez lost his self-righteous pose and became decidedly ill at ease, making no reply. William Camville's face did not lose its expression of amusement. "Why are you so interested in the death of my squire, Richard? Is it due to his connection with de Vescy—or perhaps because it is rumoured that the boy claimed to have knowledge of secret loyalties to Arthur of Brittany? Are you frightened that if Gerard was in some way responsible that it might taint his reputation with the king—and therefore your own, by reason of you being wedded to his wife's sister?"

"Of course not," de Humez replied. "My own loyalty to John is without reproach. After all, my uncle . . ."

"Yes, Richard, your connection with the constable of Normandy is well known," William interrupted in a tired voice. "But that was over twenty years ago and your uncle is long dead. And so is King Henry, who was his lord."

The sheriff's brother cast a speculative look at his companion, then added, "You, unlike Gerard, were solicitous of Richard, were you not, and stood against John when he and my brother defied Richard's chancellor? Our present king has a long memory, de Humez. Did you think to cast your lot with Arthur, so you would have no cause to worry that John might remember matters best left forgotten? Were you one of those of whom Hubert spoke as being partisan to Richard's nephew instead of his brother?"

De Humez turned white at the accusation levelled at him. Instinctively his hand dropped to the sword at his belt, then, recalling that the man at his side possessed a reputation for swordplay that was almost equal to that of his brother, de Humez changed his mind. Instead he gave William an angry glare and strode off across the bailey.

William Camville watched him go, thoughtful. What had started as an irresistible urge to bait the prig whom Gerard had the misfortune to call brother-by-marriage had turned to something more as he had spoken the words. There had been real fear in de Humez's face when William had questioned his loyalty to King John. Had he inadvertently stumbled on a truth where he had thought only to provoke irritation? Slowly William ambled back towards the keep. He would have to think more on this matter, perhaps talk privately with

Nicolaa. If there was any meat on the bones he had inadvertently stirred up, it would be best to chew it thoroughly before offering it to Gerard. And his brother's wife was a good enough chatelaine to know how best to prepare the dish.

Seven

✦┼✦

Bascot started early for his meeting with Tostig. It had rained the night before, but the sun was now trying to penetrate the cloud cover and it promised to be a fair day for the lateness of the year. The ground smelled fresh and clean, heavy with the scent of moisture and vegetation. It was an odour that pleased Bascot, one he had often dreamed of during his imprisonment in the arid terrain of the Holy Land, permeating his dreams and waking him with a fitful start of pleasure in a remembrance of home before the reality of his surroundings impinged on his consciousness. Behind him Gianni rode pillion, swathed in a warm cloak and with the hat Ernulf had given him pulled firmly down over his head.

As they descended from the high knoll on which Lincoln was situated Bascot took in the surrounding countryside. It was sparsely wooded until they reached the edge of the chase, and the ground was marshy in places and crisscrossed with rivulets, firming up only when they reached the shelter of the forest.

Bascot found his way to the place that Tostig had taken

him the previous afternoon with little difficulty and the
forester was waiting, as arranged, at the spot where the body
of the poached deer had been found. With him were two
other men whom he introduced as the agister, Copley, and
Eadric, the woodward who lived in the village on the southern boundary of Gerard Camville's chase. Eadric worked
with Tostig, and was paid his salary by the sheriff, but his
chief responsibility lay to the crown. Since it was part of his
duty to oversee any licences issued for industry within the
forest, such as charcoal burning, Tostig had asked him to attend the meeting that morning, in case he should be able to
help Bascot with his enquiries.

The agister, Copley, was a short stout man, with a florid
face and breath reeking of the stale fumes of last night's
wine. He was dressed more richly than the other two, with a
thick cloak wrapped over the good wool of his tunic and a
flat cap decorated with silver thread set atop his sparse hair.
His mood was disgruntled and he was obviously annoyed at
being asked to rise so early in the morning, but showed his
discontent only in his manner towards Tostig and Eadric. To
Bascot he was carefully deferential, mindful perhaps of de
Marins's rank and the small Templar badge worn on the
shoulder of his tunic.

Eadric, a young fresh-faced man of unmistakable Saxon
heritage with pale hair and deep blue eyes, looked uncomfortable, and kept to the rear of the company as they travelled the short distance to the village. Bascot was aware of
the complex hierarchy of forest officials, both royal and private, and of the jostling for power that occurred within its
ranks. A chase—or forest, as it was often called—brought in
a good amount of revenue to those who owned the rights, be
they king or noble. Such areas were jealously guarded
against offences by those who oversaw its management. It
was likely the young woodward was fearful of reprisal from
Copley if he was found to have been lax in his duties. Or,
since its officials were notably disliked by the general popu-
lace for their arbitrary enforcement of the rights they protected, perhaps he was just reluctant to be included in the
enquiry Bascot intended to make of the villagers.

The village was, as Tostig had said, a small one, with perhaps ten families within the fence of hurdles that bounded the compound. The reeve, headman for the village, had been apprised by the forester of Bascot's intended visit and he, along with the village priest and two others, was waiting for the Templar just inside the gate. Nearby, clustered in a silent watching group, were the other men of the hamlet, while their womenfolk huddled in twos and threes at the entrances to the small thatched cots that straggled around the perimeter of the enclosed space. Children played at the edge of a shallow pond amongst a scattering of geese, chickens and ducks. At the far end of the dirt track that bisected the compound were some storage buildings constructed of rough-hewn timber. Beyond them, over the wall of hurdles, the village fields stretched to the north, empty of grain since harvest time.

The priest, an elderly man with a completely bald head and few teeth, stepped forward as Bascot and the forest officials came through the gate.

"Greetings, Sir Bascot. I am Samson, God's shepherd to this small flock." His lined, gentle face attempted a smile as he turned and gestured to the man beside him. "This is Alwin, the reeve, and these others"—the priest's hand waved at the reeve's companions—"are Leofric, Alwin's son, and Edward, his nephew."

The three villagers looked balefully at Bascot, their manner subservient but wary. Plainly they regarded the presence of Bascot and the forest officials as an intrusion and were resentful.

Copley spoke up, his tone impatient. "Sir Bascot is not interested in the names of the reeve or his kinfolk, priest. He just wants some truthful answers to his questions. Let us get on with it."

The reeve gave Copley a sullen glare as he spoke and the priest, flustered by the sharpness in the agister's voice, made haste to invite them into a small half-timbered edifice that served as a church. The reeve and his two kinsmen followed behind.

"I have no wine to offer, good sirs," Samson said, "but there is ale, if you wish . . . ?"

"Better than nothing. Bring us some," Copley ordered before sitting down heavily on a stool placed just beside the door. The only other furniture in the one small room they had entered was a tiny altar at the far end and a wooden box used to house the priest's vestments and vessels for the celebration of Mass. On the limewashed walls crude pictures of biblical scenes had been painted, mainly from stories the villagers would most easily understand, those of shepherds tending their flocks and Jesus feeding the multitude from a basket containing only five loaves and two fishes.

As the priest turned to hurry away for the ale, Bascot stopped him. "No, thank you, Father, we do not require any of your ale. Our visit is to be but a brief one. It will not require that you deplete your small store for our benefit."

The Templar turned angrily to the agister, who was looking at him with stupefaction. "You will stay on your feet, Copley, out of respect for the good Father's office and his age. If any here should be accorded the comfort of sitting, it is he, not you, who should receive it."

Disregarding the look of outrage that settled on Copley's face, Bascot spoke to the villagers, who were now regarding him with a little less hostility and barely concealed glee at the reprimand he had given the agister. Behind them Tostig was grinning, while Eadric ducked his head to hide a smile. Gianni, who had not come in after them, stood in the open doorway, fondling one of the village dogs. The animal had declawed toes, a hobbling demanded by law to prevent any dog not belonging to a lord or forest official from hunting animals that were the sole province of the king.

Bascot addressed the reeve. "Alwin, you will know that I am here to try and discover how the squire Hubert de Tournay came to be found murdered nearby in the forest. Did any of you see him on the day he was killed?"

"No, lord," Alwin answered. "Neither did we know of his death until Sir Gerard came yesterday and told us."

"Did anyone of his age and rank ever come to the village—apart from those in the company of the sheriff?"

Again the reeve shook his head. "Only the bailiff ever comes here. And he is a man of an age with my own years."

"The boy must have come to where he was killed late in the evening of the day before or perhaps during that same night. Did you hear anything—voices or horses—out in the woods at that time?"

Again the stubborn shake of denial. Then the priest spoke up. "There are always some sounds in the forest after darkness has fallen, Sir Bascot. Once daylight has gone many creatures—foxes, owls and the like—come out to seek their prey. Unless a great disturbance was made, any slight noise would be thought just the sounds of their foraging."

Bascot sighed and stood up. "If anyone remembers anything, Father, I would be pleased if you would let me know. Tostig will get a message to me."

They all went back outside and Bascot looked around for Gianni, who had disappeared, along with the dog, from the doorway of the church. The villagers were still clustered about in clumps of two or three, watching silently as their priest led the visitors back in the direction of the gate. Suddenly there was the crash of splintering wood and the bellow of an animal; then a girl came running from one of the buildings near the pond. She was young and buxom, her fair hair streaming down her back like a ribbon of amber and, as she ran, she sobbed, stuffing her fist in her mouth to stifle the sound. She came straight towards Bascot and, when she reached him, threw herself down on the ground at his feet.

"It's my fault, lord. My fault that the squire is dead. I said . . . I said I would meet him, but I didn't go. He must have been waiting for me and . . . and got himself murdered by poachers or some other outlaws." She hung her head down, pushing her hands into the muddy earth at her knees. "It's all my fault," she said again.

Alwin went over to the girl and wrenched her roughly to her feet. "Slut," he mouthed at her. "You'll get us all in trouble with your wanton fancies. I told you to stay hidden and keep your lips sealed."

"I couldn't, Uncle." She turned and pointed in the direction of the shed, from which could still be heard an agitated lowing, multiplied now by the din of all the village dogs barking in chorus. From the shed strode Gianni, a grin on his face and a sharp pointed stick in his hand.

"That boy, the Templar's servant, he found me hiding in the cowshed. He tried to pull me out and when I wouldn't come he poked our milch cow so hard she tried to kick herself out of her box. If I hadn't of come out she'd of kicked me as well." The girl's mouth drooped in resignation. "'Sides, the boy recognised me. If not today, I'd of been found out soon enough. Someone at the castle would have remembered me talking to the squire."

Bascot looked more closely at the girl. She seemed vaguely familiar but he could not recall where he had seen her before. As Gianni came up, the boy made a series of quick hand gestures to his master, conveying that the girl had been at Lincoln castle, then hunched his shoulders and mimed a straddle-footed walk to suggest carrying a yoke laden with a heavy burden.

The girl sighed heavily. "That's right, sir. I help the milk-maids up at the castle to make buttermilk for the sheriff's table." Just for a second, pride gleamed in her eyes and her prettiness was plain. "I make good buttermilk, lord. Lady Nicolaa asks for me special to come on the two days of service our village owes each week."

"How is it that you became acquainted with the squire?" Bascot asked her.

"He saw me, sir, coming from the dairy. He kept pesterin' me and . . ."

"And you, slut, fell in with his lewdity," Alwin shouted, giving her an open-handed slap across the back of her head. The girl began crying again, tears spilling down her face and her nose beginning to run as she squirmed away from her uncle.

"Enough," Bascot said as Alwin moved to give his niece another blow. Tostig stepped forward and caught hold of the reeve's upraised arm.

"I don't think you'd be wise to do that, Alwin. Leave the girl be," the forester said. Alwin gave Tostig a look of surprise, then glanced at Bascot and, seeing his anger, reluctantly dropped his hand.

Bascot turned his attention to the girl. "What is your name?"

"Bettina, lord," she answered fearfully.

"You will come with me, and Father Samson, into the church and tell me what you know of this matter." He swung towards Alwin. "You, and the rest of the villagers, will stay here. All of you have contrived to hide information about the murder of Sir William's squire. If you do not wish to increase the sheriff's choler when he learns of your deception, you will cease this pretense. Otherwise, the consequences will be your own fault."

As Father Samson helped the sobbing Bettina to her feet and led her towards the church, Bascot stopped to speak quietly to Gianni. "Well done. Now, watch them. And watch Copley and Eadric, too. The agister is a sight too complacent with his power here not to have some knowledge of this matter. I would know more of him."

Bascot followed the priest and the girl into the church and gently shut the door behind them.

"So you think it possible that Hubert may have gone out to meet the girl and been set upon by the poachers that were roaming the woods?" Nicolaa de la Haye's mouth set in a moue as she asked the question.

Bascot nodded. "It is possible, certainly. Whether it is probable, I am not sure."

After the Templar had returned to the castle later that day he had gone to the castellan's private chamber to give his report. Nicolaa had offered him a glass of wine and set out a dish of *candi*, boiled lumps of sugar made from sweet canes in the Holy Land and transported to England by the Templar Order. A store had been put by for the guests that would soon flood the castle but, knowing how fond Bascot was of them, Nicolaa had ordered a few sent to her room. Now, seated across from her at a broad oak table, he savoured the sweet taste of the *candi*, called *al-Kandiq* by the Arabs, as it mingled with the sharp bite of the wine. The sensation of pleasure was well worth the ache he knew would settle in his back teeth later on.

"You think, then, that the girl is not telling the truth?" Nicolaa asked.

"It is not that I am questioning. Her tale seems honest enough—up to a point. She is to be married soon, to the son of a villein from another village. She is happy with her groom-to-be and did not welcome Hubert's advances, but he threatened to have her anyway, whether she was willing or no, and told her that it would be better for her to give him what he wanted without a struggle, rather than otherwise. Frightened of Hubert, and of her uncle, she said she would do as he wished and arranged to meet him at the ruins of the old hunting lodge late that evening. Then she went home and told Alwin's wife, her aunt, what had happened. The aunt told Alwin and, after conferring with a couple of other villagers, it was decided that they would keep Bettina inside and close the gates to the compound early. This they claim they did, keeping the whole matter from the priest, who is elderly and always early abed. The villagers also insist that they heard nothing from the woods that night that was unusual."

"But you think they may have decided to solve the problem another way?" Nicolaa helped herself to more wine and pushed the flagon across to Bascot.

The Templar shrugged. "It would have been a simple matter for two or three men from the village to wait for Hubert as he made his way through the woods, overpower him and string him up on the tree. They would have known that the problem he presented was not going to go away, that if Bettina did not meet him that night, he would either pressure her for another tryst, or rape her as he had threatened to do. If he had done the latter, there was nothing they could have done; he was a knight's son, she a simple village girl, a maker of buttermilk. No one would have believed her if Hubert had denied it."

"If the men from the village did murder Hubert, the poacher's presence there that same night, or early morning, was a gift of God, or the Devil, for them. It would give more credence to their story, and make it believable that he had been waylaid by outlaws. Much as Gerard supposed it to be." Nicolaa shook her head. "Is it too credible? Or just credible enough to be true?"

"I do not know, but according to one of William Camville's pages Hubert often boasted of his prowess in bedding wenches. Perhaps the only way he could sustain such a reputation was by threatening women into compliance. If that is so, then Bettina may be telling the truth."

He took another sip of wine. "But, if we take it that she is, then it tells us that Hubert was of a nature that was not above using menace to get whatever he desired. And it may not have been only women's bodies that he lusted after."

"You are suggesting that he used the threat of revealing secrets he was privy to as a means of extorting favours or possessions?"

"Yes." Bascot nodded his head slowly. "Alain, Renault and the other squires and pages did not hide their dislike of him, but when I asked them why, they became vague, saying only it was because he was disagreeable and pompous. I came away from their company feeling there was much about Hubert de Tournay they had not told me.

"And these rumours that Hubert was intimate with a faction favouring the overthrow of King John in order to put his nephew Arthur on the throne," he continued. "It may be possible there is more to this murder than a simple tale of unwanted lust and retribution."

"It could be so, de Marins," Nicolaa said, rising from her chair as she spoke. "The girl's tale will satisfy my husband, but I am in agreement with you. It does not satisfy me." She began to walk towards the door, saying as she did so, "I am afraid I must leave the matter for the moment. There are some guests recently arrived that I must make welcome."

"Do you wish me to do anything more with regard to the matter, lady?" Bascot asked, getting to his feet.

Nicolaa paused, her hand on the leather pull strap that served as a handle. "Yes, but do it discreetly. If the murderer is not of the village or to be found amongst the outlaws in Sherwood, it will do no harm to let him believe we do not intend to look further afield. Confidence often brings a loose tongue; such a false supposition may prompt someone's to wag with a freedom that has been guarded up until now."

Bascot nodded his assent, then followed her through the door and down into the hall.

Eight

❖—❖

THE EVENING MEAL IN THE CASTLE HALL THAT NIGHT
was not an elaborate affair even though there were many
guests present. Entertainments and all the special viands and
dainties that had been, and were in the process of being, prepared would be kept for the king's arrival. Bascot sat at the
table reserved for the household knights, just a little below
the dais, and studied the guests. Gerard's brother William
was seated on the sheriff's right hand, with Nicolaa and de
Humez on his left. De Humez's wife, Nicolaa's sister Petronille, had not accompanied her husband to Lincoln for the fes-
tivities, having been confined to bed with a painful ulcer on
her leg. Farther down the table were de Humez's daughter
Alinor and his son's betrothed, Alys. The boy himself, Baldwin, had retired to bed early. He was of a sickly disposition
and needed constant bed rest to maintain his strength.

The high table was being waited on by William Camville's
squires, since many of those belonging to the Haye household had been sent some days before to accompany Gerard
and Nicolaa's son, Richard, on his journey to meet King
John and form part of the entourage that the king would

bring with him to Lincoln. Bascot noted that the two eldest
of William's squires, Alain and Renault, had been given the
privilege of serving their master and the sheriff, and both
young men were performing their tasks with considerable
attention to detail. Alain, especially, took great care to move
forward at the correct moment from his place at his lord's elbow to remove William Camville's empty trencher and replace it with another for the next course, while Renault,
serving Gerard, ensured that the sheriff's wine cup was constantly refilled. At the farther ends of the table the two
younger squires, Rufus and Hugo, were serving the rest of
the company, including the ladies. Osbert and the other
pages, along with the few that still remained in the Haye
household, were kept busy bringing the various dishes and
flagons of wine to the board for the elder boys to serve. All
of them seemed to be well trained in their duties and the
meal flowed smoothly through the various dishes of spiced
herring, coney pottage and roast venison. Broth containing
onions, garlic and peas was ladled out with correctness, as
was the final course of stewed plums, platters laid with seg-
ments of cheese and dishes of the recently gathered nuts.
Once the spiced wine was served, the boys could relax a little, but not leave their post. They would stay until dismissed
and only then could they go and satisfy their own hunger.

Bascot, as he ate the meal Gianni served him, took the
opportunity to study the young people at the table above
him. Hubert, had he been alive, would have been up there tonight, taking his place alongside the others of William
Camville's retinue. Was he missed, or did his absence bring
relief to the young men who had been so outspoken of their
dislike of him? Did the other squires and pages, as Bascot
had felt, know more of his death than they had told, or was it
merely his own fancy that they were keeping something
back? Perhaps he and Nicolaa were wrong; perhaps the boy
had been led to his death by his inclination for lechery alone
and not for any other reason. He returned his attention to his
trencher, trying to quell the anger that rose whenever he
thought of the outrage of secret murder. To take another's
life by stealth was an abomination, an affront to heaven.

Death, when it came, should come cleanly, at the behest of God, not man. With a sudden surge of distaste, he motioned for Gianni to remove his platter and refill his wine cup.

IN A FINE STONE HOUSE FRONTING ON MIKELGATE, Melisande Fleming sat in front of a fire, sipping from a chased silver goblet. She was a woman of middle years, well fleshed, with heavy dark brows and an inordinate pride in the beauty of her hands, which she kept white and supple by the application of an unguent obtained from a local apothecary. Now, she moved these expressively as she spoke to the man seated on a stool opposite her.

"You are sure, Copley, that the Templar will look no further into the death of the squire?"

Copley, the agister, shook his head with certainty. "No, he will not, cousin. He seemed satisfied with the tale of the village girl. Whether he believes Alwin killed the boy himself, or locked the gates and let outlaws take the lad's life, I do not know, but I am sure that he thinks it to be one or the other."

Melisande nodded in satisfaction. She had been in some disquiet about the matter for she held the post of chief forester over the royal chase that lay to the west of Lincoln, and within which the private chase of Gerard Camville was enclosed. She had purchased the appointment after the death of her husband two years before. It was a lucrative office, one that her husband, a goldsmith, had retained for some years, and she was loath to put the security of it in jeopardy. It was not unusual for a woman to hold the position, but she had needed to employ a deputy for the actual work and Copley, a distant relative by marriage on her mother's side, was the one she had chosen. He was a pliable man, fearful of losing her favour—and the generous supply of wine she granted him as part of his remuneration—and was ever amenable to do her bidding, especially in the matter of extracting extra fees from the hamlets in her jurisdiction. She did not want the sheriff's attention drawn to affairs that were within her writ.

"You must ensure that the matter stays as it has been left,

Copley," Melisande said firmly to the agister. "Keep the villagers in their place and let them know that any further
speech with the Templar would be unwise. Remind them of
the need for pasture and pannage for their beasts—and so for
their own bellies—and that the rights to these can be granted
or taken away."

She made a graceful gesture of smoothing her skirt of
heavy velvet with the tips of her fingers, then gave her kinsman a smile that barely curved her lips. "Hunger is not a
pleasant thing, Copley. Nor is thirst. I am sure that by threatening the villagers with the former, you will ensure that you
need never experience the discomfort of the latter."

The agister ducked his head miserably in compliance and
drank deeply from his wine cup.

BASCOT DID NOT SLEEP WELL THAT NIGHT. THE TEMPER-
ature had dropped at nightfall and the small chamber he
shared at the top of the old keep with Gianni was frigid, despite the brazier that burned in one corner. The Templar had
seen the boy well wrapped in his blankets and Ernulf's hat
before snuffing the candle, but while Gianni's breathing
soon dropped into the gentle regular sound of sleep, Bascot
found himself still wide awake.

He had removed his eyepatch as soon as the chamber was
in darkness and now he rubbed the empty socket, a habit he
had acquired when alone and tired. The movement gave
some lessening of the tension he felt and allowed a light
slumber to overtake him, but it was filled with disturbing
dreams and he awoke in moments, feeling the sweat that had
broken out on his body chill like ice inside his clothes.

He knew the reason for his wakefulness. After the evening meal in the hall was over, he had paid a visit to the castle chapel where Hubert's body was laid out to rest until a
relative should come to claim it. Nicolaa de la Haye had told
him that a messenger had been sent to the squire's mother—
his father was dead—and the mother had sent the envoy
back with news that the boy's uncle would be coming to take
her son's body home.

Bascot had expected to find someone, one of the other squires or a priest, keeping vigil beside the body, but the space around the bier was empty, although candles had been lit at either end only recently. Their flickering light illuminated the chamber with an eerie glow. A cloth of dark velvet had been laid over the coffin, leaving only the boy's head and shoulders open to view, with a square of white linen spread over the face to hide the ravages of the crows. Around his neck another length of linen was loosely wound, presumably to conceal the mark of the rope that had been the instrument of his death. Against the wall, on the far side of the bier, stood a box containing the boy's clothing, boots and dagger. Bascot lifted the items out and scrutinised them. The material of both hose and tunic was expensive, marked with stains and scrapings that could have come from rough handling before the boy was dead, or on the journey back to Lincoln slung over Tostig's horse. His boots were in the same condition. The cloak was wool, a dark brown in colour, and was shredded at collar and hem. The fastening had been a simple silver gilt clasp and was still pinned to the fabric near the shoulder. The dagger was a well-made one, not ornate, but of good tempered steel. Surely, Bascot mused, if outlaws had been the cause of the boy's death they would at least have taken the pin and dagger, even if they had not had time to remove his clothes.

Finally the Templar examined Hubert's body. The squire seemed to have been sturdily built, judging by the breadth of his shoulders and the muscles that swelled in his neck. It seemed strange that, with such strength, he had not fought his attacker. Reluctantly, Bascot removed the protective cover from the face, standing for some moments looking at what was left of Hubert's visage. Someone, probably the castle leech, had sewn up the worst of the damage, but little was left to indicate what the boy had looked like. A soft ribbon had been bound under the jawbone and up over the top of the head to keep the mouth closed and hide the remnants of the lad's tongue, which, Bascot guessed, the crows would have found particularly delectable. Soft circles of lead had been laid over the eyeless sockets and his hair, a vivid chestnut in colour, had been pulled down low over his forehead to hide more of the birds' relentless feeding. Altogether there was not much left to indicate the appearance of the boy whose soul had been prematurely forced from its earthly home.

Muttering a brief prayer and asking heaven's forgiveness for his intrusion, Bascot gently moved aside the linen around Hubert's neck. The rope and the boy's clothing had been of some protection against the birds and, beneath the cloth, the mark of the rope was clear, still angry and showing starkly against the bleached hue of the surrounding flesh. The abrasion was rough and deep, running from beneath the chin and up behind his ears, ending in a large contusion on the left-hand side, which must have been made by the knot in the noose. Bascot wondered again how the boy had been taken without a struggle. Had he been threatened with a knife or a sword? Or perhaps surreptitiously given a potion that would render him senseless? Gently he ran his hands over the squire's head. There seemed to be no swellings that would indicate he had been knocked unconscious before being hanged. Again the Templar examined the rope burn, pushing the cloth a little lower. Just faintly he could see another mark almost parallel with the deeper one. It ran around the neck, from back to front, more of an indentation than an abrasion. Bascot laid his fingers in it, felt it run across the boy's larynx and, at the nape of the neck, his searching fingertips found a tiny raising of the flesh, as though it had been pinched. He pondered for some moments, then gently raised Hubert's head, searching in the dim light of the candles for visual confirmation of what he had found. The mark was there, consistent with something thin having been wrapped around the boy's neck and twisted tight, not enough perhaps to kill him, but certainly with enough force to take him out of his senses. But why? Why leave the deed half done? The murder could surely have been completed then and there without the additional need of a rope. Why this throttling twice over, when the intent, all along, must have been to kill? Perhaps the murderer had been interrupted during his grisly act and forced to delay its completion. But, if that was so, why was the garrotte not used to finish the task? What had been the need to use both cord and rope? To have done so seemed excessive and bothersome.

He examined the mark again. It would have passed unnoticed when the sheriff and his brother had stripped him and looked for some sign of a wound, missed as being part of the deeper mark left by the hanging. Hubert had certainly gone to his death without protest, but only because someone had slipped up behind him and reduced him to a state that made him unable to fight for his life.

It was this thought that kept Bascot awake that night, bringing with it an outrage at the stealth of the crime, the cowardice of it. He had spent long years in captivity, knew the helplessness that came with being a slave, unable to defend oneself from physical harm or mental torture, and he felt a strange empathy with the dead squire, losing his life without being able to put up the least resistance.

He lay awake for the rest of the night, listening to the slow tramp of the men-at-arms on night duty as they passed along the wall connected to the tower he was in, and the quiet murmur of their conversation as they stopped for a few moments' rest and a little gossip. From the bailey came only silence, broken intermittently by the lowing of a restless cow or the squawk of a goose. As he lay he wondered if he had missed anything else when he had examined Hubert's body and belongings. He would not get another opportunity to view the corpse, for soon it would be gone to its final resting place.

Sleep was just beginning to invade his restless mind when, towards dawn, the noise of men and horses stirring in the bailey awoke him. Bascot remembered that Gerard Camville had arranged for a hunt that morning. Meat was always needed for the table but, even with the annual late autumn slaughter of cattle that were too old or infirm to be fed through the winter, and the killing of deer trapped in the sheriff's buckstalls, feeding King John and all the attendant guests would demand an additional supply.

Just as dawn was about to break, Bascot heard the yelping of hounds and the strident tones of the kennel master as he called his charges to order. The Templar got up from his pallet and pushed his eyepatch back into place. Soon the horn would blow to signal for the gate to be opened and the sheriff and his hunting party would leave. Quietly Bascot slipped on an extra padded tunic over the one he was wearing, then threw his cloak around his shoulders before bending down to place a hand on Gianni's shoulder. The boy was fast in slumber, only his nose peeping out from beneath the mound of covers in which he was ensconced. Bascot hated to wake him but Gianni became alarmed if he found his master absent and did not know where he was. A fear of vulnerability left over, no doubt, from the time Bascot had found him begging for food on a wharf in Palermo.

Gianni came awake instantly at Bascot's touch, his eyes looking the question his tongue could not ask.

"It's alright, Gianni. I am going to follow the hunt. You may go back to sleep or break your fast, if you wish. I will be back by midday."

It was a measure of the boy's growing confidence that he nodded quickly in agreement and did not show any distress at being left alone. A few months before he had dogged Bascot's footsteps like a shadow and was only comfortable out of his master's presence when he was in the protective company of Ernulf or in the midst of the pack of hounds in the castle hall.

Bascot slipped out of the room and made a slow passage down the stairs, being careful of his ankle which, despite the support of his new boots, seemed more fractious in cold weather. At the stables he ordered one of the grooms to saddle the even-tempered grey gelding he had used the day before and then he left the bailey, slowly following the hunting party as it made its way in the direction of the sheriff's chase.

Nine

✦

THE MORNING AIR WAS FROSTY AND THE BREATH FROM
Bascot's mouth, and that of his mount, streamed in the cold
air like ragged plumes of smoke as they headed for the forest. The Templar ruminated on Hubert as he rode; thought
how he had only the opinions of others for the squire's character, his personality. He had been painted blackly, as a disagreeable young man, a braggart and a lecher. Had he truly
been such? Was there not a trace of good, even in the most
evil of men, some redeeming trait not immediately apparent? Bascot thought of the infidel lord in whose household
he had been held captive in the Holy Land, and at whose direction the hot iron had been thrust into his eye. Bascot had
hated him with all his might, not only for being the enemy
and his tormentor, but for the contempt with which the Saracen had regarded any of the Christian faith. Had the opportunity presented itself, Bascot would have willingly—nay,
eagerly—taken the infidel's life, even if it had been at the
cost of his own. But on reflection, and with the benefit of
hindsight, Bascot had to admit he had seen his captor show
kindness to those of his own heathen faith, and had seemed

genuinely fond of the many children he had sired on the numerous women of his harem. No doubt he had been viewed as a generous and loving benefactor by those receiving his favour.

The same could be true of Hubert, Bascot thought. He may have been a dutiful and loving son to his mother or have given a few of the women he boasted of bedding some pleasure for being in his company. Or had he been one of those individuals who loves self above all else? To whom consideration for others is never even contemplated, let alone attempted? It was possible, but there could be many other reasons why the boy had formed the character he had seemed to display, and it was difficult to make any kind of judgement of a person who was no longer alive. Perhaps the uncle that was coming to claim the body could enlighten Bascot about the nephew's nature. If just one person could be found who had liked Hubert, or whom he had perhaps confided in, it might be that the motive for this murder would become clearer.

His pondering had passed most of the journey to the sheriff's chase and Bascot entered the wood in the wake of the hunting party, broken branches and hoof prints in the mud of the track marking its passage plainly. It was the Templar's intention to visit the hunting lodge where Bettina had said she had arranged to meet Hubert. It was unlikely that the squire had been there for he had been found some distance away, but Bascot remembered that earlier that year, when he had been asked by Nicolaa de la Haye to investigate the murder of four people in an alehouse, it had been a tiny scrap of cloth found at a place far removed from where they had been killed that had led him in the right direction. It might be he would find such a guide again.

Tostig, the forester, had told him the general direction in which the ruin of the old lodge could be found, near to where the charcoal burner kept the huge mounds in which he burned his wood. A thin stream of smoke, rising almost straight up on the still air, told of the way he must go, away from the path followed by the hunting party, which could be heard farther to the south, the horns blowing almost constantly and the deep belling of the dogs signalling that a quarry had been sighted. Gerard Camville was after wild boar today, a dangerous animal to hunt, with razor-sharp tusks and lightning speed. The lair of one had been discovered by the sheriff's huntsmen and Camville was eager to test his skill against it, as well as have some of the tasty meat for the castle table. Bascot envied him his pleasure. As a Templar, he was forbidden to engage on a hunt, either with hawk or bow, but he had enjoyed those on which he had accompanied his father in the days of his youth, and the remembrance brought a smile to his lips.

Bascot came upon the old lodge almost by accident, finding the ruin in his path as he nudged his horse in the direction of the smoke. Two of the lodge's thick wooden walls were still standing, with a part of the roof clinging precariously above the join at which they met. Remnants of the foundations poked above the ground beside them, showing that it had once been a good-sized building, easily housing a large hunting party intent on celebrating their kill, or to give shelter if an overnight stay was planned. Bascot dismounted and tied the reins of the grey to the lower branches of a nearby tree, giving the animal enough slack to allow him to graze on the meagre slivers of grass at its base before he walked over to inspect the ruin.

The wood of the two remaining walls was almost sound. It had some slight infestation of insects but for the main part it stood firm to his touch and the ragged beams of the remaining portion of the roof above seemed solid. There was enough of a covered area to keep out any but the heaviest of rain or snow for a space of perhaps ten feet square. It must have been here that Hubert had intended to have his tryst with Bettina, if the girl had been telling the truth. Bascot carefully inspected the ground, but it seemed undisturbed. There was a pile of desiccated leaves blown haphazardly by the wind into a corner and underneath the moss was soft and unmarked. An old tree branch, whitened and smoothed from exposure to the weather, lay almost in the center of the sheltered space. When Bascot lifted it, the depression beneath looked to have been there for some time, with insects scuttling for cover as light and air penetrated their hiding place. If Hubert had been in this spot, he had left no trace.

As Bascot started to walk around the remains of the other walls, the sounds of the hunt increased, seeming to come nearer. His horse lifted its head and whickered softly, and Bascot went to it and rubbed a hand over its flank to calm it. If the chase came this way, he would have to ensure that he did not impede its progress. It was as he began to untie his mount that he noticed some marks in the earth near the outside edge of one of the remaining walls. He walked over to the spot and knelt down to examine them more closely. The hard-packed soil was deeply scored, two or three ruts on top of one another, ending in a flat impression like that made by the heel of a boot. Bascot looked up at the wall, then across at the faint track that led from the forest on this side. Had Hubert stood here, waiting in vain for the village girl, when he had been attacked? If someone had come up behind him, unheard and unseen while the squire's attention was fixed on sighting the maid whose body he soon hoped to enjoy, it would have been an easy matter to loop a length of cord around his throat and choke him. As the boy had struggled, kicking out with his feet, his heels could have scored the ruts in the earth, sliding uselessly as he struggled to escape the constriction at his throat. If, as Bascot suspected, Hubert had been rendered unconscious before being hanged, was this the spot where he had first been attacked? But if it was, then why had he been moved such a far distance to the oak tree where he was found?

Bascot walked a pace or two in the lee of the wall to see if there were any other indications of a struggle, some trace that would prove his tentative and unlikely assumption. The sounds from the hunt were growing louder now, but seemed to be coming from two different directions, one nearer than the other. Perhaps more than one quarry had been found and the party had split in two. The Templar was conscious of the need for haste; he did not want to get caught between the hunters and their prey, yet he did not want to leave and perhaps have any other signs of a possible assault on Hubert destroyed by the passage of dogs and horses. Making a quick circuit on the outside of the adjoining wall, he had just decided to remount when he heard the huntsman's horn blast loud and shrill from the woods that edged the perimeter on the far side of the ruin. At that same moment a huge stag burst from the trees and into the clearing. The beast paused, sides heaving. Its flanks were flecked with foam and saliva dripped from its mouth. For one second the beast's eye met Bascot's good one. Fleetingly, he saw the terror and desperation of the animal before it lowered its head, took a few faltering steps then, spurred on by another blast of the horn, sprang once again into flight. Leaping with an inordinate grace over the few remaining stones of the foundation it disappeared into the woods on the other side of the lodge.

It was as he turned to watch the vanishing deer that Bascot felt the arrow. Felt, rather than heard, for the noise of the hunt drowned out the whisper of flight the missile made before it embedded itself in the thickness of the extra tunic he was wearing under his cloak. The tip grazed the flesh covering his ribs and the cloth pulled as the shaft became snarled in the sheepskin padding of his under-tunic. Instinctively he dropped to the ground, protecting his sighted eye with his arm as he rolled into the timbers at the base of the wall. A second later a dog pack burst from the trees, led by two huge mastiffs. Racing across the open ground they continued the chase, their throaty baying echoing after them. Long moments behind were the horses, a powerful roan in the lead on which was mounted William Camville, with Richard de Humez following at some distance. Both held bows at the ready, arrows bristling in the quivers slung on their saddles. Other riders could be heard coming along the track behind them.

Bascot stood up and William's horse shied at his unexpected appearance. The sheriff's brother cursed as he fought to bring his mount under control, then changed to an oath of surprise when he realised what had caused the animal's alarm. Wrestling the startled steed to a halt, he stared at Bascot as de Humez and the rest of the hunt streamed past him.

"De Marins! What are you doing here? Did you sight the stag? Are the dogs still on its trail or have we lost him?"

Suddenly he saw the shaft of the arrow protruding from beneath the fold of Bascot's cloak. "My God, you've been pricked. How badly are you hurt?"

William slid off his horse in one motion and ran towards Bascot, bow still in hand. As he did so the two squires, Alain and Renault, came crashing with their horses through the woods a little distance from where the main body of the hunt had come. Seeing their lord dismounted and running towards Bascot, they came to a standstill. Behind them, from the woods to the south, straggled a few men on foot: a couple of huntsmen and the two foresters, Tostig and Eadric.

"I am not badly wounded," Bascot assured William. "A scratch, nothing more."

"Thanks be to God for that," William replied. "Someone must have loosed at the stag and found you for a mark instead." He shook his head. "You should know better, de Marins. A hunt is a dangerous place not only for the quarry, but also for the hunter. Even kings have been brought down by a stray arrow, unwisely loosed."

"I do not think this one was short of its target," Bascot said, pulling the shaft free of the cloth in which it was imbedded. "Had I not turned when I did, it would have taken me full in the chest."

"Even so, de Marins, it does not mean that it was intentional. The stag passed this way just moments ago, did it not? No doubt one of the others misjudged the distance and let loose beforetimes."

"I think not, my lord," Bascot insisted.

William looked intently at the Templar. "Do you have some reason for believing so? Did you see who aimed the shaft?"

Bascot shook his head.

"Then . . . ?"

"It is the direction from which it came, my lord. Your hunting party approached from the south, did it not?"

"Yes." William's face was beginning to show annoyance that the Templar was not making himself clear. "My brother was after boar. We had no beaters with us for deer, but a stag came across our path. Myself and a few others went after it while Gerard stayed with the pig. But I do not see . . ."

"My lord Camville," Bascot said, "I was on the other side of the wall when the arrow was loosed. Unless that shaft can miraculously change direction or penetrate solid wood it could not have been loosed at the deer."

"You mean . . ." William's face drew down in consternation as he realised the import of what Bascot had said.

"Exactly, my lord. It was fired from the north, not the south. I was at the edge of the wall and the arrow came from behind its protection. The deer could not have been seen from there. I was the quarry, not the stag."

Ten

+✝+

LATER THAT AFTERNOON BASCOT ATTENDED THE
Camville brothers in the sheriff's private chamber. It was a
larger room than the one his wife used as her own, filled with
spare boots, tunics, assorted bits of tack and a sleeping
bench fitted with a well-padded mattress and bolster. Nicolaa was also there, seated on a stool near the fire that blazed
in the hearth. The two brothers were on their feet, William
leaning negligently against the window embrasure while
Gerard paced the room in his restless fashion. The excitement generated in him by the hunt was still evident, seeming
to roll off him in waves as he trod from one side of the
chamber to the other. It had been he who had slain the boar,
driving his spear deep into the animal's throat after it had
killed two lymer hounds and sliced open the leg of one of
the huntsmen. Now the beast was being skinned and prepared for the evening meal.

The stag that had inadvertently strayed into the path of
the boar-hunting party had also been brought down, finally
taken when its strength had given out and the dogs, attacking
in a pack, brought it to its knees. The sheriff had good reason

to be pleased with the day's work, but the news of the arrow shot at Bascot had tempered his good humour with anger. His broad face wore a bellicose scowl as he listened to Bascot explain, as he had to the sheriff's brother, how the arrow could not have been loosed from the direction of the hunt party, and also of the other marks on Hubert's throat and how he believed that the boy had first been rendered unconscious and then carried to the tree where he had been strung up.

"You are sure you are not mistaken about the arrow being loosed at you with purpose, de Marins?" Nicolaa asked, concern in her tone. "It is not uncommon for a shaft to find the body of a man instead of a beast during a hunt. All is such confusion once the quarry is sighted."

"I wish there was some doubt, lady," Bascot replied, rubbing the spot where the castle leech had washed the small injury he had sustained with wine before binding it tight with strips of linen. "Only the hand of the Devil could have sent that arrow from the south. Otherwise, it would be impossible."

"If it was the Devil, then he certainly flies high. The wall behind which you were standing is at least twice the height of a tall man and you were only a couple of steps away from its shelter." William pondered what he had just said. "Who knew you were going there this morning?"

"No one except my servant," Bascot replied. "I have questioned him. He did not tell anyone where I was."

"He is mute, is he not?" William asked.

"Yes, but he can make himself understood by gestures for simple communications. For anything of greater import, I have taught him the rudiments of his letters and, if need be, he can write down what he wishes to impart and show it to someone who is literate. But he assures me that no one spoke to him from the time I left until I returned. He stayed in our chamber, later got some food from the kitchen and returned to our room to eat it. It was there I found him when I got back."

"Then, if this arrow shot was not chance, someone must have been watching you, seen you enter the forest and followed you to the spot," William mused.

"Or have already been in the woodland when I arrived," Bascot replied.

"You say you found traces that Hubert may have been attacked there, then taken to be hanged from the oak?" It was the first time that Gerard Camville had spoken. His voice was harsh.

"I believe so, yes," Bascot replied.

"Then it may be that you found something you were not meant to discover." He turned away to pace again. "If this is the work of those villagers, they will hang for it. And higher than they hanged my brother's squire."

"If de Marins has found out something important enough to be a threat to the murderer, what is it?" Nicolaa said in a voice that was calm by contrast to her husband's. "You are sure there was nothing else to be found?"

William answered the question. "No, there was not. We scoured the ground all around for some distance into the forest. No tracks, no disturbances, nothing."

"Well, it is a certainty that it was not an outlaw that fired the arrow at de Marins, for none would have dared to come so close with a hunting party in the woods. So it seems we must look for someone other than a brigand as the culprit. And it also appears the attempt on your life must be linked to the death of the squire in some way. If, as my husband says, you were not meant to discover those marks by the old lodge, what do they signify? It seems to matter little that Hubert was attacked and rendered unconscious in one place but finally killed in another."

"Perhaps the murderer was disturbed in his act," Bascot mused, "and had need to move away from the area. If the boy were partially strangled, it would be easy to smother him in such a state. Then it would be possible for the one deed to be done early in the evening and to hide him before hanging him some hours later. That would provide a reason for my finding the tracks to be incriminating."

"In what way?" William asked.

"I don't know," Bascot admitted. "I don't even know if I am right."

The group fell silent. Gerard refilled his wine cup from a flagon standing near the hearth then offered it to his brother. William shook his head in refusal.

Finally Nicolaa spoke. "However distasteful, what we must consider is that the person who loosed that arrow at Bascot could have been one of your hunting party, Gerard. The arrow had the mark of our own castle fletcher on it. All those engaged in the hunt used his arrows."

Her husband grunted but he let her go on. "According to what you and William have told me, all was confusion once the stag was sighted, your party splitting into two, some staying with you to bring down the boar, the others following William after the deer. Any of the men that were with either group could have slipped away, circled around the lodge and fired at Bascot, then rejoined whichever company was nearest."

Bascot shook his head. "No, lady. All of the hunters were ahead of me when I left the bailey. I followed in their wake. None would have known of my presence in the wood. They had all left before me."

"No, de Marins, all did not," Nicolaa said quietly.

Bascot's head came up sharply and he saw looks of discomfiture on the faces of the two brothers as Nicolaa went on, "My sister's husband, Richard de Humez, left after you, along with Alain and Renault. They were late rising and caught up with the main party a short time later. From what you say they must have been only a small way behind you, may even have seen you mount your horse and ride through the gate on their way to the stables."

"It couldn't have been de Humez," William said abruptly. "He was behind me when we came into the clearing, went past me on the chase for the stag."

"Was he with you when you left Gerard?" Nicolaa asked.

William thought for a moment. "I'm not sure. He must have been."

"Did you see him just before you reached the place where the old lodge stands?" Nicolaa persisted. "Or before that, as you rode after the stag?"

"God forfend, Nicolaa, you know how it is in a hunt," William expostulated. "You are keeping your eye on the dogs and the quarry, not looking to see what a rider behind you may or may not be doing." He banged his wine cup down on the table. "I do not like de Humez, but it will be a sorry day for your family, and mine, if he is found to be implicated in this crime."

"He may not be, William. It may have been one of your squires instead. Would you rather the shadow of guilt was cast on your own household?"

The sheriff's brother gave a groan at Nicolaa's words and he rubbed his hand across his brow in exasperation. "By your reasoning, I myself could have loosed the arrow. Or any of the others engaged in the hunt. I did not hear de Humez or either of my squires mention they had seen de Marins on his way into the woods earlier that morning, but they could have done so, to any one of us, or just in general conversation."

"What you say is true, William," Nicolaa replied. "And we have a scant few days before King John arrives to learn the truth of this matter. We must try, in that short time, to discover what is at the back of this boy's death and if it is something that might threaten the king, even if that threat comes from someone within our own households."

She turned to Bascot. "De Marins, where before I told you to be discreet and take your time, we must now have you investigate in the open and with haste." She looked up at her husband. "Do you agree, Gerard?"

The sheriff nodded, the thin line of his mouth compressed with distaste. Nicolaa stood up. "The boy's uncle should arrive either today or tomorrow. Question him, de Marins—find out if he has any knowledge of his nephew being privy to a plot against the king. And question Alain and Renault again—see if they told anyone that you were in the forest ahead of them." She glanced once again at her husband. "I will speak to de Humez."

Bascot got up from the stool on which he had been sitting and went to the door. As he reached to open it, Gerard Camville spoke behind him. "Let us pray for God to be kind.

It may still be that it was outlaws who killed the boy. If that is found to be the answer I will be pleased."

As he shut the heavy door behind him Bascot was not sure if the sheriff's last words had contained an expression of hope, or a threat.

Eleven

✦

THE NEXT DAY THE WEATHER REMAINED CLEAR AND cold. After the morning meal was served and eaten, a small party left the castle bail by the east gate and crossed the old Roman road of Ermine Street and entered the grounds in which the cathedral stood. Alinor had decided that a visit there would please her little brother, Baldwin, and she had asked Alys to accompany them with Alain and Hugo as escort. At the last moment, Alain had been called to attend William Camville and Renault had offered his company in his stead. As they were leaving, the page Osbert, who had taken a liking to Baldwin, asked if he could go with them. The girls had agreed and, with Baldwin seated on a small pony so that the short journey should not tire him, they had set off.

Baldwin was excited at the outing. It was not often he was well enough for more than a simple stroll in the orchard behind the fortified manor house, which Richard de Humez favoured as his primary residence, and he had begged his father to be allowed to come to Lincoln, excited at the prospect not only of seeing the king, but of visiting the cathedral. The nature of his illness, which seemed mostly to be a shortness of breath that made him weak, had caused him to be of a studious bent. He was also very devout, an instinct perhaps born of the dim realisation that it could be possible his illness would not allow him to live long enough to make old bones. With his sparse dark hair and narrow pinched face he already had the look of one older than his years. When they had arrived in Lincoln, he had gone up to the top of one of the castle towers and looked longingly at the bulk of the cathedral, its spire rising straight up into the sky beyond the castle wall, as though reaching for heaven. Perhaps it had been this excitement that had brought on a bout of his illness, for even while he had become entranced at being so near his objective, his breathing had become shallow and his throat had begun to constrict, shutting off life-giving air. He had been immediately put to bed and given a soothing drink containing poppy seed juice to calm him. A leech had been called and, after letting blood from Baldwin's arm to restore the balance of the humours in his sickly frame, had ordered that he be kept in bed until he recovered.

That had been the day after they had arrived, almost a week ago, and now he was, if not fully recovered, at least able to stand and walk a little way without discomfort. It had been Alys's idea for him to ride the pony and he was grateful to her for the suggestion. She had been his betrothed for many years now, since almost before he could remember, and she was dear to him, for she treated him in much the way his mother did, and with a sisterly affection that Alinor, for all that he knew she loved him, was not gentle natured enough to display.

As they crossed the broad swathe of road that was Ermine Street, a few flakes of snow fluttered through the air. The party were all well wrapped in cloaks, especially Baldwin, but still they felt the cold chill on the air, and when the cathedral bells rang out the office of Tierce, the sound seemed to shatter before it reached them, as though the bells themselves were frozen.

Renault was leading Baldwin's pony, with Osbert striding along beside. Alys and Alinor followed, matching their steps with each other as parishioners on their way to attend Mass thronged through the gate with them. Hugo brought up the rear, his attention seemingly focused within, a frown between his heavy straight brows. The crowd around the group was thicker than usual. Word had just reached the city that Hugh, Bishop of Lincoln, who had taken ill in London some two months before, had fallen into a decline and was feared to be near death. Hugh of Avalon was a much-loved cleric, not only for his warmth and piety, but also for the many good works he had sponsored since he had taken over the bishopric fourteen years before. He had caused lazar houses to be built, taken care of the poor, and cajoled prominent citizens into helping rebuild and improve the fabric of the cathedral, badly damaged in an earthquake in 1185. His demise, if it came, would bring sorrow to all his flock, not only to the high born, but to the low as well.

Now the people of Lincoln were assiduous in attending Masses all over the city, sending up their prayers for the bishop's recovery, fervently hoping that God would hear their pleas and save the saintly Hugh. As the little group went into the cathedral to stand with the rest of the congregation, all of the party were conscious of the seriousness of the occasion, and stood quietly as Mass was celebrated and God beseeched to turn His merciful eyes upon the good bishop. Afterwards, they drifted out into the cathedral grounds and, with Baldwin mounted on his pony, went to purchase cups of hot spiced wine from one of the stalls on the far side of the grounds. Alongside the wine stall was a vendor selling roasted chestnuts, his wares smoking tantalisingly on a grid above a brazier of charcoal. Renault bought enough for them all to have some. Washed down with the wine, they brought a warm glow to the innards.

Once the refreshments had been almost devoured, Osbert suggested that he take Baldwin and show him some stone carvings of the Nativity that Bishop Hugh had commissioned to be inserted on the facade of the north wall of the cathedral. Baldwin was eager to see them and they set off, Osbert leading the pony. Alinor, who had been watching Renault covertly, had seen the glances that he had been giving Alys when he thought no one was looking, and asked the squire if he would accompany her in following Baldwin at a discreet distance.

"Just in case he should feel ill," she said. "I know my brother does not like to be cosseted, but it would be best if he were not left alone for long. If he should weaken, or be struck with an attack of breathlessness, Osbert is not big enough to bear him up alone. It can be quite frightening."

Renault, giving her an assessing glance but nodding his acquiescence, fell into step behind her, leaving Alys with Hugo to share the last of the chestnuts.

Alinor walked slowly, allowing the Poitevan squire to catch up with her. Around them people passed, women with babes in their arms hurrying home after attending the service, merchants intent on getting back to their trade and a few clerics on errands for the church. Alinor let the crowd flow around her, keeping well behind her brother and Osbert, who had stopped beside a portion of the cathedral wall and were examining the frieze. Finally, when Renault's casual footsteps drew him beside her, she looked at him sidelong and spoke.

"You are smitten with Alys, are you not, Renault?"

"She is betrothed to your brother, lady," the squire said shortly.

"That is not an answer to my question." Alinor turned to face him. "I have seen you look at her. Even though she is not aware of your fondness for her, it is plain for others to see—if one takes the trouble to look."

"And why are you interested, lady? I am no threat to your brother's affections. Alys is chaste, and would not betray her vow to be true to him."

"I know that, Renault. It is not my brother I am concerned about."

Richard de Humez's daughter was not one to dissemble. She, like her aunt, had a forthright nature but, unlike Nicolaa, had not yet learned the wisdom of keeping a still tongue.

Alinor placed her hand firmly on Renault's arm, forcing him to a standstill. "I have heard that you and Alain were nearby when an arrow was shot at the Templar. Did neither of you see who aimed it?"

Renault shook his head, not meeting her gaze and, for a moment, the nonchalant pose he always adopted stiffened. "There was much confusion; it would have been impossible to tell who loosed the shaft."

"But you were questioned about it, were you not?" Alinor persisted.

"Yes, both Alain and I were." He relaxed a little and said mockingly, "Is it your intention to interrogate me as well?"

Alinor dropped her hand and shook her head. "No, it is not, Renault." She took a few steps, then stopped and turned towards him. "Did you know that my father was also subjected to an enquiry?"

Renault stared at her, both of them unmindful of people passing, or of the fact that Baldwin and Osbert had moved farther along the cathedral wall. The Poitevin's languid manner was completely gone. "I did not. Surely he is not suspected of such a cowardly act?"

Alinor shrugged. Her face was smooth, her cheeks rosy from the cold. Tendrils of hair had escaped from under the confines of the fur-lined hood she wore and fluttered as she moved. Her expression was one of determination. "I overheard my aunt speaking to him. She did not so much question him as probe gently about his feelings towards the king and whether he knew of any way that Hubert was involved with those who are rumoured to plot for King John's overthrow. I think she and my uncle, as well as Sir William, feel that the attempt to kill de Marins must be linked to Hubert's death, and the murderer fears the Templar may discover his identity."

Renault shook his head slowly from side to side as he pondered what Alinor had told him. "I can assure you I am not involved in any such treachery, nor did I kill Hubert for such a reason."

Alinor, light brown eyes still intent on his dark ones, said, "But you may have killed him for another."

Renault's face narrowed at her accusation but she went on regardless. "I know you detested Hubert. There had to be more than simple dislike. You and Alain both knew that he had insulted Alys, did you not?"

Renault immediately resumed his languid pose and looked away. He made no reply.

"I know you did, Renault," Alinor insisted, almost stamping her foot with anger at his lack of response. "Alys herself told me how Hubert had accosted and threatened her and so I went and questioned young Osbert, asked him if Hubert had quarrelled with anyone just before he was found dead. Osbert told me that Alain had warned Hubert that if he didn't leave his sister in peace he would be sorry for it. And Alain would have told you that he had done so, I am sure."

"Osbert should keep his mouth shut," Renault drawled.

Alinor drew herself up, anger sparking from her. "As you do, you mean? The Templar was not told of this, was he? Nor my aunt?"

Now the squire let his own temper flare. "And why should they be? Neither Alain nor I had anything to do with that bog-spawn's murder. Hubert was warned. By both of us. To have challenged him outright would have made the matter known, and damaged Alys's reputation beyond repair. He knew well enough not to repeat attempting to inflict his loathsome attentions on Alys. If he had . . ."

". . . either you or Alain would have been incensed enough to kill him," finished Alinor. As Renault's mouth set in a grim line, she went relentlessly on, "And he *was* killed, wasn't he? Secretly. Perhaps to protect Alys?"

"And your father, lady?" Renault spat at her. "If he is involved in some plot against the king and Hubert was privy to it, would that not be a much greater reason to kill him, in order to stop up that loathsome cretin's babbling mouth?" He looked at her askance, his lip curling slightly in disdain. "But then I suppose that Alain and I, both sons of knights of low station, are more expendable than a baron who comes of such high lineage as the constable of Normandy."

Alinor, furious now, rounded on him, her voice rising so that passersby looked at the pair curiously and made a wide berth around them. "How dare you accuse me of such baseness? Alys is my friend, betrothed to my brother. I only want to find the truth so that the innocent may not suffer from misguided slander."

But Renault's words had struck home. Alinor knew that her father was a fussy, fretful man who suffered from being compared with the paladin who had been his relative, but she loved him. For all his faults, he was not an unkind parent, solicitous of his ailing son and indulgent to his wife and daughter. But at the back of her mind she feared he may have been tempted into some intrigue, if only lured by the possibility of gaining lands and honours from being an adherent of any who might successfully overthrow the king. If that were so, even if he were not personally responsible for the death of the squire, he might be privy to the identity of the murderer.

Renault, seeing the conflict of emotions that flitted across her face and caused her to barb her words, took pity on her. "Alinor, do not get tangled in the strands of this riddle. Whoever murdered Hubert will not hesitate to kill again if knowledge of his identity is threatened. Let it alone, lest you put yourself in danger. Leave it to the Templar. He has the ability to defend himself. You do not."

Alinor, despite herself, heard the wisdom in his words of caution, much as she was loath to admit it. She nodded her head and when Renault offered her his arm, she took it. Belatedly they resumed their walk in Baldwin and Osbert's wake.

Twelve

✦┼✦

AT ABOUT THE SAME TIME THAT ALINOR AND HER COM-
panions were en route to the cathedral, Bascot was also leaving the castle bail. Mounted on the grey gelding, he left by
the western gate, riding in the direction of the sheriff's
chase. He rode fully armed with sword and mace, and wearing a conical helm and dark surcoat over a hauberk of mail
to ensure he would not be vulnerable to another attack by a
stray arrow. It was his intention to talk to the charcoal burner
and, from there, revisit the village where Bettina lived. He
felt sure that the core of the mystery that had led to Hubert's
murder was to be found in the forest, but he was at a loss as
to how to discover it.

Crossing the Fossdyke, he barely felt the coldness of the
morning or noticed the random snowflake that dropped and
melted on the warmth of his horse's flank, except to reflect
fleetingly that Hubert's lust must have been high to have
sought a tryst with Bettina in such dank weather, even
though it had been reasonably mild on the night he was
killed. Still, he thought, ardour does not cease when winter
throws its blanket over the earth, and the young are robust. A

warm cloak and a bed of leaves would be just as snug as a cold secluded cranny within the castle walls. As he entered the chase, he bent his mind to his task, trying to envision the forest as it would have been on the evening when Hubert had met his death. The woodland was alive with movement at all times of the year, not only with wolves, deer and boar, small animals and birds, but with men as they chopped and hewed, hunted and gleaned, reaped a harvest of meat and berries for the pot or gathered wood for building and burning. Most of these activities were lawful, carried out either by agents of the lord who held the land or by peasants given permission from their master. But there were many in the forest that were not there by right, men and women judged by society as outside its law, forced to steal in order to keep hunger at bay.

Although it was late in the year, there would still be a few peasants grazing a goat or a pig in the forest, or collecting bracken and wind-felled wood. This was a territory they knew, all the tracks and pathways as familiar as the lumps of straw in their beds. Their own livelihood and health depended on such knowledge and they would be well aware of any intruder, be it four-footed beast or two-legged man. Unless Hubert had possessed the skill to move through the denuded branches of the trees with the stealth of a spectre, someone must have seen or heard him. It was Bascot's task to find out who.

As he neared the site of the old hunting lodge, the snow began to come down a little harder, still in tiny delicate flakes, but swirling now, drifting in circles as it was driven by a slight wind that had arisen. At the ruins of the old hunting lodge, the ground had hardened with the drop in temperature. The churned-up tracks made by the passage of the hunt were hard with rime, the mud glistening with frozen moisture. Bascot passed them by, heading in the direction of the thin trails of smoke from the charcoal burner's fires that were visible above the tops of the trees.

Bascot travelled only a short distance before he came to a large clearing. In it were three huge turf-covered mounds, each about nine feet high. Built up from the inside of a shallow pit, they were a construction of wood piled about a central tripod of tall branches, which was then covered with a thick layer of soil and sod. At the top of each was an iron disk, covering the hole through which the stacks were lighted by means of dropping in a handful of burning embers. Ventilation slits were carefully placed around the perimeter of each mound, at intervals of approximately three feet. When the smoke from these slits turned a clear blue it signalled that the charcoal was ready. The whole process took about three or four days, and constant attendance was needed to monitor the fire and repair any cracks that might appear in the outer covering of turf.

One of the stacks in the clearing had apparently already served its purpose, for it had been allowed to go out and was dismantled. Some charcoal still remained in the depths of the base, waiting to be put in bags and taken for sale. Both of the other mounds were still burning, the nearest one emitting smoke that was an almost translucent haze. At this one, a tall gaunt man clad in a rough goatskin jerkin was on a ladder placed against the side of the stack, carefully blocking the vent holes so that the lack of air would extinguish the fire. At the next stack a young man, similarly dressed and enough alike the other to be his son, was engaged in filling in cracks in the turf covering. Both looked up at Bascot's approach, but only the younger one looked startled.

The Templar dismounted and tethered the grey to the branches of a tree at the edge of the enclosure, near to where a crudely built cart with iron-plated wheels stood. In a small pen a donkey peered inquisitively at the newcomers. Bascot's horse snuffed discontentedly at the acrid smell of burning but, being a reasonably placid animal, chose to ignore it and began to push his nose hopefully at the rough grass near his feet. The Templar walked over to the mound at which the elder of the two men still kept to his task and approached the bottom of the ladder. As he did so, another boy, a younger version of the other two, appeared at the doorway of a roughly constructed shack, a dog at his side, and stood watching.

"Are you John Chard?" Bascot called up to the man on the ladder.

"I am," was the laconic reply.

"My name is Bascot de Marins. I have been sent by Sheriff Camville to enquire into the murder of a young man in the forest near here. I need to ask you some questions."

The man made no reply, nor did he seem in awe of Bascot's rank, or the fact that he was armed. He continued to concentrate on his task. Bascot felt his temper rise, but held it in check. He knew only too well how deep ran the resentment of those who had to answer to a master. Charcoal burning was a filthy job, demanding that the stacks be watched day and night to keep the fire under control, and it was dangerous, too, for when the stack was finally cool enough to extract the charcoal there was always the possibility that it would burst into flame and consume not only the wood, but the charcoal burner as well. There was little profit in it either, for despite the skill that the procedure required, and the demand for charcoal for braziers and the forges of smiths, there was little remuneration to be had, especially after the licence to operate had been paid.

Bascot walked over to the youngster standing at the door of the hovel. At his approach, the dog emitted a low tentative growl, which soon subsided when the boy administered a sharp cuff to the animal's head.

Bascot gestured to Chard and spoke to the boy. "Go up on the mound to your father and tell him that I will wait only long enough for him to descend his ladder before I use my mace on the sides of his stacks. Then he will either talk to me or I will take him to be questioned by the sheriff."

The boy, eyes wide in his dirty face, nodded quickly and ran to the mound and scampered up the ladder. After pulling urgently on the back of his father's jerkin he whispered Bascot's message. The charcoal burner turned and gave the Templar a stare of sullen resentment, but did as he had been told, and shambled over to stand in front of his tormentor. Chard's face was just as dirty as his son's, his hands and nails black and ingrained with a dirt that had been there so long it would never wash off. The goatskin garment he wore gave off a pungent smell and was stiff with old sweat and grime. Giving his young son a push and telling him to go up on the stack and continue with the task of stopping up the vent holes, the charcoal burner at last grudgingly gave Bascot his attention.

"You have heard of the death of a lad, a squire in William Camville's retinue, found hanged in a tree not far from here?"

Chard gave his head a slight nod.

"Where were you the night before he was found?" Bascot's tone was sharp.

"I'm here every night," Chard replied. "My sons are too young to be left with the care of the fires. I have to do it."

"Did you hear or see anything of the dead boy on that night?"

"No." The answer was surly.

Bascot drew a deep breath and tried to summon up patience as he walked to the stump of a newly hewn tree and sat down. He decided to try a different tack.

"Who takes the charcoal to sell?" he asked.

"My eldest son," the charcoal burner replied with a jerk of his head in the direction of the bigger of the two boys, still perched atop the middle mound and watching them both fearfully.

"Did he go to Lincoln that day?" Bascot asked.

Chard nodded his head. "He did. And returned before sundown. He and my younger boy were in the compound through all the hours of darkness."

Bascot called up to the boy. "Did you see or hear anything unusual on your journey?"

Before the lad could speak, his father interrupted. "He did not. I told you. We were here all that night. No one came near nor by."

Bascot stood up and drew the short sword he carried in his belt. He walked over to the stack that the charcoal burner had been plugging and dragged the top of his knife across the top of one of the squares of turf that formed its cover. Almost immediately a little puff of smoke appeared. He turned to Chard. "I have little inclination to be lenient with you, burner. You are insolent and uncooperative. Your very manner tells me you have something to hide. Either you tell me what it is willingly, or I take you to the sheriff and let him force it out of you. The choice is yours."

Still the charcoal burner stood silent, his wide mouth set in a stubborn line. The dog began to whine. Bascot, his patience at an end, stepped forward and said, "Very well, Chard. You have made your decision."

At these words the elder son, from his perch atop the smoking mound, let out a yell. "No! Tell him, Da! For the sake of Our Lord, tell him."

Chard looked up at his son. "Shut your mouth, Adam."

"No, Da, I will not." The boy scrambled down and came to stand by his father, resolution on his thin grimy face. "I did see summat that afternoon," he said to Bascot. "Just as I was coming home. A horse and rider were ahead of me on the path. There was a girl, too, up behind, on the pillion."

Chard interrupted once more. "This has nowt to do wi' us, Adam. If the sheriff can find someone to blame he will, whether they be guilty or no. You are putting your head in a noose, and mayhap mine and your brother's as well."

"No, burner, you are wrong," Bascot told him coldly. "If you are innocent, you have nothing to fear."

The charcoal burner gave him a scornful look of disbelief, but said nothing. Bascot left him to his doubt and turned once again to the boy. "Did you recognise either of these people? Did you see where they went?"

The boy hesitated for a moment, glanced at his father's face, and answered with a deliberate shake of his head. "No, sir. And that's the truth. I could tell they were my betters by the fineness of the horse and the cloak the girl wore. If they were bent on a loving spree they would not take kindly to the likes o' me spying on 'em. So I stopped the donkey and waited for a spell. Once they had disappeared up the path, I took a different track to get back here."

"Did you get a look at the girl's face?"

Adam shook his head. "She had her back to me and the hood on her cloak was up."

"Nothing else?" Bascot asked, disappointed.

"No, sir. That's all."

The charcoal burner relaxed his stance now, a look of resignation on his face. Bascot spoke to him once more. "I will ask you again, Chard—did you hear anything later that night—a scream, a shout for help, anything?"

The man shook his head in negation and his eldest son did, too. Even the little one, still crouching down by the dog, moved his head sideways in agreement with the others in his family. Bascot knew he would get no more out of them.

Thirteen

+

HUBERT'S UNCLE, JOSCELIN DE VETRY, ARRIVED LATE
that afternoon. He was a corpulent man of middle height
with a mane of dark curly hair frosted with grey. His face
was fat, creased with lines that seemed to show a genial tem-
perament but his eyes, for all their sparkle, were busy as he
looked inquisitively about him. The clothes he wore were of
good quality; his cloak was lined with fur and there was a
finely set piece of amber surrounded by silver filigree on the
side of his cap. On his arrival, Nicolaa de la Haye's steward
provided him with refreshment in a corner of the hall and
sent to inform his mistress of the man's presence.

De Vetry's manner to the castellan was courteous, but not
overly respectful. He was, he explained, only Hubert's uncle-
by-marriage, his wife being the sister of the mother of the
boy.

"You will know that Hubert's father is dead," he said,
"and since all his other male relatives are away from home,
it was thought best if I came to escort the boy's remains back
to his mother so that she may bury him."

He went on to add that he also had business in Lincoln

that could be transacted during the day or two he would stay before he returned home. There followed a careful explanation of his own antecedents: that although he himself had been gently born of a father who had been an impoverished knight, his mother had been the daughter of a prosperous goldsmith in Boston, and that he followed the same trade. It was of matters pertaining to this that he had reason to see one or two of the goldsmiths in Lincoln.

"I will not say it is for the sake of expediency that I combine my sad duty to my wife's nephew with monetary concerns, but travel is hard at this time of year and I do not wish to make the journey more often than is necessary."

"I trust Hubert's mother will not be too distressed at the condition of her son's body," Nicolaa replied, feeling distaste for the man and his smugness. "I instructed my messenger not to tell her in too great detail how the boy met his death, but I fear the state of his flesh would be a shock to any mother."

De Vetry sat up straighter in his chair, his complacency falling away. "Condition? I was told by my wife that he had met with an accident in the forest. I—we—assumed a fall from a horse while hunting, or some such. What happened to him?"

Nicolaa told her visitor of how Hubert had been found and what the crows had done to him. "He has been decently wrapped and covered, of course, but if you could find a way to keep his mother from too close an examination of her son's body, I think it would be better for her peace of mind."

De Vetry was shaken. "Of course, of course," he muttered, quickly drinking down the remains of his wine. As Nicolaa motioned for one of the servants to refill his cup, the goldsmith struggled to regain his composure. "Then he was . . . he was . . . murdered, you say?"

"I think it most unlikely that he could have bound and hanged himself from so high a branch without assistance," Nicolaa said dryly. "My husband believes that he surprised some poachers and was slain by them."

De Vetry seemed to relax a little at her words but he still

looked at her doubtfully. "Is that what you believe, lady? And Sir William, is he of the same mind as your husband?"

"Suffice it to say that the matter is being looked into," Nicolaa replied. She rose from her chair. "But even though I advise that his mother does not see the boy's body, some member of the family must view the remains, for piety's sake. I am sure that you, de Vetry, will be willing to perform the task."

The goldsmith rose hastily to his feet. Nicolaa felt a perverse satisfaction in watching the colour drain from his face. "Yes, of course, lady. You are right. It is only proper that I do so."

"Then, since the hour grows late, I suggest you do it now. Afterwards the body may be placed in a coffin ready for transport when you have finished your—matters of business."

Calling to her steward, the castellan gave de Vetry over to his care, directing her servant to take the merchant to the chapel where Hubert's body lay. She fancied that de Vetry would, in a few short moments, have a more proper respect for the death of his wife's nephew than when he first arrived.

Bascot arrived back in the castle bail late in the afternoon. He took his horse to the stables and gave it into the care of one of the grooms, then started to cross the ward in the direction of the armoury so that he could divest himself of hauberk and helm. Before he had taken more than a few steps Gianni ran up to him, face alight with pleasure at his master's return. Behind the boy, standing in the doorway of the barracks was Ernulf, and the familiar figure of Roget, captain of the sheriff's town guard. Both men raised their hand in greeting, Roget brandishing a wine skin.

"*Hola*, de Marins. Come, join us and wipe the dust of the journey from your throat. I have brought a good vintage for you to try. It will fare you better than the horse piss that Ernulf keeps in his store."

Bascot nodded his acceptance of the offer and continued

on his way to the armoury. Inside, Gianni helped him out of his hauberk, struggling to lift the chain mail shirt onto a stout wooden crosspiece kept for the purpose. Bascot resisted the temptation to help him. The mail weighed almost as much as the boy himself, but the lad took pride in his abilities and the Templar had decided to encourage him in this regard. It had taken Bascot much soul-searching to determine the fine line between indulging the boy and teaching him responsibility and, despite his affection for his servant, he knew that it would be a disservice to allow the lad a laxity that could lead to selfishness.

When they walked back into the barracks, one of the men-at-arms told them that Ernulf and Roget were in the small room that the serjeant claimed for his own, and Bascot went to join them. The doorway was covered with a heavy leather curtain and the Templar drew it aside so that he and Gianni could enter. The two soldiers were seated at a small table, sharing a jack of wine. Roget hooked a stool from beneath the table for Bascot to sit on, while Gianni scuttled to a corner and settled himself on a pile of neatly folded blankets.

Roget filled a mazer with wine for Bascot and the Templar drank it down thirstily. The captain had been right in his boast; it was good, full ripe on the tongue and warm in the gullet.

"So, de Marins, Ernulf tells me you were skewered by an arrow while roaming about in the wildwood looking for brigands. Is life here in Lincoln so dull that you must always be hunting a murderer?"

Roget laughed as he finished his jest, a full-bodied chuckle that came from deep in his throat. He was a fearsome looking man, tall and strongly built, with the scar of an old sword slash nearly bisecting one cheek from temple to chin. He had once been a mercenary and was reputed to be uncaring of either man or beast, as well as a lecher and a hard drinker, but Bascot found him good company and knew that, for all his faults, he was a capable soldier and loyal to Gerard Camville.

"I think a murderer must be easier to find than wine as good as this, Roget," Bascot responded. "Where did you steal it from?"

The captain gave Bascot a gap-toothed grin and laid a finger alongside his nose. "I can smell out a good wine just as well as I can scent a willing woman, Templar. *Le bon Dieu* blessed me with a nose for both."

They each had another cup of wine, then Ernulf told Bascot that Hubert's uncle had arrived in Lincoln, come to escort his nephew's body home.

"Is he much grieved?" Bascot asked.

Ernulf gave him a scornful look. "That one? The only thing that would bring sorrow to Joscelin de Vetry is a loss of his silver."

"Was the boy of his own blood, or related by marriage?"

"Son of his wife's sister. De Vetry is a pompous blowhard. He was gently born on his father's side, but his mother was the daughter of a goldsmith. Never fails to remind everyone of his father's lineage while adorning himself with enough jewels to weigh down an ox cart."

Ernulf chuckled as he added, "Seems Lady Nicolaa turned him, if not his gold, a bit green, though. She barely let him get his foot in the ward before she sent him off to see the mess the crows had made of his wife's kin. The steward told me that afterwards the goldsmith had urgent need to rush to the privy."

Roget offered to refill Bascot's cup but the Templar refused, preferring to wait until he had eaten some food. Rousing Gianni he sent the boy to the kitchen to bring him some cold viands and bread.

As the youngster scampered off, Ernulf's face became serious. "I didn't want to say this in front of the boy, Bascot, but you were foolish to go out alone this morning. You've already had one attempt made to kill you, yet you invite another. Why didn't you take a couple of my lads with you? Never hurts to have a guard at your back."

Bascot shook his head. "I will learn nothing from the villagers, or any other peasant, with a show of force, Ernulf. It only makes them herd together, like a flock of sheep, and seals their lips from fright."

"But what if the sheriff is right and it was poachers who killed Hubert?" Roget said, his mobile face wearing a sombre expression. "Brigands like that have only one thing to fear, that of getting caught. They will kill you, or each other, without a flicker of conscience. And they will laugh at your stupidity."

Ernulf nodded his head in agreement with the captain's words, but Bascot refused to heed the warning. "I will have to chance that, Roget. It could be that the answer to who murdered the boy is to be found in the forest. I will only know for certain whether it does or not if I make a search for it. And this morning, my roaming, as you call it, was worth the risk. I may have sighted a very small glimpse of the truth."

He related to Ernulf and Roget what the charcoal burner's son had told him. Both listened intently until he had finished. "The male rider must have been Hubert, but if the female the boy saw was wearing a fine cloak, it does not sound as though it was Bettina. Unless Hubert had brought it for her as an enticement," opined Ernulf. "Could it have been another wench, perhaps one more compliant than the dairymaid?"

"It may be so, and I must admit that I hope it was," Bascot replied. "I would have sworn Bettina was telling me the truth. If she lied, she was most convincing. Of all the people I have asked about the dead boy, she is the only one I have been inclined to believe. Unless she was forced to the tale by her relatives, I would not have thought her corrupt."

"*Mon ami*," Roget said sadly, "all men—and women— are corrupt. It is not a fine art to know that; it is to judge the degree of iniquity that is difficult. And those with the fairest face and form often have the blackest hearts. It is a sorrow, but it is true."

Ernulf nodded in morose agreement and held out his wine cup for replenishment. Bascot thought on the mercenary's words, reminded of the last time he had been involved in a matter of unlawful slaying and how he had been so easily gulled by a pretty countenance and a soft manner. Was it happening again? Was the dairymaid lying to him? And if she was not, and she also was not the girl the charcoal burner's son had seen with Hubert, then who was?

Fourteen

❖❖❖

NEAR THE NORTHERN TIP OF SHERWOOD FOREST, AND A good few miles from Lincoln town, a ragged band of men, women and a few small children were gathered around a barely smouldering fire. Above the almost dead embers some thin strips of venison were roasting, threaded on a wooden skewer. It was the last of their store. Hunger was beginning to make itself felt once again and the hopelessness of despair was etched on all their faces. A tattered canopy of leaf-bare branches still shielded them a little from the stark winter sky above, but the smell of snow was in the air and they were cold. All the men were fugitives, brigands who had, in one way or another, broken the law and fled from the harsh penalties of justice. The women, tied by bonds of marriage or kinship, had chosen to flee with their men rather than face a life of poverty alone. But hunger is still hunger and is not eased by sharing it. Dusk had not yet fallen but most of their number were already asleep, too weak to stay awake. The women were huddled together, the children in their midst, getting as much shelter as they could from bracken piled against the trunk of a fallen tree. One of the children, a babe of barely twelve months, began to cry and his mother soothed him by pushing a rag soaked with ale into his mouth. Soon there would not even be any ale, for the last of the brew they had husbanded so carefully was almost gone.

"We'll have to go back to Camville's chase," said Fulcher, handing the child's mother one of the strips of venison. It was little enough, but she could chew it until it was soft enough for the babe to swallow.

"Go back there?" Talli burst out. "Has hunger mazed your senses?"

"No," responded Fulcher, "but it soon will, unless we get something to eat."

He looked around at the little band. The strips of venison had come from the chunks of meat taken from the deer they had poached, but even though it had been bolstered by the addition of boiled hedgehog and a few dried berries, it had not lasted long when shared amongst them. Rustling noises came from the forest around them as small nocturnal animals began their nightly quest for food and in the distance the lone howl of a wolf sounded. Fulcher shuddered. They were helpless in the face of winter's onslaught.

"There's deer enough in Sherwood," Berdo said. "And not so much chance of getting caught." The dying glow from the fire lit up his face, catching the stub of all that remained of his left ear, clipped for stealing. "There's more cover to hide from the foresters, for one thing and, for another, we don't have to cross the river to bring the meat back."

Talli nudged his companion. "You know why we can't take a deer in Sherwood, and it's nothing to do with the foresters."

Berdo seemed about to say more, then decided against it. Fulcher gave him a glare. "Spit it out, Berdo. It's me that Green Jack's got an argument with, not the rest of you. That's what you're thinking, isn't it?"

Berdo looked up. Fulcher was their leader. They had been together for two years now, ever since the day that Fulcher had helped him and Talli escape from the confines of the sheriff's gaol in Nottingham. He was strong, and he was

clever, but what he said was right. It had been Fulcher who
had fought with the leader of another band in Sherwood.
And Green Jack—so called for his ability to move through
the greenwood with no more noise than a leaf rustling on a
twig—had been there longer than Fulcher and had more
men under his command. Fulcher and his band had been
penned into this small northeastern corner of Sherwood for
months, finding themselves stopped by an arrow or a sharply
flung stone if they attempted to move deeper into the forest.
That was why they had been forced go farther afield than
Sherwood to find meat. The feud between the two outlaw
chiefs would end only if Fulcher turned over the leadership
of his band to Jack or if Fulcher left the area entirely.

Berdo leaned forward, speaking earnestly, encouraging
his leader to pretend to disappear. "It'd be easy to do,
Fulcher. If you was to hole up somewheres and stay out of
sight, Jack would think you'd gone for good and let the rest
of us join up with him again. We could even sneak you some
food if you needs it. It'd only have to be until the cold
weather is past, then, in the spring, we could get together
again."

Fulcher leaned across the fire and grabbed the front of
Berdo's filthy jerkin, pulling him forward so that the thief's
face was close to the embers. "Do you think I'm going to
hide from that vermin? Let him think I've turned tail and
run? I'd rather roast in hell."

Talli laid a placating hand on the arm of his leader. "Easy,
Fulcher. Berdo don't mean it. He's hungry, that's all, and his
stomach is talking through his mouth."

Reluctantly Fulcher released Berdo, who slumped back
onto his haunches, resentfully rubbing his face where the
heat from the fire had scorched it.

"Maybe you and Jack could call pax, Fulcher," Talli suggested. "Just for the winter. Let one of us go and talk to him,
see what he says."

Fulcher hawked and spat into the fire. "You know what
he'll say, Talli. Same as I would if I were him. Leave me and
join his men and he'll see that you get a share of whatever
they can steal or beg. You can go if you want. I won't stop

you, nor blame you. It's your sister and her boy over there that's starving and you want to see them fed."

Fulcher rested his elbows on his knees and stared into the fire. Finally, he straightened up. "I'll make your choice for you, Talli; for all of you. Tomorrow I'll go alone to Camville's chase and try to snare some game. If I don't, I won't come back. Then you can go to Jack for help, or to the Devil for all I care."

With these last words he rose to his feet and strode off into the darkness. Talli looked nervously at Berdo. "He's sure to be caught. That lad that was hanging in the tree will have been found by now and Camville's soldiers will be all over the place looking for whoever put him there."

Berdo shrugged and rubbed his fingers over the remains of his ear. "If he's taken, he's taken; if he's not, he's not. Either way we'll get some grease for our innards, if not from Fulcher, then from Green Jack."

TOSTIG FINISHED INSPECTING THE BUCKSTALL THAT Gerard Camville had instructed his huntsmen to erect for the enclosure of deer destined for slaughter, then mounted his horse and rode to John Chard's camp. As he approached the compound he heard the burner's dog whining. The animal was on the far side of one of the dome-shaped mounds, paws edged close to the body of a man who lay facedown on the ground. Tostig knelt beside the animal and turned the lifeless form over. It was the charcoal burner. The broken shaft of an arrow protruded from his chest and there was a look of surprise on his face. He had been dead some hours, for his body was as cold as stone.

The dog became agitated now, backing away from Tostig, its declawed feet clumsy as it scrabbled round the side of the mound. The forester followed, trying to coax the animal to return, but the dog kept up his lopsided gait and disappeared into the shack that had been the charcoal burner's home. Tostig went to the door and pushed back the flimsy curtain of bound reeds that covered it. As he stepped inside, the dog began to growl, belatedly trying to protect another body that lay on the floor. It was Chard's older son, Adam. His throat had been slashed from ear to ear. In his hand was still clutched a stout branch with which he must have tried to protect himself. On the other side of the shack his little brother lay in a similar condition, mouth set in the rictus of a silent scream above the gaping wound in his throat. Blood was spattered over the boys' clothing and on the beaten earth of the floor. Of what had once been the charcoal burner's family, only the dog remained alive.

Tostig went outside, took a few deep gulps of air, then dragged John Chard's body inside the hut to join those of his two sons. After securing the door of the shack against predators, he left the camp. The dog set up a mournful wail as the forester rode off.

BASCOT WAS IN THE TEMPLAR LINCOLN PRECEPTORY when one of the castle guard was despatched to apprise him of the forester's discovery. He had been there since the previous evening, having come to deliver a request from Nicolaa de la Haye for the Order to supply the castle with extra spices, mainly cinnamon, for the king's visit. D'Arderon, the preceptor, was a man of mature years who had spent almost the whole of his adult life in the Templar Order. He had welcomed Bascot warmly, genuinely pleased to see him. The older Templar knew that Bascot's imprisonment in the Holy Land had caused doubts about the rightness of the Templar cause in his younger comrade's mind, and that it had also seriously damaged his trust in God. This lapse had been exacerbated when Bascot had returned to England and found that all of the de Marins family—father, mother, brother—had perished in his absence. But d'Arderon believed it to be only a matter of time before Bascot would, as he put it, "unravel the confusion of his senses" and once more take up his sword and join his comrades in the battle against the Saracens.

It had been time for the evening meal when Bascot had arrived at the preceptory and d'Arderon had invited him to join the company at board. There were three ranks in the

Templar Order and their status was denoted by the colour of the surcoats that they wore; knights in white, serjeants and men-at-arms in black or brown, and priests in green. Bascot had taken a place with his fellow knights, enjoying a welcome feeling of ease. Here were men who lived as he had done, scrupulously obeying their vows of poverty, chastity and obedience. The rules were rigorous, but simple. Duty was the prime mandate, to keep oneself fit and able to bear arms in order to protect pilgrims and, if the opportunity arose, to slay the infidel. Templars were not responsible to any earthly magnate, be they monarch or prince, their only obedience outside the Order to the pope in Rome.

Bascot had taken his seat amongst the others, nodding to a few old acquaintances and introducing himself to those he had not met before. The meal was a hearty one, for this was one of the three days of the week when meat was allowed, with good-sized chunks of lamb in a rich brown broth and an assortment of winter vegetables stirred in, followed by plates of cheese and marchpane. Although they were all monks, the usual stricture regarding diet that was laid on nonmilitary religious orders was not applied to the Templars because of the necessity of maintaining their strength for battle. While they ate, silence was mandatory, only a reading of scripture by one of the Templar priests to be heard above the clatter of bowls and eating knives.

Afterwards, Bascot stayed for the recreational hour when the Templars were allowed to gather in the chapter house for general conversation until it was time for the service at Compline. Besides the preceptor, there were only four knights in residence at the moment: two who had just joined the Order and would soon be on their way to Outremer, one recently returned from the Holy Land after fulfilling a vow of atonement that had involved a promise to serve with the Templars for ten years—an arrangement that had been allowed by the Order on receipt of a gift of land from the penitent knight—and one lately arrived from Spain with despatches for d'Arderon. Old battles were refought, former acquaintances remembered and the politics of the struggle against the Saracens discussed, along with the hope of a good response to the call Pope Innocent III had made the year before for Christendom to undertake a new crusade.

Bascot enjoyed the evening and it had not taken much persuasion by d'Arderon to convince him to spend the night in the preceptory dormitory. Since it had been necessary that he and Gianni give up their small chamber in the older of Lincoln's two keeps to guests that had come for the king's visit, they were now sleeping in the barracks alongside the men of the garrison. Bascot knew that Ernulf would see Gianni safely in bed for the night and felt able to indulge himself in another cup of wine and more talk with his comrades.

It had been late when he had rolled himself up in his cloak and lain down on one of the hard pallets that lined both sides of the Templar dormitory, dimly lit all night by small oil lamps as commanded by the Order's rule. Around him the other knights were also preparing for bed; the creak of leather and small clangs of metal the only noise as they took off the outermost of their garments and lay down still almost fully clothed, another rule that was scrupulously obeyed. Soon the large chamber was quiet, only the sounds of regular breathing and the occasional snore disturbing the silence. Bascot lay awake for a time, considering the path that lay before him. He felt pulled in two directions: Gianni and the boy's welfare on the one hand, his vows to the Order on the other. The boy was dependent on him, had been since the day Bascot had saved him from starvation in Sicily, and Bascot admitted to himself that he would be reluctant to part from the lad, had come to regard him almost as a son. But Gianni was growing older, would soon be of an age to fend for himself, and in the meantime Bascot knew that if he left to rejoin the Templars, Ernulf, without family or child of his own, would care for the boy as well, if not better, than Bascot was able to.

As for the Templar Order, Bascot was beginning to feel a pull to return to its ranks. He had been happy here this evening, had experienced a sense of belonging that he did not feel among the household knights in the Haye retinue, despite his liking and respect for Lady Nicolaa. When he had arrived in Lincoln almost a year ago, he had been angry, at

God and at himself. Then he had wished only for solitude, a place to try and forget all that had happened. It was for that reason that the Order had sent him to Lincoln and Nicolaa de la Haye. She had, at the request of the Templar preceptor in London, provided him with shelter and food so that he could have a space of time not only to recover his health and strength, but perhaps also his devotion to God and the Order. Now he wondered if he was, as had been hoped, beginning to do just that.

Or was he merely wishing for an easier path to follow? Staying on in Lincoln would invite responsibilities, not only for Gianni but in the matter of earning his keep. He knew that Nicolaa would be only too happy for him to retire from the Order and take up a post among her household knights, for she had hinted as much. He knew she valued his talents, had already taken to using him as a deputy in the many instances that required not only a man of knight's rank, but also literacy, a rare commodity among the upper strata of society, and one that he possessed. There was also the matter of his successful apprehension of the alehouse murderer some months before. That he had felt satisfaction at his success and that both Nicolaa and her husband had been grateful to him had been obvious. And now she had once again set him to probing into a matter involving a secret slaying. Could it be that a fear of failing to solve this new riddle of death was the cause of his feeling such a strong pull to return to the Order? Was he experiencing, perhaps, not a return of faith but apprehension about the extent of his own abilities?

He burrowed deeper into the covering of his cloak, murmured a prayer for guidance, and then fell into a deep sleep. It was out of a dark dreamless void that the chaplain's bell for Tierce woke him. The other Templar knights in the dormitory had already left their pallets to celebrate the earlier religious offices, and Bascot got up from his own bed and went to join them in the round chapel that was the hub of the preceptory, his confusion still unresolved.

It had been just as he was leaving the chapel after Mass and preparing to return to Lincoln castle that the man-at-arms sent by Ernulf had arrived and told of Tostig's grisly discovery at the charcoal burner's camp. The report was accompanied by a request from Nicolaa de la Haye to return as soon as possible. D'Arderon, who had come to bid Bascot farewell, listened gravely while the man-at-arms was speaking, his face concerned.

"I know you are under duty to Lady Nicolaa at present, de Marins, and must give her your assistance in this matter," the preceptor said. "But don't let it be so long before you come to us again. You belong here, with us, not out in the forest chasing murderers. The Order needs you, and so does God."

Bascot acknowledged the sincerity in d'Arderon's words and bade him a reluctant farewell before he turned his mount towards the gate and followed the man-at-arms back to Lincoln castle.

EARLIER THAT MORNING FULCHER HAD EMERGED FROM the verge of that part of Sherwood Forest that abutted the banks of the Trent and crept in the predawn light down to the water's edge, pulled out a small skiff from its hiding place in the overhang of undergrowth and poled himself across the river. He had been in Gerard Camville's chase just as the pale winter sun was striking its first shards of light across the tops of the trees, and inside the sheriff's buckstall a short time later. There were several deer trapped in the huge pen, ones that had been lured there by the mounds of tasty ivy and holly piled inside into leaping over the low fence, only to find their exit blocked by a deep ditch at the internal base of the barrier. Fulcher, straddled above them in the boughs of a tree that overlooked the pen, surveyed the frightened animals below him and chose a small female roe deer that looked to be in her first year. Fitting an arrow to his bow, he took her in the neck with one shot and leaped down into the enclosure to claim his prize. The rest of the deer, smelling blood, shied away to the far side of the buckstall, clustering together and milling about looking for a means of escape. Fulcher quickly removed the arrow from the dead doe, then slung the carcass up on his back before traversing the ditch and climbing the fence, throwing his burden down on the other side before jumping over himself. He stood still for a moment, testing the quietness of the forest before he once again heaved the dead deer up on his back and began to retrace his steps to the river's edge.

He was breathing hard by the time he saw the glimmer of water ahead of him. Since leaving Talli and Berdo at the camp the night before he had travelled three miles to where the skiff was hidden, then another two to get into Camville's chase. The lack of food combined with the loss of a night's sleep had sapped his strength, but he knew he had to make it back across the river before he stopped. Once on the other side, he could hide the carcass, and then get Talli and Berdo to help retrieve it. He slowed a little and shifted his burden, took a deep breath and prepared to trot the last few hundred yards.

The small boat could just be seen bobbing quietly among the reeds when the first arrow struck the ground ahead of him. A second later he heard the baying of dogs. He was able to take two more steps before another arrow flew over his shoulder and thudded into the tussocky grass at his feet.

"Halt, or you'll be deader than that deer!" a voice yelled. The barking of the dogs sounded closer now and Fulcher turned to see two mastiffs flying towards him, heavy jaws agape and slavering as they ran, teeth gleaming wickedly against their dark fur. Behind them, at the edge of the fringe of trees he had just left, were two foresters, their green tunics blending with the darkness of the foliage at their backs. Both had bows, nocked and drawn. Between them was another forest official, mounted on a large roan gelding.

"Yield!" the mounted officer called. "Or I let the dogs have you."

The mastiffs were nearly upon him, the larger of the two in the lead, his powerful haunches propelling him forward with the speed of an arrow shot. Fulcher had no choice. "I yield," he called loudly, dropping the deer and throwing up his arms.

It seemed an eternity before a shrill whistle halted the dogs. Fulcher could smell their fetid breath as they pulled up abruptly at his feet, fur bristling and teeth bared. Slowly the foresters moved towards him, grinning, enjoying his obvious fear of the dogs.

As the men came closer Fulcher saw that all three wore an emblem decorated with a royal crest on the front of their tunics.

"A good day's hunting, I would say," said the mounted officer. He leaned down in the saddle to look at Fulcher. "I am Copley, agister for King John. Although this is not my bailiwick, I think the sheriff will be pleased to learn that I have caught a poacher in his chase."

The agister leaned back and gave a mirthless chuckle, his florid countenance gleaming with a sheen of sweat despite the chill of the morning. "I would say he will be even more appreciative if it is proved I have also caught a murderer."

"A deer I may have killed, but I have murdered no man," Fulcher proclaimed, trying to ignore the dogs, which were tensed and seemed ready to spring at the sound of his voice.

"So you say, brigand, so you say," Copley said, still grinning. "But it would not be unexpected for a man in your position to lie, would it?"

The agister did not wait for Fulcher to respond, but ordered the bowmen to bind the outlaw and bring him and the deer to Lincoln castle.

Fifteen

+—+

JUST AFTER MIDDAY THE WEATHER WARMED SLIGHTLY and rain began to fall, gently at first, then with more intensity until it became a driving sleet that covered the streets with an icy slick that made walking difficult. Despite the weather, all of Lincoln was aware of what had happened that morning and people gathered in twos and threes under eaves or in one another's homes to discuss how the charcoal burner and his sons had been found murdered and that an outlaw had been taken for poaching the sheriff's deer.

In her house on Mikelgate the goldsmith's widow, Melisande Fleming, sat discussing these matters with Hubert's uncle, Joscelin de Vetry. They were well known to each other, both being in the goldsmith trade, and were also connected from earlier times, from not long after de Vetry had married his wife and Melisande had been looking for a comfort that her elderly husband could not provide. They had been lovers for a time, but not in love, and when their lust had grown cold they had ended the liaison, but had remained friends. This suited them both, for each had a mercenary bent that made them easy confidants.

Now, in the small solar above the hall of Melisande's house, they were seated comfortably in chairs that possessed both arms and padded cushions, sipping an amber-coloured wine from Spain that the goldsmith's widow had ordered opened for their enjoyment. The chamber was richly appointed, the light from beeswax candles reflected in gleaming points of light on the silver of their goblets, and draughts were kept at bay by a profusion of fine tapestries on the walls. Under their feet a coverlet of sheepskin graced the floor before a fireplace of smoothly dressed stone, and the wood burning in the grate filled the chamber with a warm glow.

"So, you will be taking your nephew's body home tomorrow, Joscelin?" Melisande asked.

De Vetry sighed heavily. "Aye. It will not be a pleasurable task to bring the corpse to his mother. She is of an agitated nature at the best of times. What she will be like when she hears of how her son met his death, I shudder to contemplate."

"But you said you requested that the coffin be sealed. Is there any need for her to know the more distressing details?"

"No, but they are sure to be bruited abroad by gossiping tongues. I would rather she heard them gently, from a member of her family."

Melisande nodded in agreement. "That is a caring thought, my friend. It is a shame the boy was killed at all."

"Yes, but he was a careless youth, heedful only of his own pleasures, and greedy for them. I told him more than once that he might one day end up in trouble if he did not curb his impulses, but he would not listen. And now he is dead, murdered, most likely by someone he angered beyond toleration." De Vetry sighed again. "For all his cunning intelligence, he was a stupid boy."

Melisande reached over and placed her hand comfortingly on her companion's knee. "And his stupidity was most likely the cause of his death, Joscelin. You must not blame yourself."

As the goldsmith murmured his acceptance of her condolences, they were unaware that their conversation was being overheard. Outside the chamber door, which was slightly ajar, stood Melisande's daughter, Joanna, a young woman

just past her eighteenth summer. She was not pretty, being
rather too plump for beauty, but her eyes, when not red
rimmed from crying, were of a luminous quality that gave
her the look of a startled doe. Now, listening to the conversation going on in Melisande's chamber, she stuffed the corner of her sleeve into her mouth to stop herself crying out.
Hubert was dead and her whole world was crashing into
pieces around her.

IN A CHAMBER NOT FAR FROM MELISANDE'S HOUSE, in
the top storey of Lincoln castle's new keep, another young
woman was in distress. Alys had gone to the room she was
now sharing with three other girls to sit and think. Neither
Alinor nor the others were there, and she was glad of their
absence, for what Hugo had told her had alarmed and frightened her.

She had, from its onset, noticed the morose mood that
had occupied her young cousin for the last few days. At first
she had thought it was due to a reprimand for some prank or
other, or perhaps for being negligent in his duties, but when
he had continued to be dejected, an attitude so different from
his normally cheerful bonhomie, she had become concerned, especially as he seemed to become more depressed
when in Alain's company, for he had always respected and
admired her brother. That morning, after attending Mass,
she had watched for him among the crowd and pressed him
to walk with her in the castle herb garden, saying she had
need of his company as an escort. He had followed her in an
abstracted manner, not seeming to feel the cold bite of the
wind that had been a harbinger of the sleeting rain which
soon followed. Alys had wrapped her cloak tightly around
her and pressed him to tell her what it was that was distressing him so.

"There is something wrong with you, Hugo," she had
said. "Do not deny it, for it is obvious. Please tell me, so that
I may help you."

Her soft caring tone had made the boy stiffen at first, then
he had flung himself down on a stone bench that was placed

in the lee of the wall. Pulling at a late-blooming sprig of mint, Alys had thought he was going to be stubborn and not answer her, and she sat down beside him in an attempt to cajole him further. But there had been no need. Seeming relieved, he had spoken first.

"I don't see how you can help, Alys, but I must tell someone before I burst with it. I dare not even tell a priest, for fear that somehow Alain will suffer."

"Alain?" Alys felt her mood swing from concern to alarm. "What has Alain to do with what is troubling you?"

Hugo looked up, confused. "But I thought that was why you asked what was the matter, that you, too, suspected . . ." The squire shook his head in dismay and sunk his head into his hands. "Oh, I should not have said anything, anything at all."

Alys touched him gently on the shoulder. "But now you have, Hugo, and you must tell me what it is. If it concerns Alain, I have a right to know. I am his sister and, like you, I love him. I would do nothing to hurt him, even if to do so meant hurt for myself."

Although her words were brave, her dismay had intensified as she had listened to the tale that Hugo had to tell. It had been about the night that Hubert had met his death, and how her cousin suspected that Alain, and perhaps also Renault, was responsible. "We were all sleeping on the floor of the hall," he had said, his voice tremulous, "wrapped in our cloaks, along with a lot of other guests. I couldn't fall asleep—the man beside me was snoring so loud I thought he would choke—and I saw Alain get up and leave the hall, quietly, so as not to disturb anyone. Some time later, maybe two hours or perhaps three, Renault followed him."

"But that does not mean . . ." Alys started to protest.

"They did not come back for a long time, Alys," Hugo interrupted her. "It was early in the morning when they returned. I know it was because just a few moments later the cathedral bells rang the hour of Prime. They had been gone nearly all the night."

"Did you ask Alain where he and Renault had been?" Alys said.

"Yes," Hugo replied miserably. "But he lied. He said he had only got up once, to relieve himself at the privy, and had returned almost immediately. When I tried to say I had seen him, and Renault, he just laughed and said I must have been dreaming." The boy gave her an agonised look. "I wasn't dreaming, Alys. They *were* gone all that time. And it was during those hours that Hubert must have been killed."

"But why would Alain or Renault want to harm Hubert?" Alys said, fearful of the answer, fearful that her brother had discovered how Hubert had shamed and threatened her. "I know they didn't like him," she went on bravely, trying to convince herself as much as her cousin, "but Hubert was not liked by many people. That is not a reason to do him harm."

Hugo took his cousin's hand and held it. "Alain knew what Hubert had done to you, Alys. Hubert taunted him with it, daring Alain to challenge him, saying that if he did he would tell all the world you are unchaste. There was nothing Alain could do, except . . . except . . ."

"Murder him?" Alys said tearfully. "Oh, Hugo, Alain would never do such a thing. It is dishonourable, treacherous. I don't believe it. And even if I did, it would have been unnecessary. Hubert tried to force me to bed with him, but I did not. There was no truth in his cruel taunts."

"But Alain would not have known that Hubert was lying," Hugo replied. "Not unless he asked you. And he would never have done that. It would have implied he thought you welcomed Hubert's attentions."

"I still don't believe that Alain would commit secret murder, Hugo. I cannot."

"I don't want to either, Alys," her cousin replied, his despondence deepening. "But before the Templar came to question us, Alain told all the other squires and the pages that we were not to volunteer any information, that we were to protect each other. What else could he have meant except that we were to lie for him?"

This revelation shocked Alys, convincing her more than the fact that Hugo had witnessed Alain and Renault's absence from the hall that her brother had something to hide. Alain had always been an honest person, valuing truth and loyalty above all else. Only a terrible secret would make him veer from such a path. Were her fears that her brother had killed Hubert now to be proved true?

There had been no words she could find to console Hugo. They had sat together in silent commiseration until disturbed by one of the kitchen maids come to pick some of the mint that Hugo was mindlessly shredding between his fingers. As she sat in the chamber, Alys thought that always, ever after, she would associate the smell of mint with death.

Sixteen

✦✤✦

GERARD AND NICOLAA'S SON, RICHARD, ARRIVED HOME that night just as the company seated in the hall had finished listening to a troubadour that Nicolaa had hired to play for the king during his visit. The minstrel was a woman, not so uncommon an occurrence as it had once been before Queen Eleanor had ascended the throne and given her patronage to anyone, male or female, who had the ability to compose and sing well. The troubadour's name was Helena, and she was from Portugal. Not only was she an accomplished jongleur, she was young and beautiful. Seated on a stool before her audience, she had just plucked the last notes of a soulful melody from her lute when the door of the hall was flung open and Richard and two other people came hurriedly in, all appearing tired and dishevelled.

"Richard!" Nicolaa de la Haye, with an unaccustomed loss of composure, stood up from her chair and gazed in surprise at her son. Gerard Camville pushed his chair back, rising swiftly and with an alacrity that belied his girth.

"All is well, Mother," Richard Camville called out as he came into the hall and made his way through the throng of people to the table on the dais where his parents sat, the young man and woman who were with him following close behind. The heir to the castellanship had his father's broad shoulders and heavy thighs, but he was taller and more loose-limbed. The red hair that marked him as a Haye shone like a flaming beacon when he pushed back the hood of his cloak. "I have been sent by the king to tell you of his progress and on what day he will arrive," Richard said when he reached them. "King John bids me convey to you his warmest affections and tell you he will be in Lincoln in three days' time. I have left the squires and pages of our household in his care and they will return with the royal party."

He then introduced his companions. "This is Godfroi de Tournay and his sister, Marie. But before I explain why they are with me, we need food and drink. We are all chilled to the bone and our hunger would put a starving man to shame."

Nicolaa signalled to a servant and mulled wine was brought, as well as a huge platter of cold meat, bread and cheese. Room was made at the high table for the three newcomers and they gratefully slaked their thirst before helping themselves to the food.

As he ate, breaking off chunks of white crumbly cheese and devouring it with mouthfuls of cold venison, Richard explained that King John had wanted to send his parents a personal message and had entrusted it to him. "I also have a letter from the king in which he asks you to inform him if it seems that he will arrive before William of Scotland." Richard looked up and smiled, his strong white teeth flashing as he did so. "He is most anxious not to seem too eager, and would rather that Scotland waits on England's pleasure than the other way around."

Nicolaa nodded. "He has nothing to fear. King William is but one day's journey from Torksey. A messenger from the Scottish entourage arrived this morning."

She looked around at the others seated on the dais, all of whom were straining their ears to hear what Richard had to say; some openly, others more surreptitiously. Beside her husband, his brother leaned in a nonchalant pose, and beyond him Richard de Humez listened quietly, attempting to seem preoccupied with his cup of wine. On her other side, her niece Alinor openly showed her interest while Alys, beside her, looked only at her brother and Renault, who stood in attendance behind the Camville brothers.

Nicolaa decided it would be wise to defer any more discussions of the king until there were not so many listening ears. She swerved from the subject by asking, "And your companions, Richard? Have they, too, brought messages from the king?"

Richard became more solemn. "No, mother, they have not. Godfroi was with me in the king's camp and, it is true, came with me to bring King John's letter, but that was only until we came to Boston."

Now Godfroi leaned forward and spoke to Richard's parents. He was tall and compactly built, with short black hair and a clean-shaven chin. His eyes were as dark as his hair. There was a look of intensity about him that was enhanced by the grimness of his tone. "Richard and I decided to break our journey at Boston where my elder brother, Ralph, has his manor house. There we learned, from my sister, that a member of our family had died. In short, lady, Marie and I were half brother and half sister to Hubert, whose body I believe his uncle, Joscelin de Vetry, has come to take home."

His sister now spoke up. "His mother is distraught, Lady Nicolaa. She lives with us still, preferring Ralph's protection to that of her own family. When the news of Hubert's death came, both Ralph and Godfroi were away and only de Vetry remained to come for my half brother's body and bring it back to her. When Godfroi arrived she begged him to let me accompany him to Lincoln so that her son might have a woman's tender care on the last journey he will make on this earth."

Nicolaa gave the girl a searching glance. "You were fond of Hubert, then?"

The girl did not drop her gaze. "No, lady. Not especially so. But I do care for his mother and Hubert was, after all, a son of my own father's loins. It is my duty to comply with my stepmother's wishes."

Nicolaa nodded and spoke to her husband. Gerard

Camville had stayed silent throughout this exchange, leaning back in his chair and listening with watchful eyes. Musi-
cians with rebec and viol were playing quietly at the back of
the hall and the company, after the initial excitement of
Richard's arrival, had resumed conversing with each other
and holding up their goblets for scurrying servitors to refill.

"I think, Gerard, this matter would be best discussed
privily, do you not agree? Afterwards, Richard can give us
the king's messages."

Camville grunted and rose to his feet. He was by nature a
taciturn man, and an indolent one, content to let his wife deal
with any demanding matters that arose. Reluctant though he
was to leave the comfort of the hall and become embroiled
in yet another discussion of the squire's murder, he recognised the need for his presence.

"De Marins should also attend," he said to his wife
shortly; then, to his brother, "And you, too, William. This
matter touches both of us."

Nicolaa sent Alain, who was standing rigidly behind Gerard's chair, to find Bascot and direct him to attend her without delay. Then she made her excuses to the company and
they all left the hall.

BASCOT CAME AWAY FROM THE MEETING WITH GODFROI
and Marie de Tournay with a feeling that he was now more
familiar with the character of the murdered squire. The boy
certainly did not seem to have many redeeming qualities.
Quite the reverse in fact.

Like Joscelin de Vetry, the brother and sister had not been
aware that Hubert had been murdered, or that his body had
been desecrated by crows. Nicolaa had explained that she
had not wanted to cause the boy's mother undue anguish and
had therefore left the details of her son's death untold when
she had sent her message.

"I fear she will be much distressed," she said. "De Vetry
intends to have Hubert's coffin sealed, but even so, some explanation will be required."

"I will tell her," Marie said firmly, although her eyes were awash with unshed tears. In appearance she was very like her brother, with dark eyes and hair, but there the resemblance ended. The intensity that was etched on every plane of her brother's face was lacking in Marie. She was strong, but not unbending, and there was compassion in her voice when she spoke of her stepmother.

"My father married Hubert's mother when he was elderly," she had told them, at which William Camville nodded. It had been at Fulk de Tournay's request that he had taken Hubert to train for knighthood. Soon after the boy had become a part of William's household the elder de Tournay had died, after suffering many long months from a wasting fever.

"Our mother had been dead for some years when my father married again," Marie had gone on to explain. "The household had long been in need of a woman's hand, for I was too young to take charge. Hubert's mother is kind, too kind, perhaps. When he was born she was overly protective of him, cosseting him and keeping him by her when he should have been out from under her skirts." Marie shrugged. "It made him petulant. When he was not given something he wanted, he would run to her, begging her indulgence. She never refused him. Even when he told lies or stole some trifling object—which he did quite often—he was never punished. And my father was too ill by then to take him under his hand. My brothers attempted to chastise him when he would do some mischief, but"—Marie gave an impatient sigh—"his mother always defended him, giving him a tidbit to eat and telling him he was not to be upset at their angry words. It was hopeless."

"By the time he went to your household, Sir William, his nature was set in ways that were not commendable," Godfroi added, his face wooden. "But he is our blood kin and his murder must be avenged."

Gerard Camville, pacing the room as was his usual habit, had listened to them in silence. Then, tersely, he told them of the murder of the charcoal burner and his sons and how an outlaw had been taken while poaching the sheriff's deer.

"It is more than likely that brigands are behind all of these deeds. If the one that has been captured did not carry out the acts himself, I will warrant that he knows who did," the sheriff said. "He will admit to no crime other than taking the deer, but I will get the truth from him before I am through. If he killed your half brother, you may rest assured he will pay—and pay dearly—for the doing of it."

As he spoke the words there was no doubt in anyone's mind that the sheriff would carry out his promise. Gerard Camville was known for his brutality. The outlaw would not be spared any pain before he faced his final moments.

Bascot had left the room with the de Tournay brother and sister, leaving Richard alone with his parents and uncle for their private conversation. It was obvious that Marie was exhausted. The hurried journey in winter weather and the distress of the news she would have to convey to Hubert's mother had taken their toll. Leaving her in her brother's care, Bascot asked if he could meet with them in the morning when they were both rested, to discuss if there could be any other reason for Hubert's murder besides a chance encounter with outlaws.

Seventeen

ƒULCHER WAS BEING KEPT IN A SMALL HOLDING CELL
near the barracks. His wrists were still pinned to the sturdy
branch that Copley had ordered his men to place across his
shoulders and he was slumped on the dirt floor, head bowed
and eyes glassy. He was so near to unconsciousness that he
paid no heed to the two men who were beating him, nor to
Roget and Ernulf, who stood watching.

"He is either stupid or fearful of a greater punishment,"
Roget said to the serjeant. "My men have been at him for the
best part of the morning and still he will not admit that he
had any hand in the murder of the boy."

Ernulf made no comment. He was here only at Lady
Nicolaa's request. Inflicting pain on a person unable to defend himself was not something for which he had much liking. He knew it was necessary at times, but fair battle was
more to his taste than this torturing of a helpless man, however great his crime.

The two men who had been systematically beating the
outlaw were members of Gerard Camville's town guard, of
which Roget was captain. They were both evil tempered and

surly, and seemed to enjoy their task. Their smirking grins had produced an angry knot in Ernulf's gut. He longed to escape the dimness of the small windowless cell, lit only by a few flaring cressets set in sconces on the wall. The smell of blood and sweat permeated the air.

"Perhaps he is innocent of the boy's death," Ernulf said. "Although even if he is not, he is a rare man not to admit it after a beating like that."

Roget gave Ernulf a sideways glance. The scar that ran down the side of the captain's face puckered as he mused on the serjeant's words. "That is my opinion also, *mon ami*," he finally said. "The sheriff will not be pleased at my lack of success, but I do not think we will get any further with this miscreant. Guilty of taking the deer he may be, but of the other . . . I am beginning to doubt it."

With a brief command to his two men, Roget stopped Fulcher's punishment and told them to leave. When they had gone, laughing as they did so about how great a thirst their exertions had built up, Roget went forward and released the outlaw's wrists from the pole. Fulcher slumped to the ground, eyes shut and breath shallow. Between them, Roget and Ernulf lifted the comatose brigand onto a straw pallet and threw a threadbare blanket over him.

"I'll send one of my men with food and water, although I think perhaps it will be futile," Ernulf said, leaning over and feeling the pulse in Fulcher's throat. "He is still alive, but barely. Your men did their work a little too well."

Roget regarded the outlaw, the bruises that swelled his face, the split lips and grotesquely puffed eyelids. The rough tunic he had been wearing was split in several places, blood seeping through the torn cloth like sap bubbling from the cracked bark of a tree. Roget gave a Gallic shrug of his burly shoulders. "Perhaps. But if he dies, it may be a mercy. He will hang whether he killed the boy or not. It is the penalty for poaching and the sheriff will be only too pleased to inflict the punishment."

The two men walked to the door and went out into the bail. Ernulf threw the iron bolt that locked the door from the outside. Pulling a wineskin from his belt, Roget took a large mouthful and passed the flask to the serjeant. Above them the sky was darkening into evening. The air was cold and clear. Around them the bailey was settling down for the night, and the muted sounds of servants finishing their tasks for the day drifted towards them—the clank of a bucket, the mournful protest of a cow being penned in for the night, the call of the castle guards as they changed shifts.

The captain took another swig from his wineskin, his brow furrowed in thought. "Something bothering you, Roget?" Ernulf asked.

"I am wondering how it came to be that it was Copley who caught the wolf's head we have in there. The sheriff's chase is not in his bailiwick, is it?"

Ernulf shrugged. "No, but as agent for the chief forester he has a right to be in any part of the woodland. All belong to the king, even Camville's chase. And the chief forester is the king's officer and so, therefore, is Copley."

"I do not mean that, my friend. What I mean is that Copley is renowned for his love of wine, not for his attachment to duty. Not that I find fault with that, of course," Roget's mouth split in a wide grin, revealing teeth that were still sound, but gapped in places. "But does it not strike you to wonder why Copley, who finds it such a great effort to carry out his normal responsibilities, should suddenly engage in extra labour by patrolling a part of the forest where he has no reason to go? And then, while he is doing this, he has the great good fortune to stumble across an outlaw poaching the sheriff's deer? It seems to me most strange."

Ernulf pondered Roget's words then reached for his companion's wine and took a deep draught. "Strange it may be," he said, "but I cannot see anything untoward in it."

"Think, Ernulf, think! The sheriff looks for an answer to the riddle of who killed the squire. Lady Nicolaa also looks for this. They ask questions, set the Templar to ask more. Suddenly, they have the culprit—a brigand provided by Copley. That *chien* in there"—Roget nodded in the direction of the cell—"will hang for taking the sheriff's deer. Once he is dead, it takes only a little step of the imagination for everyone to believe he also killed the squire. Who is to prove different?" Roget's eyes sparkled as he propounded his theory. "It is a tidy answer. Me, I do not believe providence smiles so easily."

"Nor do I, Roget," Ernulf replied musingly. "Nor do I." He handed the wineskin back to the captain. "I think I will have a private word with Bascot. And with Lady Nicolaa."

THE SMELL OF BLOOD HUNG IN THE AIR AS GIANNI passed through the western gate of the castle bail. Today was the eleventh of November, St. Martin's day, and the traditional time of the year to slaughter animals too old or infirm to warrant being fed throughout the winter. Within the castle, in the town, and out in the villages dotted around the countryside, cattle, sheep and swine had been butchered during the last few days and their carcasses readied for preservation by salting or smoking. But first there would be a feast of fresh meat, to celebrate the saint's day, and Gianni felt his mouth water at the prospect.

Resolutely he put the thought of food from his mind. He had met with no difficulty from the guards on the gate as he had passed through. There were many people coming and going—tradesmen, merchants, villagers, servants and a few guests—so that he had been able to slip past unnoticed. He set out towards the Fossdyke and, as he walked, turned over in his mind what he had heard that morning.

He had been present when his master had talked to the dark-haired young knight called Godfroi, and his sister, Marie, and had heard Bascot asking them if they had any knowledge of their half brother, Hubert, being involved in a plot to depose King John from his throne. Godfroi had been angry at the accusation, but the Templar had calmed him, saying it was a rumour that must be looked into before it spread and was acknowledged as truth. The girl, Marie, had added her plea to Bascot's words and Godfroi, still surly, had assured the Templar that if Hubert had, by some chance, been involved in such machinations, then it was without the knowledge or agreement of the rest of his family.

"My brother and I are as loyal to the king as my father

was to Richard, and Henry before him," Godfroi had insisted. "Never has any of our family betrayed their liege lord, not even when Stephen took the throne from his cousin Matilda. We kept to the oath we had sworn to her father, and helped Henry retrieve his inheritance." Marie had placed a hand on her brother's arm, showing her support.

"And your kinsman, Eustace de Vescy—the boy spoke of his involvement, and that Hubert was privy to plans that were being made," Bascot said.

Now Godfroi had laughed out loud, more amused than angry. "If de Vescy was ever forming such a plot—and I, for one, am sure it is untrue—such a great lord would hardly divulge his schemes to a stripling related to him only by the meagrest thread of blood. Were it not so serious, it would be laughable."

Bascot had then sent Gianni to fetch more victuals from the kitchen. The Templar had met the brother and sister just after early Mass and they had taken seats in a corner of the hall to break their fast. Godfroi had proved to be a prodigious trencherman, especially when fuelled by anger, and he had quickly devoured all that Gianni had set before them, including the small loaf of fine manchet bread reserved for those of higher rank. Even though Marie had denied being hungry, Bascot hoped that another plate of food might tempt her to take some nourishment.

It was as Gianni was returning from the kitchen that he heard something that had interested him. He was in the covered walkway that connected the building that housed the cook's ovens with the great hall, and had been forced to step aside into the entryway to wait for a gap to appear in the press of servants running to and fro with platters of food. A little way behind him, two merchants of the town had been standing, conversing quietly in low tones. Presumably they were there on matters of supplying provisions to the castle and were waiting to speak to the Haye steward. At first Gianni had taken no notice of them, but then the context of their discourse had intrigued him and he had edged closer, hoping to hear more, counting on the dense throng of scurrying servants to conceal the fact that he was listening. He had stood some minutes thus, then slid silently away before his eavesdropping became obvious.

Now, as he crossed the Fossdyke, dodging carts laden with supplies and mounted travellers bound for Lincoln or the Torksey road, he ruminated on his decision to leave the castle without his master's knowledge. It was the first time he had ever done such a thing, and was an action he had never even once contemplated from the day the Templar had rescued him from starvation. But his reasons were simple. He knew that his master was beginning to feel a desire to rejoin the Templar Order. When Bascot had returned to the castle after spending the night at the preceptory, it was obvious how much he had enjoyed the visit with his former comrades. He had spoken longingly to Ernulf of old friends he had met and the battles they had discussed. At first Gianni had been angry and felt betrayed, but he had not let it show, for he knew that would hurt his master and be harsh repayment for all the largesse the Templar had bestowed on him. But, if his master should go back to the Order, Gianni would be forced to fend for himself, and he was ill equipped to do so.

At Lincoln castle he had a place he belonged and where food and warm clothing were in plentiful supply. But if the Templar went away, there would be no more use for his servant within the castle walls. Ernulf might take pity on him and feed him for a while, but it was more probable he would be thrown out of the castle gates, his only option to beg on the streets. To ensure that such a fate did not overtake him, he must make himself valuable to others besides his master. If he could uncover some information that would lead to finding out the identity of the man who had murdered the squire, and do so without the Templar's help, then Lady Nicolaa might realise his worth, perhaps even give him a place in her retinue. Under such influential patronage he need have no more fear of being homeless and hungry.

This was the reason he had decided to steal away from the Templar, to try to find out if the gossip he had overheard that morning was the truth. The dairymaid, Bettina, would be able to tell him, or one of the other people in the village.

Gianni was sure the priest of the hamlet, Samson, was literate. There had been scraps of parchment and a quill pen on a shelf in the tiny chapel where Bascot had spoken to the villagers. Since Gianni had been taught to read and write by the Templar, he could, through Samson, ask the questions that would prove the validity of the tale he had overheard. If it was true, then he was sure he had discovered a lie that had been told. He remembered when, earlier that year, he and his master had tracked down a murderer in Lincoln town, and how the Templar had come upon the truth by unmasking the lies that had been told; and the manner in which one lie had led to another, and yet another, until all was revealed. Perhaps he could do the same thing now, on his own.

As Gianni left the Fossdyke and struck out across the marshy land to the west, he hastened his steps. It was a long way to Bettina's village and he would need to get there and back again before the Templar found he was missing. As he ran he pictured in his imaginative young mind the accolades that would be heaped on his head if he was successful in his quest. Already he was gaining fast in literacy, due to the lessons the Templar had been giving him. After today, he would be praised not only for his learning, but also for his quick mind. One day soon, he assured himself, he would be trusted with tasks of importance, perhaps even, in time, become a *secretarius* to Lady Nicolaa herself. His inability to speak would be of little significance, he would be prized as a servant of the highest rank, and it would all be due to the conversation he had overheard that day.

Eighteen

✢

THE HEAVY WAIN THAT BORE HUBERT'S COFFIN STOOD near the eastern gate of the bail with Godfroi de Tournay, Nicolaa de la Haye, Gerard Camville, and their son Richard all gathered to bid Marie and de Vetry farewell on their sad journey. Godfroi fussed with the dun-coloured palfrey his sister was to ride, checking the set of the saddle and asking Richard if he was sure the horse was placid enough to warrant no danger to Marie.

"We are only going as far as the river, Godfroi," Marie protested. "From there de Vetry has hired a boat to take us to Boston. It will be an easier journey than by road and I shall have no need of a mount. This one will do very well for the short distance to the quay." She shook her head in impatience. "Tell him, Joscelin, that there is no need for concern."

The goldsmith moved forward, ignoring the look of dislike on Godfroi's face. "I shall ensure that both your sister and the body of poor Hubert come to no harm. I will be with them all the way."

Godfroi did no more than nod his acceptance of the goldsmith's words, then made a point of ignoring him, turning to make conversation with Richard. Across the ward, the squires and pages of William Camville's retinue were again at practice with the quintain, ignoring with youthful exuberance the sharpness of the cold wind and spatters of freezing rain that tossed around their heads.

To one side, Bascot and Ernulf stood watching the cortege prepare to depart, while Richard de Humez and his daughter, Alinor, overlooked the group from the shelter of the keep's entryway. Young Baldwin had remained in his chamber, the weather being too inclement for him to venture outside, and his betrothed, Alys, had stayed with him to keep him company. Those servants who were going about their duties in the great expanse of the ward steered a wide path around the wagon, attempting to avoid the truculent gaze of Gerard Camville as they passed by.

Nicolaa placed her hand soothingly on Marie's arm. "Do not fret about your brother's concern," she said quietly. "It is just his distress about this matter that rises to the surface. He will calm when he hears that you have arrived safely in Boston. I have instructed one of my men-at-arms to accompany you and return with all speed to let us know you have done so."

"Thank you, lady," Marie said, her dark eyes filling with sudden tears. With an effort, she stemmed them and said, with a quaver in her voice, "I must admit my own temper is frayed. Telling Hubert's mother how he met his death will not be easy. And I fear that she will want the coffin opened. I do not know, in all conscience, how I can prevent that. If she insists, it may well be that the sight of his poor body will be too much for her. She is not a very strong person and he was, after all, her only son and dear to her."

"A child's death is never easy for a mother," Nicolaa responded. "But God will give you guidance, child, if you ask for it. Our prayers are with you."

Marie nodded in acquiescence and mounted her palfrey. As she did so, a pair of riders entered the bail, a woman mounted on a fine black mare caparisoned in red and blue, and a man astride a dark bay alongside her. Both were wrapped in heavy cloaks, the woman's hood trimmed with soft fur. They rode up to the funeral party and the man has-tened to help his companion alight from her mount.

As the pair approached the small gathering, Ernulf let out a low chuckle and said to Bascot, "The Fleming woman has picked a poor day to seek an audience. Lady Nicolaa is not overfond of her at the best of times and I am sure she will give her short shrift on such a sad day."

Bascot looked at the pair, recognising the agister, Copley, but not the woman who was with him. He asked Ernulf who she was, and the serjeant explained, "That is Melisande Fleming, chief forester for Lincoln. She is also heir to her late husband's gold manufactory, and is ever trying to curry favour with Lady Nicolaa, hoping she can persuade her to use her influence with the king to bring more offices and commissions Melisande's way. She is a greedy woman, the Fleming widow."

"And Copley, the agister," Bascot asked, "is he connected to her in some way other than holding his office from her?"

"They are related," Ernulf replied. "Cousins of some distance, I believe, but it is said Copley hopes a closer rela-tionship will develop. If he were to wed Melisande, the contents of her coffers would pay for enough wine to drown himself in." The serjeant shook his grizzled head. "But the fool has little cause to hope. There are many men in Lincoln who sniff at the widow's skirts, but she keeps them all dangling, like fish on a line. I doubt she will marry again. She is too fond of her wealth to give it over to the control of a husband."

Bascot watched as Marie and de Vetry settled themselves on their horses and the men-at-arms of the escort took up positions in front and behind the cortege as it slowly exited the bail through the east gate. After they had left, Gerard Camville, with his son and Godfroi, walked over to the prac-tice ground to watch the squires at their exertions, leaving Nicolaa to walk back to the keep with Melisande and Copley at her elbow.

"Come, de Marins," Ernulf said, "let's go and find some-thing hot to warm our bellies. And a pot of ale to wash it down."

Bascot readily agreed and, for the first time that morning, noticed that Gianni was not with him. He was so used to the boy dogging his every step that he had assumed the lad was waiting nearby, out of the coldness of the wind. But his servant was nowhere to be seen. Bascot shrugged it off. The lad was showing some independence lately and it was most likely he had found a task that would give him an excuse to stay indoors and keep warm. Hunching his shoulders against the swirling flakes of snow that were hesitantly beginning to fall, Bascot felt that he could not blame the boy for doing so.

AT ABOUT THE SAME TIME AS BASCOT AND ERNULF were eating a tasty rabbit pottage and drinking their ale, Gianni was beginning to wish he had not embarked on his venture alone. He began to realise how foolish he had been. Even if his suspicions were confirmed and proved to be pertinent, how could he prevent the villagers from alerting the man about whom the questions had been asked? He was only a boy, and a servant, with no authority to enforce their silence. Nicolaa de la Haye would not praise him; she would castigate him for his stupidity. The Templar might even be so angry at his interference that he would cast him back out into the streets to beg for his bread. Besides, the distance to the village was greater than he remembered and the solitude of the forest was frightening. He felt his heart begin to hammer with trepidation as he became aware of how far he was from all that was familiar. No, he had been wrong to come on this fool's errand alone. He was *pazzo*, he said to himself in his native Italian. Daft in the head and an *idiota* as well. He must return to Lincoln, and return at once.

He was quite near the village now, but hastily turned back on the path to retrace his steps. He had gone only a short distance when he heard a rustling sound from somewhere behind him. To Gianni, the forest was as much a foreign country as England had been when he first came. All his young life had been spent in a city, and he knew the smells and sounds that could threaten from a dark alley or a shadowy doorway as well as he knew the fingers of his own hands. But here, among the towering shafts of tree trunks and the grating noise of winter-stripped branches swaying in the wind, it was as though he were in an alien land. He began to panic. Was the noise he heard just some small harmless animal, or was it something larger, like one of those ferocious wild pigs that the lords hunted with dogs and spears? It could even be a wolf. Fear coursed through his veins as his imagination leaped. In his mind's eye he could see fangs, dripping with saliva, reaching for his throat.

He tried to hurry, heedless of the direction in which he was going, such was his sudden desperation to get back to the familiar walls of Lincoln castle. Completely gone were his dreams of the morning envisioning how he would be commended for his cleverness, how he would solve, all on his own, the mystery of who had murdered the squire. The turmoil of his thoughts was interrupted when he suddenly found himself on an unfamiliar path and was unsure of the way he should take. How he wished he were back in the soldiers' barracks with the reassuring bulk of the Templar at his side. Taking a deep breath, he tried to calm himself.

It was as he stood thus, small body tensed with concentration, that the noise came again, closer this time, and louder. Before he could turn to see what it was that threatened him, the world went black as a rough sack was thrust over his head and his flailing wrists were caught in a vice-like grip. His efforts to free himself were short-lived. Within the space of a breath, his hands were bound and he was thrown up onto his captor's shoulder.

IT WAS WARM IN THE CHAMBER WHERE ALYS SAT READING to Baldwin. A brazier burned in the corner and heavy rugs of wool and sheepskin had been placed on the floor to exclude drafts. Baldwin was wrapped in a blanket from the knees down, and seated in a cushioned chair with a high back. He listened in contentment as his betrothed read from a Psalter, her voice stumbling slightly when she came upon an unfamiliar word. Alys had come late to literacy, unlike Baldwin and his sister, Alinor, who had both been taught to read at a young age. There were still many nobles who could not read or write, but as realisation of the enjoyment and power that literacy could bring became more commonplace, it was becoming the fashion to have children of both sexes taught their letters by a household cleric or priest.

" 'I will lift up mine eyes unto the hills, from whence cometh my help.' " Alys's light, even tone faltered a little as she read the passage aloud, then seemed to fade altogether as she continued, " 'My help cometh from the Lord. . . .' " At these last words, she bent her head and broke unashamedly into tears.

Baldwin quickly removed the wrappings from his knees and came to her side. "Alys, what is it? Are you ill?"

The young boy, sick so often himself, was ever solicitous of illness in another, and he put his thin arm around the girl's shoulder and lifted her head with his hand. Her eyes swam with tears, but she shook her head. "No, I am not ill; at least, not in body."

"Then what is the matter?" Baldwin stroked her hand tenderly. Although she was older than he by four years, he seemed the more mature, the long hours spent in bed with his recurring sickness having given him ample time to reflect on the nature of life and its troubles.

"I cannot tell you, Baldwin," Alys said. "It is a terrible matter, but it was confided to me by another and I do not wish to break a trust."

"A trust is indeed a heavy honour," Baldwin agreed, going across to a table and bringing her a small goblet of spiced cordial from a jug that stood there. "But if the burden is too great, it will be easier if it is shared. You know that I will not break any confidence you divulge to me."

Alys sipped at the soothing drink and regarded the slight figure in front of her. She had always been a little in awe of Baldwin, in a way she was not of either his parents or his sister. He was so learned, and so pure, and his faith in God was of a strength rarely found in priests, let alone her elders. Her fears for Alain and the worry about his guilt had consumed her ever since she had spoken to Hugo. She had a need to confide in someone who would be able to tell her what, if anything, she could do to protect her brother, someone to allay her fear for him. Baldwin was kind, he was to be her husband one day, and she knew him to be trustworthy. Taking a deep breath, she told him what Hugo had said and about Hubert, stumbling over the part about the day the squire had propositioned her, but telling it all just the same.

Baldwin listened until she finished, his only reaction a frown as she told of Hubert placing his hand upon her breast, but he gave her a reassuring smile and nodded for her to continue. When she was done, he neither censured her nor did he reprimand her for keeping the matter secret. His trust in her honesty was complete.

When she was done, he poured himself a cup of cordial and resumed his seat, pulling the blanket over his legs before sitting silent and deep in thought for some minutes. Alys waited, used to the way he would mull over facts before making a judgement, and feeling a sense of relief in the telling, as though the weight of a millstone had been taken from her back.

"There is no proof in this story that your brother had anything to do with Hubert's death," he said finally and, when she started to interrupt him, held up his hand. "Although it may be that he lied to your cousin, the reason could be entirely different from the one Hugo ascribes to it. And there is only one way for you to find that out, Alys, and that is to ask Alain yourself."

Alys leaned forward, gripping him by the hand. "I cannot, Baldwin. Alain will be angry with Hugo, and Hugo will be angry with me for breaking his confidence. Besides, if Alain and Renault did have anything to do with Hubert's death, they might not admit it, even to me."

"Then I will ask your brother on your behalf, and I will also ask that he swear on his honour to tell me the truth."

At the dismay in Alys's face, Baldwin reassured her, and stroked the hand that held his so tightly. "You are to be my wife, Alys. It is my duty to sustain you. If Alain is innocent, he has nothing to fear. If he is not, then we will ask God for guidance in the matter. We must trust in the Lord, Alys. Have you not just read that He is our keeper? He will show us what is to be done."

Nineteen

✦✛✦

As it came up to the hour for the evening meal
Bascot realised that Gianni had been missing for a long time.
He went in search of the boy, looking in all the likely places
he was to be found and enquiring if anyone had seen him.
Finally he went to Ernulf and asked if he would question the
guards that had been on duty at the castle gates that morning.

"Perhaps he left the castle precincts on some errand or
other and, if he did, they may have seen him leave," Bascot
said. "Although it is unlike Gianni to go anywhere without
telling me, it is possible he may have done so. But if he did
go out into the town or the cathedral he should have been
back long ago. He would not miss the evening meal. I have
been to the kitchens. The cook has not seen him, nor have
any of the scullions. If the last food he had was when we
broke our fast this morning, he will be sore hungry by now."

Ernulf took the matter as seriously as the Templar. "Aye,
you're right. The lad likes his victuals. He would not willingly miss a meal. I'll ask my men if any of them have seen
him."

When their enquiries were all answered in the negative,

they searched the castle more thoroughly, going through the stables, the armoury and all the outbuildings, even poking about amongst the huge sacks in the food store in case Gianni had crept in there for warmth and fallen asleep. The hour for the evening repast came and went, and still there was no sign of him.

"I am certain some mischief has befallen him," Bascot said to Ernulf as they stood in the middle of the bailey under a sky now almost fully dark. "It must have done. There is no other explanation."

The serjeant nodded, his seamed face as worried as the Templar's. "It's too late tonight to search anymore. But if he does not turn up by morning, I'll have my lads scout around outside the walls and over the Fossdyke. He is not within the bail, else we would have found him, so he must be somewhere outside."

Bascot acknowledged the truth of the serjeant's words and added, "If he is, Ernulf, he is not there of his own volition. Of that I am certain."

Not ONLY GIANNI MISSED THE EVENING MEAL. AT THE hour when trestle tables were being erected in the hall and laid with clean linen cloths, Nicolaa was sitting in her private chamber listening to her nephew Baldwin tell what he had discovered that afternoon from Alys, and how he had questioned both Alain and Renault.

"They both swore to me they had nothing to do with Hubert's death, Aunt, although Alain did go out that night with the intent of waylaying him and giving him a sound thrashing for his treatment of Alys. Renault was privy to his purpose and, when Alain did not return, he followed to find out what had happened. But Alain could not find Hubert. He knew the squire had left the castle by the western gate just after sunset, riding one of Uncle William's sumpter ponies and, since Hubert had been bragging earlier of a wench that he said was panting for his company, both Alain and Renault assumed that he had gone to keep a tryst with the girl. They expected him to return before curfew was called. Alain waited just outside the main gate until the gateward's horn was blown to signal that the entrance would be shut, and then he and Renault kept watch for Hubert from inside the ward, thinking he would use the postern gate when he returned. They stayed there until the early hours of the morning and it was nearly dawn before they returned to their pallets in the hall. That is their explanation of why they were gone for most of the night. When the squire was discovered murdered, they decided it would be best to say nothing of their vigil, lest they be suspected of something in which they had no part."

Baldwin's tone was earnest as he continued, "I am certain they are telling the truth, Aunt, for they swore that it was so on my holy relic of St. Elfric's finger bone." Baldwin's pale face was shining with perspiration. The anxiety Alys's revelation had caused, and his subsequent interview with the two squires had distressed him, and he could feel his chest tightening in the way it did before one of the attacks of breathlessness overtook him. With difficulty, he held it in check, determined to finish the task he had set himself before he gave in to the ailment.

Nicolaa had listened carefully to what Baldwin had told her, and how he had come at his own suggestion and at the request of both Alain and Renault to ask her advice on what they should now do. She also saw the familiar signs of her nephew's affliction start to show itself, and called for one of her servants to come and help him to his chamber.

"Be assured I will deal with this, Baldwin, and also be certain that if they are telling the truth, they will not be reprimanded, except perhaps for the misdemeanour of not being forthright with their elders. But now you must rest. Leave the matter with me and do not speak of it to anyone else, and caution Alys that she must do the same."

Baldwin accepted his aunt's directions gratefully and went to his chamber, leaning heavily on the arm of the servant, his breath labouring as he went. Once he had left the room, Nicolaa sat back down at the table she used for dealing with correspondence. She would need to tell Gerard and William what Baldwin had related to her, but first she needed to think. Were the two squires telling the truth? Baldwin was very sure, but he was an honest soul, to whom swearing a falsehood on a relic would be anathema. But she knew that such an act of blasphemy was not uncommon; it had been perpetrated many times, even by kings. And the boy wanted to protect his betrothed, Alys, from the pain she would feel if her brother were found to be guilty of such a heinous act as murder. Finally, she took up a sheet of parchment and drew forward the quill and inkpot that were always on the table. Tomorrow would be time enough to tell Gerard and his brother of Baldwin's tale. For tonight she would keep it to herself, safely recorded and hidden out of sight.

GIANNI HAD NOT RETURNED BY MORNING. BASCOT AND Ernulf had sat up nearly all the night, in case the boy should appear from some cranny in the castle grounds that had been missed in their search. When dawn came both the Templar and the serjeant were haggard and worried.

Ernulf sent some of his men to search the area outside the gates and down into the town. Those men-at-arms who were off duty volunteered their help to swell the ranks of searchers. Gianni was popular with the men, not only because he accepted his inability to speak with equanimity, but also because he was an orphan, a condition that plucks at the hearts of all men who follow the profession of soldier. Again the buildings in the bailey were thoroughly checked, servants questioned once more, menials that came from outside the castle for daily work within its walls were asked if they had seen Gianni on their journey, and even the pens containing fowl and sheep were inspected.

It wasn't until just after mid-morning that one of the guards on the wall came running to where Bascot and Ernulf were making another search of the old keep. "We've found someone who saw a lad that might have been Gianni, serjeant," the soldier said. "A carter, bringing a load of wood for the cook's oven. We've told him to wait until you can speak to him."

"Where did he see this boy?" Bascot asked, following as

the man-at-arms set off back in the direction from which he had come. Ernulf was right behind him.

"That's what's strange, Sir Bascot," the soldier replied. "The man said the lad was on the other side of the Fossdyke, going into the forest. What would Gianni have been doing out there?" The man-at-arms gave the Templar a sidelong glance. "It's possible the carter is mistaken. It may have been some other boy he saw. He doesn't know Gianni by sight, only said he'd seen a youngster that looked about his size."

The carter was waiting with his load of wood just inside the entrance to the west gate. He was sitting patiently, leaning against the pile of logs at his back, chewing on a piece of straw. When he saw Bascot, he straightened a little, but did not get down from his seat.

"The boy you saw, what did he look like?" Bascot asked shortly.

"Didn't get a right good look at him, sir. Wouldn't have noticed him at all except it seemed strange for a little lad like that to be outside the city walls all on his own at this time of year." The man chewed ruminatively on the straw, not noticing Bascot's impatience. "He wasn't very tall," he finally said, "and was as skinny as a sapling. About ten or eleven years old, I'd say. Had a peculiar hat on his head, like a soldier would wear on a march in cold weather. Couldn't see what he looked like 'cause the hat hid his face and hair. But he was skipping along right merrily and kept looking over his shoulder."

"What time of the morning was this?" Bascot asked, sure from the description of Ernulf's hat that the boy the carter had seen had been Gianni.

The carter looked up at the sky. "A little earlier than it is right now. I was just coming with my load; allus do on the same two days of the week. The wood's part of my fee as tenant to Lady Nicolaa. . . ."

"Did you see him go into the forest?" Bascot interrupted, impatient with the man's slowness.

The carter shook his head. "Had no reason to watch him, did I? He was headed that way and I gave him a passing glance, that's all. I had to get on with my load, the traffic on the Fossdyke gets heavier the later it gets, and I got work to do when I get back to my byre. Besides, it was Martinmas; there was to be a feast later on, I didn't want to miss that. And right enjoyable it was, too; my old pig came up with a good load of fat. I can still taste the tripe my old woman made from his innards, well toothsome it was. . . ."

Bascot turned to Ernulf, ignoring the man's pleasurable reminiscences. "I'll need a couple of your men, Ernulf, to search the woods. Why he was out there, only the Good Lord knows, but if he spent the night in the forest, he will be in dire straits from the cold. I pray to God he's still alive."

Ernulf nodded and called to a couple of his men to follow as he and Bascot started off for the stables at a run.

It was as mounts were being saddled that a priest from St. Mary Crackpole, a church at the lower end of Lincoln town near the Stonebow gate, came puffing up to the door of the stables. He was young, with a round face and a head of hair that was pale and sparse. In his hand he clutched a small and dirty piece of parchment, and he struggled to catch his breath as he leaned his portly frame on the edge of the wide stable door.

"Sir Bascot? I am Father Michael, priest of St. Mary Crackpole. I have come to see you on a matter of importance."

Bascot barely paid the man any attention, thinking the cleric had come on some errand to do with the housing of guests during the king's visit. Many of the visitors were to be given beds in properties owned by the church. "I have no time now, Father," Bascot replied. "Go to the hall. Lady Nicolaa's steward or her *secretarius* will be pleased to attend you."

The priest shook his head. "No, you do not understand, I have a message, given to one of my parishioners this morning. It is for you. And I believe it is urgent."

The priest paused and inhaled deeply as his breathing slowed. "It mentions the brigand Sheriff Camville is holding prisoner, and a boy. Perhaps the lad that one of the men-at-arms on the gate told me you are looking for."

Bascot's head snapped up and Ernulf spun around from

where he was adjusting the girth on one of the horses. "What is the message?" Bascot said tersely.

"It is a written one. Here, on this piece of parchment." The priest held out the soiled scrap of vellum to the Templar.

Bascot unrolled it. Only a few words were printed in the middle of the torn and jagged square, the writing ill formed and the ink thin and splodgy.

If you wants the boy alive bring Fulcher to the crossing by the oak at None. Come alone.

At the bottom was a rough sketch of a wolf's head.

"Who gave this to you?" Bascot asked the priest.

"As I said, one of my parishioners—"

"A man known to you?" Bascot's tone was sharp and short.

The priest nodded. "It was handed to him this morning as he entered the church for Mass. The man who entrusted it to him said it was to be given to one of the priests, and given quickly, as there was a life at stake. He made particular mention that the priest who received it was to be told that it was for the Templar monk who serves the sheriff of Lincoln. My parishioner naturally thought that someone was ill, maybe dying, perhaps one of your brethren. He brought it to me directly."

The monk looked uncomfortable as he saw the anger building in Bascot's face. "It was unsealed, Sir Bascot. I did not know its import when first I read it, but the message itself speaks of evil threats. I came as fast as I could."

"What does it say?" Ernulf asked. Since the serjeant was not literate, Bascot read it out and showed him the drawing that had been added. His friend's face hardened with an anger that matched his own.

"The man who gave this to your parishioner, what did he look like?" Ernulf barked at the priest.

"I do not know," the priest admitted. "I was told he was a rough fellow who was standing by the door of the church. After I read the message, I went to look for him, but he was gone."

"Where is this crossing, Ernulf?" Bascot asked the serjeant.

"Can only be the one where the Trent borders the sheriff's chase. There is a slight curve in the river there, to the west. An easterly spur of Sherwood Forest comes down hard on the other side."

Bascot strode to the door, looking up at the sky as he tried to put his thoughts in order. Rain had begun to fall, and the grey lowering clouds that had earlier hung in the sky like dirty pregnant sheep had coalesced into a solid mass the colour of old pewter. It was now late morning, None just a little more that two hours hence. An hour's ride, even in such inclement weather, should bring them to the spot that the message had designated.

Bascot moved back inside the stables. Ernulf, the man-at-arms, the priest and a pair of grooms were all watching him. "Ask Sheriff Camville if I may see him directly, Ernulf, if you would, and also Lady Nicolaa. I will be in the hall directly."

As the serjeant turned to go, Bascot moved as quickly as his leg, now aching from a night without rest and the activities of the morning, would allow, to where the chest that held his belongings stood. Inside, along with his own spare tunic and the only other pair of hose that Gianni owned, was his Templar surcoat. He laid it carefully on the pallet beside the chest before calling to one of the grooms to bring him his helm and shirt of mail from the armoury.

Twenty
✠

GIANNI LOOKED CAUTIOUSLY AROUND HIM. THE CAMP
to which he had been brought was quiet, the trees that encircled the clearing looming overhead in the early morning
gloom like a great ill-fitting ceiling. Wisps of fog drifted
eerily through the branches, the shapes flat as though a giant
hand had pressed them. Sleeping bodies lay everywhere,
some entwined together for warmth, others rolled into a
foetal ball as though wishing never to leave their womb of
sleep. In the middle of the clearing the remains of the fire
that had been lit the night before barely smouldered, only
tiny wisps of smoke reluctantly puffing as the embers underneath finally died.

The boy tried to see if there were any guards posted, but
the darkness was too deep at the edge of the trees. Cautiously he stretched out his legs and, when his movement
was not detected, he tested the security of the rope that
bound his leg to the bole of a nearby tree.

He had been brought here the day before, after the captor
that had scooped him up in the sheriff's chase had run with
him thrown over his back for what seemed to Gianni like a

long distance. Then, after being bundled into a boat and fer-
ried a short way on water, he had been foisted up again on
the shoulder of the man and carried through trees whose
branches had slapped at his back and shoulders before he
was dumped roughly on the ground and the sack that had
covered his head removed.

The clearing had been brighter then, with the fire burning
energetically from well-seasoned wood that emitted little
smoke. Over the flames a carcass of a deer had been roasting, the fat sizzling as it dripped into the fire, sending off a
delicious aroma that caused Gianni's already churning stomach to push bile up into his throat. There had been a lot of
people in the clearing, mostly men, but a few women also,
all roughly dressed and dirty. Little notice was taken of his
arrival until the man that had captured him, and still held
him by the arm, dragged him through the press towards another man who sat up higher than the rest, on a rough chair
carved from wood and decorated with garlands of ivy.

"This is the Templar's servant," his captor said to the man,
and Gianni at last looked up and saw that the person who
had taken him from the forest was one he had seen before,
the day he had gone to the village with his master. It was Edward, the reeve's nephew. "Strolling through the woods all
by himself, he was. I thought as how he might be of some
use to you, Jack. Perhaps get a bit of silver if that Templar
monk wants him back bad enough to pay for his return or, if
not, maybe to use as a servant for yourself."

The man in the chair had looked down at the prize he had
been brought. He was not a big man, but his appearance
caused Gianni to feel a frisson of fear. Like the chair, his
person was decorated with stems of ivy, most of the leaves
brown and curling. The vines were wound around his arms,
threaded through his belt, and a circle of them was woven
into the pointed cap he wore on his head. His face, like most
of the other men who had started to crowd around, was
bearded, his a thick dense thatch of a dark golden colour that
curled tight to his jaw and down his neck until it disappeared
beneath the ragged collar of the scarred leather jerkin he
wore. From beneath eyebrows that were as scant as his beard

was thick, eyes of dark hazel looked at Gianni, the intense stare reminding the boy of one of the hawks in the mews at Lincoln castle when it was inspecting a gobbet of meat offered by the falconer.

"The Templar's servant, you say, Edward?" the man called Jack said. His voice was quiet, but there was menace in it.

"That's right, Jack. I thought him a right good catch to bring you." Edward's voice was puffed up with pride in his accomplishment.

Jack leaned back, his hand resting on the thick oak staff that leaned against the arm of his chair. For a long moment he stared at Edward, and the silence grew in the clearing as he did so. Gianni could sense fear begin to grow in the man beside him, evidenced in the nervous twitch of Edward's fingers where they gripped his arm.

Still the man called Jack did not speak, and Edward began to stutter nervously. "I didn't do wrong, did I, Jack? No one followed us, I swear. I thought you'd be pleased, but if you're not, I'll get rid of him. He'll just disappear, like he was never born."

When his words brought no response, Edward dragged Gianni to his feet and would have thrown him back over his shoulder, but suddenly the stave that had been carelessly lying beside Jack's chair moved so swiftly it was a blur. It came up in his hand and cracked down on the back of Edward's neck with a blow that brought the reeve's nephew to his knees, Gianni tumbling down with him, almost into the fire.

"I did not tell you to bring him here," Jack said, "but now that you have, you'll wait my command to take him away."

Edward nodded as best he could while he tried to regain his senses. Struggling to his feet he mumbled, "Aye, Jack. I'm sorry."

Around him the crowd of people relaxed, some of the men shaking their heads in disapproval of Edward's folly, others whispering together, smiles on their faces. Gianni could see now that there were children amongst them, including a couple of small ones still in their mother's arms.

All of the people—men, women and children—were clad in rags of one sort or another, most of them layers of old clothing tied on with other scraps of cloth, or bits of rope; a few more fortunate ones had belts strapped around their middle. Head coverings ranged from hats made from torn pieces of animal fur to crude caps fashioned from the bark of a tree. All the faces were dirty, grimed not so much from lack of water but ingrained in skin that had been exposed to the elements for too long.

Jack's hawk eyes turned to Gianni. "What's your name, boy?" he asked.

Gianni made the sign he had made so often in his life to show that he was mute, lifting his bound hands, then opening his mouth and pointing a finger to it while shaking his head.

"Can't speak, eh?" Jack said. "But since you've still got a tongue in there, it's the way you were born, not from punishment."

Gianni nodded. He could never remember being able to speak, although he had tried to do so many times, and had finally accepted that he never would, that God had fashioned him that way at birth. Jack looked at the boy's clothing, noticing the serviceable wool of his hose, the thick padding of his tunic and the stout boots on his feet. Ernulf's hat was no longer on Gianni's head; it must have come off when Edward had grabbed him, or was still in the sack that had been thrust over his head. Gianni cringed. He knew well enough that, even without the hat, his clothes were far better than those worn by most of the people crowded around him, and he also knew it would be the work of moments for him to be stripped bare and his garments distributed amongst the women for their own use or for that of their children.

Jack's mouth split into a grin as he saw the fear in Gianni's eyes, revealing broken teeth that were the same colour as his beard, a dirty yellow. "Frightened, aren't you, boy?" he said. "And well you might be, for we've no liking for those who live at ease behind castle walls and dine off fine meats, even if they are only servants." He leaned forward, his head thrusting down, reminding Gianni again of a predatory bird.

"You'll do well to remember that while I decide what to do with you. Try to run and I'll give you to the wolves. After we've removed your finery, that is."

This remark brought guffaws of laughter from the people crowded at Jack's side, including Edward, who had now recovered from the blow he had been given and was joining in the merriment. Jack motioned to one of the men beside him. "Take the boy over to the edge of the clearing and truss him. Not too tight, mind. We don't want to damage his clothes for those that will have them. Eventually."

Another burst of laughter followed this remark as Gianni was roughly hauled up and dragged to a tree on the far side of the fire. A rope was tied to his leg and fastened to the tree and his feet were bound with pieces of well-worn leather to keep company with his tied hands. There he was left, hungry and thirsty, while his captors sat just a few yards away from him, eating and drinking their fill as they discussed his fate.

"YOU *WILL* TELL ME WHO HE IS, JOANNA, FOR YOU WILL rue the consequences if you do not!" Melisande seized her daughter's arm and shook her, then threw her down onto a wide padded settle that stood against the wall. The girl stayed where she was, lying on her side and rubbing her arm, looking up at her mother with eyes filled with scorn.

"What of the identities of your own lovers, mother? You are not so free with their names as you wish me to be with mine, are you? Even when my father was alive you had others to warm your bed. I saw you, and more than once." The girl threw up her head and glared at Melisande. "Like mother, like daughter. I have my secrets, too. And I will keep them."

Melisande drew back her hand and slapped her daughter across the face, just once, but hard. The mark of her fingers stood out on the girl's flushed cheek like a stain of blood. Then the goldsmith's widow shook her head and moved away from the girl, walking across the room to take a seat in one of the padded chairs near the fire. She leaned her head back on the softness at her neck and heaved a sigh.

"You do not know your own foolishness, girl," she said heavily. "Yes, I gave my favours to men other than my husband, but not before I was married, and never recklessly even then. I want you to marry well, and no decent man will take a bride who has tossed her skirts for all and sundry, not even if I dower you with all the gold I possess."

"I have not lain with 'all and sundry' as you put it!" Joanna expostulated. "I am not a harlot!"

Melisande shook her head sadly, rose from her chair and went over to her daughter. Gently she placed her hand under Joanna's chin and lifted it, and then looked straight into her eyes. "Not a harlot, perhaps, but not a newly plundered virgin, either."

When Joanna would have protested, Melisande continued, "I can see it in your eyes, girl. In the way you walk, the manner in which you lace your gown. You have lain with a man and more than once or twice." She shook her head again. "I would not deny you your pleasure, Joanna; I only wish you had possessed the sense to wait until you had a husband to shield your good name before you indulged your fancy. There will come a day when you will regret what you have done, and regret it dearly."

Her mother's words, so softly spoken, took the anger from Joanna's face, and her defiance as well. Sullenly she hung her head and looked at the floor.

Melisande turned and walked to the chamber door. There she stopped and turned. "I hope you have not been foolish enough to fall for the glib persuasions of a man who is already married or, God forbid, one of those prancing young lords up at the castle. But, whatever the case, you can tell your paramour that if there is a bastard child I will not acknowledge him, or her, as my grandchild," she said. "If you do not give up your lover, I will send you to a nunnery. The choice is yours."

GERARD AND NICOLAA WERE WAITING FOR BASCOT when he entered the hall. They had been engaged in a conference with Tostig and a couple of other Camville foresters when Ernulf had come to tell them what had transpired. Immediately they had broken off their discussion and given their attention to the plight of Gianni and the involvement of the sheriff's prisoner, Fulcher.

The sheriff was pacing back and forth when Bascot joined them, his face drawn into a scowl as Nicolaa greeted the Templar and offered her commiserations for the abduction of his servant.

"It must be outlaws that have the boy, for the drawn likeness of a wolf's head can mean nothing else. Ernulf tells me Gianni was seen alone, going into my husband's chase. It must have been while he was on that journey he was captured. But what was his purpose for such a venture?"

"I do not know the answer to that, lady," Bascot replied. "I only know that I must get him back. To do that I must ask that you release Fulcher and let me take him to the place they have designated."

"Never!" Camville growled. "Even if you give them what they want, they will kill the boy anyway, and you as well, if they can. It is a risk that cannot be taken."

"Sir Gerard," Bascot said, "I ask this as a boon from you. The boy is very important to me, more than a servant. He is like my own son." The admission cost him dear, for although he had come to realise the depth of his feelings for Gianni, he had never before admitted it out loud, even to himself. "If you will grant me this favour, I pledge that I will leave the Templar Order and become your liegeman. It is all I have to offer; if you would have my life I would surrender that as well." To reinforce his sincerity, Bascot dropped to one knee and bowed his head.

Nicolaa, knowing how much the words had cost this reticent and solitary man, stepped forward and laid her hand on Bascot's shoulder. "There is no need to humble yourself, de Marins. You have already given my husband and myself more service than was required for your pallet and sustenance. While we would relish your joining our retinue permanently, neither Gerard nor I would wish you to do so under duress."

She turned to her husband, who had stopped his restless

pacing and was standing motionless beside her, a cup of wine forgotten in his hand. "Do you agree, husband?"

Slowly, Camville nodded. "I shall give you your boon, Templar, without restraints," he said. "You shall have Fulcher as bait for this carrion, but you will not go alone. Ernulf and I will follow, with some of the castle guard."

As Bascot made to protest, the sheriff held up his hand. "We will keep out of sight and wait to see what they do. If they have the boy and truly intend to exchange him for the outlaw . . ." Camville shrugged and did not finish the sentence. "Once your servant is safe we will take the brigand back and perhaps catch a few more of these wolf's heads in the doing of it." He looked up from under his heavy brows at Bascot. "If they do not have the boy, they will already have killed him, de Marins, and will attempt to kill you also, once they have their confederate. We will be there to see that does not happen."

There was a resolution in the sheriff's face that told Bascot he would brook no argument and the Templar had to admit that Camville's reasoning was probably correct. He knew he would not get the imprisoned brigand to use as a ransom unless he agreed to the sheriff's plan, and if Gianni was dead—he felt his breath squeeze in his chest at the thought—he would wish to kill as many of the outlaws as his sword could reach, Fulcher amongst them. He nodded in acquiescence to Gerard Camville.

It was not even the half part of an hour later when Bascot set out. The rain was now falling heavily, being driven in gusty sheets by a fitful wind that blew from the northeast. Fulcher, hands bound and a rope around his neck, was mounted on a sumpter pony, with Bascot astride the grey he was accustomed to use, and holding the end of the rope that secured the brigand. Beside the Templar, Tostig rode, bow slung across his shoulder and arrows in his waist quiver, to guide Bascot to the spot by the river that was to be the place of the meeting.

Behind, in the bailey, Gerard Camville was mounting the big black stallion that was his destrier. The sheriff was in full armour, as was his brother William, who was waiting for one

of the grooms to lead out his own deep-chested roan. Another knot of riders was also gathering—Richard Camville,
Ernulf, Roget, a handful of men-at-arms, and the squires
Alain and Renault. Bascot gave Fulcher a prod in the back
with the point of his unsheathed sword and the outlaw, still
weak from the beating he had received from Roget's men,
kicked the pony into a shambling trot, preceding the Templar out of the west gate. The sheriff watched them go,
waited until he heard the cathedral bells ring out the hour of
Sext, then spurred his horse to follow.

Twenty-one

⊷

IT HAD BEEN ALMOST DUSK BEFORE THE OUTLAWS gathered around the man in the chair ceased talking. Gianni had watched them intently. He could not hear what they were saying but the days he had spent begging in Palermo had made him practiced in recognising people's attitudes from the way they stood or gestured with their hands. From the manner in which a person walked, or held their head, it was possible to judge if they would be generous or not, if they would be angry at being importuned or merely ignore the outstretched hand with blank eyes, if they would look guilty for being without alms to give, or self-satisfied because they had more than the beggar. The same had been true of the other rag-wrapped urchins with whom he had shared the small piece of wharf where he had slept and taken shelter. Some had been fearless in their harassing of the merchants, ship owners and sailors that worked or came to trade at the wharf, knowing which ones would be pricked by shame and throw a coin and which ones would respond with a curse or the kick of a boot. But others, Gianni among them, had been too small and frightened to try such tactics, resorting to a helpless whine or cringing tears to wring the price of a piece of stale bread for their efforts. Even amongst themselves it had taken stealth and guile to hide any successful result of their begging. They were friends only when all were hungry. As soon as any alms were given, the recipient would quickly secrete the pittance he had been lucky enough to gain or, if not quick enough to hide it, to swallow it, whether bread or coin, knowing that, if it were the first, it would fill his stomach and if it were the second, it would be safe from the rough clutching hands of the others until he could void it in secret.

It had taken Gianni only a few moments to forget his fear of the dark circle of trees surrounding him and remember those days, and to realise that the outlaws here in the forest were no different from those he had known in the time before the Templar had come. Resolutely he pushed thoughts of wolves and other nameless terrors from his mind and concentrated on studying his captors.

It had been apparent from the first that the man seated on the chair was their leader, even as the burly miserable-tempered boy Alfredo had been the self-appointed captain of the band of urchins in Sicily. And this man was the same type as Alfredo, too, a bully, but clever with it, using sharp words and stinging blows to rule those whose mind and body were not as quick or as strong as his own. The reeve's nephew, Edward, had called the man Jack, but Gianni thought of him in his mind as *Diabolo*, like the devil he had once seen painted on the wall of a small church where he and some of the other smaller boys had sometimes begged food from the priest in the chapel. The picture had imprinted itself on Gianni's mind. It had been just inside the entrance, a painting of a huge figure grinning down at the writhing bodies of the unshriven souls at his feet while he poked them with the pitchfork he held in his hand. Curling spirals of flame had risen up around the satanic figure, enfolding the head and body in loops and whirls of hell-smoke, just as the man called Jack was wreathed in the strange winding of stems and dead leaves. And, just like the *Diabolo* in the mural, this Jack pushed and prodded at the people gathered round him with his heavy staff, chastising as he saw fit and commanding their obedience.

Finally one of the brigands had been summoned to come forward to where Jack was seated. Reverently the man had lifted up a little box and taken from it a small pot and quill, and a piece of dirty and much-scraped parchment. The paper and quill he handed to Jack, then laid the box carefully across the leader's knees and held the pot ready while Jack dipped the pen and wrote on the parchment. The band of outlaws looked on admiringly as Jack penned some words on the paper. Gianni doubted whether any of them were literate, which was another means whereby Jack had them in his thrall. Then the paper was rolled up and given to one of the band. Jack pulled him close and whispered in his ear; the man had nodded and hurried off into the forest.

There had been some cheering from the group as the man left, and Jack had called loudly for ale, and the male members of the band had joined him eagerly in a cup while the women began to serve up to their menfolk and children the meat that had been roasting over the fire, dishing it out wrapped in some of the dead brown leaves that littered the forest floor.

Gianni's mouth had watered as he watched the meat being torn from the skewers that held it. He was both hungry and thirsty, and felt fear clutch his bowels again as he wondered what they were going to do with him. The Templar would be searching for him, he knew, but he would not look in the forest. He would look through the castle, then the town, but it would not occur to him to look outside the city walls. Why had he been so foolish as to think of going to the village? He had betrayed his master's trust and now he would pay for it. He wondered if he would be starved, for there seemed little food to go around. If the note that had been sent was to ask Sir Bascot for payment for his return, it would not profit them to feed him. If the Templar agreed to pay the ransom, a day or two without the food they could ill spare would not harm him, and if Sir Bascot refused to pay, then the food would be wasted on a useless hostage. Gianni shivered. Would they kill him if his master would not pay?

Or would they, as Edward had suggested, make him a servant to *Diabolo* Jack? With visions of that thick stave coming down on his back every time he failed at some task, Gianni was not sure which fate would be worse.

RICHARD DE HUMEZ LOOKED ACROSS AT HIS DAUGHTER, then swivelled his eyes to meet those of his sister-by-marriage. His expression was a mixture of anger and fear. He had come to Nicolaa's chamber at Alinor's request, had waited with impatience while some matter of great urgency was dealt with by Nicolaa in the hall, then had sat in growing amazement as he had been told the reason why Alinor had asked for this private meeting.

His daughter's voice broke into his racing thoughts. "I know, father, that you were not in favour of John taking the throne and would have preferred Arthur. I heard you saying so, to mother. I even heard her trying to dissuade you from any rash action that could jeopardize your position with the king. You were not quiet. If I heard you, so could others."

De Humez looked from one to the other of the two women. They were more alike than just niece and aunt. His wife, Petronille, Nicolaa's sister, was dark, as he was himself. But Alinor had inherited the redness of hair and high colour of her Haye antecedents. She had also inherited their stubborn and outspoken high-handedness, and was as he remembered Nicolaa to be in her youth, before time had moulded her forthright temper to include a modicum of diplomacy. He thanked God it had been the soft-spoken second Haye sister who had been chosen for him to take as a wife, even if her dower had been much smaller. He wished that Petronille was here now; she would have calmed the stormy scene he could see coming before it had even begun.

"What you heard being discussed between your mother and myself was private, Alinor. It was an opinion expressed by many nobles at the time, not only by me, and has nothing to do with you. I am greatly displeased that you have bothered your aunt with such ramblings."

De Humez tried to put as much anger as he could into his

voice, but knew his headstrong daughter would take little notice, and tried to console himself with the knowledge that Alinor believed she was protecting him rather than putting him in danger.

"Alinor has not been a bother to me, Richard," Nicolaa said, trying to speak calmly in an attempt to soothe the ruffled feathers of her sister's husband. "She is only concerned to protect her family—which is my family also—against any slander that may arise. The king has a long ear for any hint of unrest about him. I would that he heard none about any of our kin and will do whatever I can to ensure that he never does."

Slightly mollified, de Humez took a sip of watered wine from the cup that Nicolaa handed him, and said, "There is no rumour to forestall. I have no connection now, and never did have, with any support for Arthur supplanting John."

Nicolaa took a mental breath and forced herself to smile. She had a liking for her brother-by-marriage even though she knew him to be querulous and vacillating. He was an indulgent husband and father, but he was also indecisive and prone to be sanctimonious. His would be a willing ear for any plot that would increase his own aggrandisement, as long as he felt the danger to his position would not be too great. A little like King John, she reflected briefly, the very monarch de Humez, she was sure, had not willingly supported. This time her smile came naturally. She had an affection for John, too.

"It is the matter of Hubert's death, Richard. Even though Gerard has done his best to ascribe the squire's murder to outlaws, there is much rumour being bruited abroad that it was for political purposes—that Hubert was privy to a plot against John and was killed because he threatened to expose those involved. That is why Alinor came to me, and why I asked to have speech with you. If you voiced your . . . opinion . . . about John to anyone other than Petronille, if you even so much as hinted that you would be willing to support a plan that would topple him from the throne, you could be implicated. Not only in Hubert's death, but in a treasonous plot."

As the blood drained from de Humez's face, Nicolaa allowed her voice to stiffen. "I am fortunate enough to have the king's favour. That is due to the proven loyalty of my family and myself in the past. But my husband, as you know, does not have the same regard from the king. If it were to be suggested that not only one husband of the Haye sisters, but two, are rumoured to be disloyal . . ." She let her voice trail off deliberately, watching de Humez closely, then spoke with tones of ice. "Are you sure that you have not spoken of what you call only 'an opinion' to any other than Petronille? That any knowledge that Hubert might have had of treason would not have included your name? Be very sure, Richard, of your answer."

De Humez shook his head, put down his wine cup with shaking hands. His face was ashen. "I swear to you Nicolaa, I have not, would not—I am loyal to King John. On my oath, I swear it."

Nicolaa observed him closely as he made his protestation; saw the concern in Alinor's face as she, also, searched her father's expression in an attempt to detect the sincerity of his words. It was possible de Humez was telling the truth, but had there been a slight falter in his voice? Had he been unwise enough to let an indiscretion slip in company that was dangerous? Some word that perhaps was not meant, but could be taken as truth?

"I believe you, Richard," she said at last. "And I will do my best to protect your name, and that of my sister and her children. But remember this, just as a candle carelessly dropped on a scrap of straw can be the beginning of a conflagration, so can one ill-judged word bring ruin on the one that utters it. If any hint of this comes to the king, and your name is involved, let us pray that his affection for the Hayes will prompt him to disregard it."

GIANNI HAD WORKED ALL NIGHT AT THE KNOTS THAT had bound his feet and hands. Under cover of darkness and the blanket of mouldy leaves that had been thrown over him he had managed to untie them, then refasten them with a loose wrap that would easily slip undone. He knew that it would be useless for him to try to escape into the forest. He did not even know in which direction to run if he had the chance. But he had learned what they intended to do with him, and he would be ready if an opportunity for escape presented itself.

Carefully he rolled onto his side and looked through the gloom towards the dying embers of the fire. Only one man sat awake, the small skinny one who had brought him some food earlier and was now keeping watch over the encampment. He had said his name was Talli and even though he had tried to be rough with his captive, he had seemed to have some sympathy for him. Gianni had given him the wide-eyed scared look he had used so often when he had been a helpless urchin begging for food, and Talli had softened slightly, bringing him a tiny strip of venison to chew on and a wooden bowl of water to drink. It had been as Gianni was gnawing thankfully on the meat that Talli had hunkered down beside him and told him what was to be his fate.

"Hungry, weren't you, boy?" the brigand had said as he watched Gianni devour the food. "Well, if all goes right, you should be back in the castle by this time tomorrow and able to get yourself some better fare."

Gianni had given him a tremulous smile and put a hopeful look on his face. The outlaw had nodded. "Yes, that's right. If your master does what he's told, then that's what'll happen."

Talli had leaned closer to Gianni, his eyes gleaming out from the dirt that stained his flesh. "Green Jack's a clever one, he is. See, him and Fulcher don't like each other. Fell out over Fulcher not wanting to join Jack's band when we first come to Sherwood. Well, now Fulcher's in the sheriff's gaol, and the rest of us come here to Jack, so there's no grudge anymore, see. And if Jack can get Fulcher free, then he can come here as well. Be Jack's man, like. And Fulcher's a good man to have. He has a right true aim with a bow and there's not a fear of man or beast in him. Ah, I'll be glad to see him again."

Talli had fallen silent then and Gianni had ducked his

head and given him another imploring look. In response the outlaw had patted his shoulder and said kindly, "Don't worry. Your master will come for you, Jack's sure of that. Edward said the Templar values you highly. He's bound to come. All he has to do is bring Fulcher to Sherwood and then Jack'll change you for him. That's what Jack wrote on the parchment."

A look of wonder came over Talli's face. "Imagine that, being able to scribe words." The outlaw had leaned close to Gianni. "No one knows where Jack come from, but if he can do that he must have been more than just a serf, mustn't he? Perhaps he was the son of a merchant or even a cleric." The little brigand shook his head. "His crimes must have been serious ones for him to have ended up here."

Talli had said no more, just thrown the leaves over Gianni, and then taken up his vigil by the fire. Gianni had curled up, pretending sleep as he worked at the knots. Whatever happened tomorrow, he would ensure he was as prepared as possible for any chance that came to escape from the clutches of *Diabolo* Jack.

IN BALDWIN'S CHAMBER OSBERT PACED ABOUT EXCITedly as he told his friend about Gianni being taken hostage by outlaws and how the Templar was going to try to get him back.

"The sheriff has taken a force of men-at-arms to assist Sir Bascot, and Sir William, Alain and Renault have gone as well. Ah, I wish I were old enough to have joined them." Osbert almost danced with glee as he pictured the battle that he was sure would take place on the banks of the Trent.

"It will be a great coup if they can get Sir Bascot's servant back and capture some of the outlaws as well," Baldwin agreed, his pale face shining as he, too, envisaged a clash between the two forces. "I hope Alain has a chance to show his mettle," he added. "It would make Alys so happy to think that her brother has proven his worth. She has had much lately to plague her. . . ."

He broke off, realising that he had almost given away the

secret about Alain and Renault's absence on the night of Hubert's death but, to his surprise, Osbert did not question the unspoken words. Instead he came and placed his hand on his friend's shoulder. "It is alright, Baldwin. All of us pages and squires know about the suspicion that has fallen on Alain and Renault. We made Hugo tell us when Rufus saw them going into Lady Nicolaa's chamber and Hugo was waiting outside."

"They didn't do it, you know, Osbert," Baldwin asserted. "They swore to me on a holy relic that they were innocent. No one would endanger their immortal souls with such a lie."

Osbert gave his friend a comforting grin. "Of course not, Baldwin. I am sure they told you the truth."

Footsteps sounded outside the door and a servant entered, bringing a round wicker basket full of charcoal to feed the brazier that was kept constantly burning in Baldwin's chamber. As the man deposited the receptacle on the floor, Osbert gave de Humez's son a covert glance. He hoped his friend was right and that Alain and Renault were innocent, even if it was only so that Baldwin's faith in human nature should not be destroyed. But privately the young page doubted that the two squires were free from guilt. Unlike Baldwin, he knew that if there was enough at stake, men would swear on the most holy of relics, be they saints' bones or the blood of Christ, and still not tell the truth.

Twenty-two

⊹I⊹

FULCHER COULD BARELY KEEP UPRIGHT ON THE BACK OF the pony as they approached the place designated for the exchange for Gianni. He was a strong man, but the beating given him by Roget's men, combined with the distance they had travelled through the needle-sharp pricks of rain, had rendered his body almost useless. Only the point of Bascot's sword nudging the space between his shoulder blades had kept him from sliding to the ground.

Finally, a low word of warning from Tostig gave Bascot the signal to bring his mount to a halt. The forester moved his horse close to the Templar and pointed through the mist of rain. There, a few score yards distant, was the river and, at the water's edge, a large oak tree, its branches bare of leaves.

"That is the place, Sir Bascot," the forester said. "I should leave you here. The instruction was for you to be alone when you brought the brigand." Tostig gave a furtive glance over his shoulder. Behind them the trees were thin, with a stand of coppiced hazel crouching like a hunkered dwarf at their base. Nearby, a few desiccated red berries still clung to the branches of a rowan tree, providing the only splash of colour on an otherwise desolate landscape. Downstream, beyond the oak, a willow tree curved gracefully on the eastern bank of the Trent as it wriggled slightly in its course to the Humber estuary. No horses or riders could be seen. Across the river the thick mass of forest was silent.

"I am sure the sheriff is not far behind and will put men both above and below the spot where the oak grows," the forester said. "Give him a little time to get them into position, then move up. I will go and join them. May God grant you good fortune."

With these abrupt words the forester turned his horse and within a moment was gone, the rain-darkened flank of his horse disappearing like a wraith into the curtain of mist.

Fulcher, who had finally tumbled from the pony when they halted, knelt motionless on the ground, head hung on his chest and breath coming in great shuddering gulps. He got reluctantly to his feet when Bascot prodded him with his sword. The Templar felt no pity for the man; his whole being was intent on freeing Gianni, on discovering if the boy was safe and well. His mind dare not dwell on the possibility that the lad could be injured or dead and might perhaps be lying deep in Sherwood for the wolves to find. He thought only of the boy as he had last seen him, alive and happy, and concentrated on keeping that image in front of him.

As they neared the tree, Fulcher stumbled forward on his feet, leaving the pony behind. Bascot scanned the forest on the other side of the river as best he could, cursing the loss of half his vision. The oak was dripping moisture onto the sodden mass of fallen leaves at its base; the very air was drenched with wetness. The river itself was in full spate, water rushing in tiny wavelets against the drooping grasses and reeds at its edge as the flow in midstream eddied into small currents that broke and ran before they were fully formed. Bascot knew that the Trent was a river that had a tidal bore which had the capability of becoming frightening at full intensity. When it rose to its peak it was called the Aegir, after a Norse sea giant, and he had been told of the damage it could do. Although the bore usually only swelled to full power in the spring, it had been known to happen after a heavy rainfall, and he prayed that it would not let loose such a monster today, not if he was to get Gianni across from the other side.

When they reached the base of the tree, Fulcher once again fell to his knees, then rolled over onto his side and lay like a man dead. He had not spoken one word throughout the journey, had not seemed interested in his fate then, nor did he now, with closed eyes and scant regard for the water that streamed down upon his bruised and ragged figure. Bascot eased his horse away from the brigand, the better to see around the trunk of the huge tree, and flexed the fingers of his left hand before easing the strap on his shoulder that bore the weight of his shield. Water dripped from the end of the nose guard on his helm, running in streams from the rim of the conical steel cap he wore over his hood of mail. He felt the dampness of moisture that had gathered under his eye-patch and shook his head to free it and his sighted eye from obstruction. His surcoat was wet through, only the padded leather gambeson he wore underneath his hauberk saving his skin from the dankness, and raindrops glistened on the hilt of his sword and the mane of his horse. The animal also shook its head, and emitted a loud snort in protest at the weather, but it made no other movement except for an impatient lift and kick of a hind leg, after which it stood still, seeming as wretched as its surroundings.

For nearly half the part of an hour Bascot stood there, watching and listening. The river was narrow at this point, perhaps thirty or forty yards across, and looked shallow. Bascot thought it was likely to be fordable here, the place having perhaps been used in the past for toll passage and so was the reason it had been called a crossing in the note sent by the brigands who had Gianni. His thought was prompted by the remains of a raft-like construction standing near the river's edge, a collapsed pile of broken planks from which a short hank of rope, ancient and rotting, lay coiled in the reeds. Nonetheless, traversing the narrow expanse of water might soon prove difficult for, as time passed, the roar of the river grew in magnitude and the rush of the current swifter, as though it was in turmoil. Then, through the growl of angry water, the Templar heard what sounded like a shout and he saw a movement among the trees opposite him.

"Ho! Templar!" The call came from a man standing at the edge of the screen of trees. He was dressed in murky brown and had a bow strung and at the ready in his hands.

Bascot raised his arm to show that he had heard and edged his horse closer to the bank.

"Bring Fulcher over," the outlaw called to him. "We will give you the boy once our comrade is safe on this side."

Bascot took his time in answering. Behind the lone man he could discern what seemed to be the shapes of one or two other men, but they were well concealed in the trees and he could not be sure that what he saw was anything more than the blurring of tangled bushes distorted by the screen of rain.

Finally he made an answer. "Where is my servant? I will do nothing until I see him alive and well."

A few moments of silence passed before there was some stirring in the undergrowth and two figures appeared at the edge of the clear space where the archer stood. Bascot recognised one as Edward, the nephew of the reeve at the village where he had questioned the dairymaid. The other was Gianni, his hands tied in front of him and his arm firmly held in the grasp of the reeve's nephew. It appeared his feet had been hobbled also, for he stumbled as he came into sight and moved forward with small hesitant steps.

Bascot felt his stomach contract at the sight of the boy. He looked so small and slight beside the bulk of his captor, his head bare, curls a dark wet rumpled mass and eyes peering intently in Bascot's direction, as though he could send him a message with his mind.

Bascot nodded once, then tugged on the rope that was tied to the brigand lying on the ground. Fulcher groaned and struggled to his feet, then spoke softly.

"Templar, it is not me that Green Jack wants; it is you and the fine ransom you will bring. Do not trust him. Once I am on the other side, he will slit my throat and take you captive. Have a care."

Bascot looked down at the outlaw. "Green Jack? Is he the leader of these men? The one who sent me the note?"

Fulcher nodded. "It can be no one else. This is his stretch of forest."

"I do not understand. You say he will kill you. Are you not a *compagno* to this Green Jack? Why else would he risk such a venture as stealing my servant if he did not value your life?"

Fulcher grinned, his mouth distorted by the lumps and bruises that littered his face. "I do not know how it came about, but I do know that Green Jack values no life but his own. If he lets me live, he knows I will kill him."

The outlaw gave a slight shrug of his shoulders. "It is of no matter to me, Templar. I will either die here or dangling from a rope by order of the sheriff. I would rather have taken Green Jack to hell with me, but if I do not have his company perhaps the Devil will greet me easier." He gave a deep sigh. "It is up to you; do as you will."

Bascot eyed the river. It was a short space across and it looked as though it would not reach the height of his horse's shoulders at the middle. He could drag Fulcher across by securing him to his saddlebow, but the danger came on the other side, where he would be surrounded by the outlaws he was sure were secreted in the forest behind Gianni and the men on the bank. For all that he was equipped with mail and sword, if there were too many of them, it was likely he would be overcome. If Fulcher spoke true, and he was the target of this whole escapade, then both he and the boy would be at the mercy of this Green Jack, despite any effort of Camville, or his men-at-arms, to save them. For himself, it would be a matter of fighting, but Gianni would be helpless and, if the brigands were attacked by the sheriff's men, he could easily be killed in the resulting battle.

Bascot looked again at the rotted planks and threadbare rope. The sight reminded him of a day when he had been barely more than a toddler on his father's fief on the south coast of England. There had been a boat that day too, lying on the shingled beach that was not far from the keep that stood high on the headland, a watching post for invaders from the sea. On the day he remembered, he had been with his father and two older brothers. He had been carried aloft on his father's shoulders as they had taken the path down to the beach, but when they had arrived on the shore, he had been placed in the boat and his father had rowed the little craft out a short way into the small bay that curved around the landing place. His two brothers had stood on the strand, watching, their faces alive with merriment. Bascot had not understood their amusement, but recalled how he had joined in their laughter as they watched him being taken out into the midst of the waves that rolled in from the sea.

When they were a short distance from the shore his father had shipped the oars and let the boat drift. He had pulled Bascot up onto his knee and said, "You are a de Marins, Bascot. You come from a long line of ancestors who have fought and earned glory from battles upon the sea. Always our keeps have been within sight and sound of the ocean. It is our protector and, at the same time, our enemy. To be a true son of our line you must live up to our name of de Marins— the mariners—and that means you must learn to be as one with the sea, not only to swim in it, but to feel its strength, learn its comfort and respect its terrors. And there is only one way to do that, my son, and that is to meet it as though in battle, to both conquer it and care for it as though it were your serf."

With these words, Bascot's father had thrown him over the side of the boat and into the water. The Templar still remembered the shock of the waves closing over his head, how he had sunk down, his breath involuntarily held as he watched tiny bubbles of air that had been trapped within the folds of his small tunic float to the surface. Then he had tried to breathe and water had flooded into his nostrils, gushed into his mouth as he had opened it in a vain attempt to take in air, and he had felt the saltiness of the water sting the back of his throat and make his stomach heave. Without thought, he had pushed upwards, pumping his legs furiously in a desperate attempt to reach the light shining on the surface above him. When his head broke through, he took great gulps of air, unconsciously working his arms in conjunction with his legs to keep his body afloat.

As his vision had cleared and his breathing steadied he

had heard his father's great booming laughter. "Well done, my son. You are a true de Marins, just like your brothers. Now you have all fought the sea and made her your servant. She is the hardest enemy you will ever fight, but she is also the greatest ally in all of the world, and you are worthy of her."

After his father had pulled him back into the boat and taken him to join his brothers, Bascot realised that both of them, too, had been subjected to the same treatment. That day he had been proud of himself, and of his family, but in later times he had wondered what his father would have done if he had not been able to swim. Would he have been left to drown, or been saved and then shunned as an outcast?

Bascot looked across at Gianni. He loved the boy like a son. No ordeal was necessary to prove that. Somehow he would get the youngster away from the outlaws and back to the safety of Lincoln castle, even if it cost his own life to do it. He looked once more at the river. Perhaps the trial his father had put him through had not been wasted. At the moment, the river gave the brigands an advantage, but there might be a way that he could use it for his own purposes and so turn the stretch of water, as his father had said, into his ally rather than his foe. A mirthless smile stretched his mouth. How his father would have applauded his notion.

Twenty-three

❖

IN THE PRIVACY OF HER CHAMBER NICOLAA DE LA HAYE was engaged in a diversion that was rare for her. She was pacing. Her thoughts far outstripped her feet as she slowly walked from one side of the room to the other, then back again. Not only was her mind on the rescue of the Templar's servant, but also on her conversation with her son, Richard, the previous evening, as well as the murder of William's squire and the impending visit of King John.

Perhaps the private speech with Richard was the most disturbing. Although he had assured her that John was in an ebullient mood rooted in joy of his new young bride, Isabelle of Angouleme, her son had warned her that the king was as suspicious as ever of those about him. Constantly he probed for information about his vassals, asking questions that barely veiled his mistrust of their pledge of fealty, and often lapsed into a broody silence that made those about him uneasy.

"Of this meeting with the Scottish monarch he can have no cause for alarm," Nicolaa had said to her son. "William is completely cowed. He will keep his pledge to pay homage to John."

"I do not think it is Scotland about which the king frets, Mother, but about his nephew, Arthur. Dead Geoffrey's son was long a competitor for the crown of England and John still sees the boy as a threat. Anyone foolish enough to voice even a whisper that Arthur should have the crown in John's stead will soon lose his head, and it would not be parted from his body in a quick manner, either."

Nicolaa's steps increased their speed as she continued to walk back and forth. There would be little means to keep the death of Hubert from the king's knowledge. It had been done in too spectacular a fashion for the news not to be known to all the inhabitants of Lincoln. And with the tale of his death would come the rumour of the boy's intimacy with a conspiracy that favoured Arthur to take John's place. Nicolaa had much affection for John, but she knew how suspicious he was. Not even his esteem for her could prevent his viewing not only her husband, but also her brother-by-marriage, de Humez, and perhaps even Gerard's brother, William, with distrust. And where John distrusted, he destroyed.

Again and again she went over the squire's murder. The method of the deed was not one she would have attributed to Gerard; a simple sword thrust would have been more in keeping with her husband, and the body left carelessly where it fell. Neither would any of his hired ruffians, like Roget, have acted in a dissimilar way. But she knew how much Gerard hated John. Had he become involved in a plot against the king and Hubert become privy to it? Had her husband ordered the boy despatched to dam up his overflowing mouth?

And her brother-by-marriage, de Humez—was his assurance of innocence in the matter of the boy's death a truthful one? And his attempt to convince her that he was not involved in any treasonous scheme to supplant John—could she believe him? It was difficult to be completely sure. Even William could be considered suspect; perhaps the boy had overheard something in his lord's household and had paid the ultimate price for his snooping. And were the murders of Chard and his sons tied to the squire's death? And if so, how? Had they been privy to the identity of the person who had slain Hubert? Was that the reason that they, in turn, had been killed?

She pondered on the two squires, Alain and Renault. She could see neither of them as murderers. Alain might have given Hubert a terrible beating if he had found him that night, but if either had been intent on killing him, it was more likely to have been done during practice at swordplay, or with a lance. Easy enough to pretend a misjudged stroke had caused his death by accident and both squires were skilled enough at arms to do so. Hubert would have been an easy target if they had been so inclined.

Another thought struck her, just as unpleasant as the last. Could the two squires have left the hall that night with the express purpose of killing Hubert, and were only using the story of his offensive behaviour with Alys as a cover for their real reason for wanting the squire's death? Was it William, instead of her husband and de Humez, who was involved in a plot against the king and the boys knew it? If that was so, then the two squires, mimicking the barons who had murdered the exasperating Thomas à Becket for King Henry, could have reasoned that they were doing their lord a favour by ridding him of the troublesome squire. Henry had professed that he had not been guilty of ordering his barons to kill the archbishop, but few had believed him. Was it possible William was now caught in a similar snare?

Reluctant to accept such a possibility she pushed her mind away from thoughts of treason and once more ruminated on the manner of the squire's death. Perhaps the hanging had not been intended as a warning. Could it be possible that, instead, it spoke of a need for revenge? If the desecration by the birds had been intended, then it had certainly slaked a need to humiliate the boy in death that the murderer might not have been able to achieve while Hubert lived. Or had it only been made to seem so, and the apparent vengeance was in itself misleading?

She sighed in frustration and paused in her reflections, pouring herself a cup of cider spiced with cinnamon, a beverage she preferred to wine. As she sipped it, she thought that her time would be better spent in sending up a prayer for the safe deliverance of de Marins's mute servant than in expending her energies in useless speculation. Resolutely she pushed the matter from her mind and set herself instead to work on composing a letter of welcome to be sent to the Scottish king the following morning.

JOANNA, MELISANDE'S DAUGHTER, WAS IN HER MOTHER'S fine stone house in Lincoln. Melisande was not at home, having left early that morning to attend a meeting of the goldsmith's guild to discuss plans for presenting a gift to King John on his arrival in the town. The servants, too, were all gone on various tasks for their mistress around the city, except for the young girl who tended the brood of hens caged in the yard at the back of the house.

Joanna peered out of one of the two casements that brought in light to a chamber on the upper storey of the widow's home. The room served as her mother's solar and, like the rest of the rooms, was liberally strewn with the expensive tapestries, cushions and furs that Melisande loved. But Joanna had no thought for the comfort that surrounded her. She strode nervously from one window to another, then to a brazier that stood in one corner of the room, heaped with glowing coals, where she warmed her hands with a wringing motion that had more of nervousness in its movement than a wish to bring heat to her cold flesh.

Anxiously she listened for the church bells to ring the hour of None, knowing, as most of Lincoln town did by now, that this was the time when the Templar would be at the riverbank to try to obtain his servant's release. Once she heard the bells, Joanna would go to the castle, for when news came as to whether the exchange of prisoners had been successful, it would first come there. She needed to know that her lover was safe and, despite her mother's warning, did not intend to give him up. Only death could force her to do that.

GREEN JACK WAS PERCHED IN THE TOP OF A TREE SOME little way from the spot on the riverbank where his men were holding the Templar's servant. He had a good vantage point and, despite the bareness of the leafless branches, would not easily be spotted in his clothes of russet brown twined with the half-dead vines. His vision was exceptionally keen, especially for long distances, and he scanned the area surrounding him, looking for the sheriff's men. He knew they would be there, to the north and south of the old oak, but, hopefully, not on both sides of the river. Although he had instructed the Templar to come alone, he had not expected that command to be obeyed, especially when he had no doubt that Gerard Camville would be involved in the rescue. The sheriff would dearly love to capture even a few of Jack's men and there was no doubt as to the fate of any who should be so luckless as to end up in Camville's merciless hands.

Although Green Jack knew the dangers of using the boy as bait, he had been unable to resist the temptation of luring the Templar into the forest. But he had been careful not to stretch the risk to his own person too far. He was some little distance from the crossing he had specified and had sent the men most expendable from his band to be in the forefront of the danger. Berdo, Talli and Edward, the reeve's nephew, were with the boy; the first two Fulcher's men and of no importance, and the last too stupid to be of any further use even if he should not be captured. Jack had given instructions to the archers he had sent with them to withdraw into the forest if it looked as though the plan to capture the Templar was going awry.

The Templar. The thought of having one of the men who wore that hated red cross in his, Jack's, power brought a surge of emotion to his loins that was almost lascivious. How many times had he dreamed that he would one day humiliate one of them, and in just such a manner as they had

done to him so many years ago when he had been no more
than a lad, a stupid young boy who had idolized their holi-
ness, their strength, their dedication. Whenever one or more
of the supposedly virtuous knights had chanced to appear on
the streets of Nottingham where he had lived as a child, he
had rushed to watch them ride by on their gleaming horses,
imagining the valiant deeds they would perform in the Holy
Land, and the infidels they would kill in defence of the pilgrims they protected.

Now his thin lips curled in wry amusement of how feeble-
witted he had been to believe the stories that circled the
Templars like halos of glory. Holy monks who fought for
Christ it was said, but they were no better than mercenary
soldiers, lower even, for what they did was not for monetary
profit, but for love of their own vanity, and to promulgate
their sordid vices. He could still remember the day he had
managed to scuttle through the gates into the yard of the
Templar preceptory in Nottingham, how he had hidden behind some bales of hay and watched a few of the knights at
sword practice. They had seemed like giants to him rather
than mere men, wielding flashing blades of light as the
swords arced up and down, thrusting, cutting, parrying. So
intent on the dazzling display had he been that he had not
heard the brown-robed serjeant approach him from behind,
nor been aware of his discovery until a hand clad in a gaunt-
let of leather had clamped down on his shoulder. Then he
had been swung from his hiding place and tossed out onto
the edge of the practice field as lightly and easily as if he had
been a flea thrown from a dog.

"It seems we have an intruder in our midst," the serjeant
had called, and the knights had ceased their swordplay to
come and look at Jack, who had crunched himself into a fearful ball at the serjeant's feet. From his vantage point, too
frightened to look up, all he could see were the dusty boots of
the men around him, and the hems of their surcoats.

"Is he armed?" one of the knights had asked jocularly.
"You had best search him, Eubold. He might be a Saracen in
disguise, with a scimitar concealed beneath those rags he is
wearing."

"No, no," another knight had said. "He is more likely to be one of their eunuchs, come to see how whole men comport themselves."

Much laughter had followed this, then another knight called, "Perhaps we should see for ourselves. Strip him, Eubold, let us see if he truly has any balls, or if it is as de Limenes says and he has been parted from his manhood."

Jack had tried to struggle to his feet but the serjeant, Eubold, had dragged him up by the hair of his head and quickly divested him of his tunic and hose, then dangled him by his heels in front of the watching knights.

"It seems, lords, that he still has all the equipment God gave him at birth," the serjeant had said, laughing along with the rest as he gave Jack a shake that made his head flop and his senses spin in a sickening circle. Even now, he could still hear their laughter and the scorn with which they had jested about his exposed genitals.

"Ah, well," said the first knight who had spoken. "I did not really suppose he was lacking proof of his manhood, else he would not have been brave enough to sneak in here."

"What shall I do with him, lords?" the serjeant had asked.

"Throw him on the dung heap," answered one of the knights lazily. "Or whatever you will, Eubold. Just make sure he is gone from here and knows beyond doubt that he is not to come into the preceptory again."

The spectacle of his humiliation had now lost the knights' interest and most of them turned away and resumed their sword practice. The serjeant had tossed Jack into the air, catching him by the shoulders as he fell. Then the soldier carried him to the back of the preceptory and flung him, and his clothes after him, into a pile of pig dung that was heaped outside a pen containing about a dozen of the animals. He had watched in amusement as Jack had tried to scramble to his feet and rescue his clothes, the foul-smelling muck sticking to him more and more with every movement. When he had finally pushed himself clear of the heap of excrement, the serjeant had put his boot to Jack's bare arse and kicked him all the way to the door of the compound. There the guards that manned the gate had laughed as he had run out into the street, where passersby had first looked in amazement at the naked lad, then backed off as the smell of the ordure reached them. From a distance they had tittered with amusement as he had struggled into his clothes and run all the way home.

To Jack, that day had been branded in his memory and his adoration for the Templars had turned to hatred. It had also marked the beginning of the time when his life went sour. His father, a seller of mediocre quality parchment, had died the very next week, his only legacy to his youngest son an unfinished teaching of the rudiments of his letters. A few days later his stepbrother, older by some ten years, had decided he did not want to bear the cost of feeding the brat his father had sired in old age, and had thrown Jack out of the family home and told him to fend for himself. Hunger had forced Jack to steal, and then steal again, until a narrow escape from being caught while robbing an angry pie merchant had led him to take refuge in the greenwood. Through all those years, and the ones that followed, he had never forgotten the humiliating incident in the Templar preceptory, or the irrational belief that the Order had somehow been the cause of all his misfortune. How many times had he fervently prayed for heaven to give him an opportunity to take his revenge? Now his prayers had been answered and requital was at hand. And, if providence smiled on him further, not only would he have the Templar in his power, but also that thorn in his side, Fulcher. His mouth stretched into a smile as he contemplated such a coup.

Twenty-four

✦

GODFROI DE TOURNAY HAD NOT ACCEPTED RICHARD
Camville's invitation to join the armed party that was following in Bascot's wake. He had given the condition of his
horse as an excuse for declining. The animal had indeed become slightly lame on the last leg of the journey from
Boston, but Godfroi had checked on him earlier that day and
had found the tenderness in his mount's foreleg almost disappeared. He could, in any case, most probably have secured
the loan of a horse from the Camville stables, but had left
Richard before his friend could offer one.

The real reason he had refused to accompany the sheriff
and his men had been that he had wanted some time alone,
to think. Ever since he had spoken to the Templar and had
been told of the suspicion that Hubert had been involved in,
or had knowledge of, a plot against the king, his mind had
been in a whirl. Although he had vociferously denied the
charge to the Templar, and to Richard Camville when the
sheriff's son had asked about it, both denials had been a lie.
Inwardly he cursed his dead half brother. Hubert had plagued
them all his short life, always whining and complaining, and

now, even in death, his well-remembered nasal voice threatened the peace of his family. Godfroi got up and replenished the wine cup from which he had been drinking with the contents of a flask kept beside the bed in the small cramped chamber he was sharing with Richard. As he took another swallow of the vintage, Godfroi thought back to the time, some months ago, when Hubert had been on a visit to his mother at the de Tournay manor house in Boston. William Camville had often given the boy leave to go home for a short space—most probably glad to be rid of him for a while—but this time neither he nor his brother Ralph had been aware of Hubert's presence until it was too late.

They had been ensconced in an upstairs chamber when he had arrived and it was not until Ralph had gone outside to use the garderobe that they had discovered Hubert lingering outside the door. Their half brother had made out that he had just arrived and been preparing to knock when Ralph had opened the door, but both Godfroi and Ralph had wondered afterwards if he had been listening to their conversation. Hubert's play of innocence had reassured them and they had thought of it no more. But Godfroi was thinking of it now, and cursed his half brother once again.

He got up and strode to the arrow slit high in the wall that served as a window for the chamber. His vantage point looked south, the direction from which King John would come. His thoughts raced, trying to untangle the reason for Hubert's murder. Had the lad, as he and Ralph had at first suspected, eavesdropped on their conversation and discovered that they were privy to a plan being hatched in the northern part of the kingdom to overthrow John and place Arthur on the throne? If that conversation had been the basis for the barely concealed innuendos Hubert had apparently been so fond of spouting, it was likely that the murderer was someone who had also been party to the plot, and had killed their half brother to still his wagging tongue. If that was so, had Hubert been murdered soon enough, before he had revealed Godfroi and Ralph's names to any who would betray them?

Godfroi felt cold sweat break out on his brow, from where it dripped and ran into his eyes, as he thought of what his fate would be if the king became aware of their treachery. That the proposed plot had come to nothing would matter little. John was not like his dead brother, King Richard. He did not have a forgiving nature, nor did he trust lightly. Godfroi swallowed the rest of his wine, then poured himself yet another cup. He must hope the de Tournay brothers' secret had died with Hubert and prayed, with all his heart, that his half brother's murderer would not be caught.

To THE NORTH OF THE OAK WHERE BASCOT WAITED with Fulcher, Alain and Renault were crowded close behind William Camville on the western side of the river. Sherwood was a vast forest, spreading over a good portion of Nottinghamshire, but its eastern edge splayed out like an inkblot, touching the banks of the Trent in more than one place, as it did in the area they were now in, where the forest abutted the river for a stretch of roughly two miles. Its writ was in the province of the sheriff of Nottingham but it was unlikely he would complain about their trespass for, not only was he a friend of Gerard's, he would also welcome the capture of any of the brigands that continually plagued his territory.

The small group led by the sheriff's brother also included Roget, Tostig and the young forester Eadric; the woodsmen having been ordered to accompany them so that they could help guide William's men through the forest. Tostig was mounted, with Eadric riding pillion behind him. Both men carried bows. They had all forded the river just moments before.

"We must try to work our way close to where the Templar is without signalling our presence to the outlaws," William said. "We must catch them before they retreat into the forest. Our mounts will hamper us once we are amongst the trees and we will be sure targets for any arrows loosed from their cover. Are there any trails, Tostig, that we can use?"

"None that I know of, my lord," Tostig answered.

William Camville shook his head in irritation and Renault, who had been studying the stretch of riverbank that wound to the south of where they stood, said, "My lord, the river is shallow as it runs close to the bank on this side. Could we not walk our horses in the water for a space? It would cover any sound of our approach and would get us nearer to the Templar."

William considered this, then asked Tostig how far it was to the spot where Bascot was to take Fulcher.

"A little under half a league, my lord. But the river turns close to the place, and to the outlaws' advantage, for it curves eastwards. If we are in the water, we cannot get too near before we will be seen. And the river deepens at the bank not far from here. It would be treacherous for the horses."

William hunched forward to lean with both hands on the raised front of his saddle and gaze at the turbulent expanse of water. "A good thought, Renault, but unfortunately one we cannot use. We must make our way through the forest and lead our mounts; otherwise, their passage will be heard long before we are seen."

"My lord Camville," Eadric spoke up hesitantly, "I know the woods on this side a little better, perhaps, than Tostig, for I was in the employ of one of the king's agisters for Nottingham before I came to Lincoln."

William swung around to the young woodward. "If you know something that may help us, speak up," he commanded.

Eadric's fair face flushed with embarrassment, but he answered the baron without hesitation. "There is a path, lord, only a little way from where we stand. It is a deer track, but a well-used one. We would still have to lead the horses, but could make much better time than by a winding course through the trees."

"Good man," William said. "That is the way we will go. And we will have to hurry. It will be dusk soon and I would lief have these outlaws secure in our hands before darkness falls. Lead on, Eadric."

BASCOT GAZED ONCE MORE ACROSS THE RIVER AT Gianni. The boy was still staring at him intently, his gaze locked to the place where Bascot stood. The Templar let his eye stay on the boy a moment and, as he did so, he saw

Gianni raise his shoulders in a peculiar hunching motion, then let them drop. As Bascot watched, the boy did it again. The reeve's nephew, Edward, who still had hold of Gianni's arm, shook him for the movement, but the boy defiantly did it again, earning himself a cuff on the ear from his captor. Bascot saw Edward's lips move in what must have been an admonishment to stand still.

Gianni was trying to convey something, Bascot thought. Because the boy was mute, they had long conversed by means of hand or body signals, even after Bascot had taught Gianni to read and write. But this movement was one which he had not used for a long time, not since those early days when the Templar had first come across the boy. It had been an instinctive gesture, both as a measure to sum up courage and, at the same time, a tensing of the muscles to withstand any blow that may have been aimed at him. It had always presaged the lad's intention to run, to flee whatever threatening situation he found himself in. He had done it often in the first days of being in Bascot's company, and it had slowly lessened as the Templar had earned his trust. Afterwards, many weeks later, Bascot had teased him about it, especially when he had given the boy some task that was disagreeable, such as the painstaking job of polishing his mail with an abrasive mixture of sand and vinegar. It had been a long time since he had seen Gianni hunch his shoulders in that particular way, preparing for flight. But he was doing it now, trying to tell his master something. Bascot hoped he was interpreting it correctly.

Bascot hauled on the rope still attached to Fulcher and pulled the outlaw upright. "Can you swim, poacher?" he asked.

The brigand looked up in surprise and nodded.

"How well?" Bascot asked.

"My father was an eeler. I could swim before I could walk."

"And do you know this stretch of the river?"

"As well as the palm of my own hand."

Bascot leaned down. "I will give you your chance to take this Green Jack to hell with you, or to escape, if that is what you prefer." At the look of distrust that appeared on Fulcher's lacerated face, the Templar went on. "I do not give a damn if you were responsible for the squire's death, nor do I care if you take deer that belong to the sheriff, the king, or even God. I care only to get back my servant, unharmed."

Under cover of his shield Bascot withdrew the short dagger he had at his belt and held it up. "This is yours if you do as I say. I will put it in my boot and you may take it when the time is right. Betray me and you will find it in your throat."

Fulcher looked at the face above him, the leather eyepatch glistening with water, the one sighted eye so pale a blue it seemed transparent. Slowly the outlaw nodded in assent. "For a chance to see Green Jack sent to his grave I would face the jaws of hell twice over."

Bascot straightened, a grim smile on his face. "Then tell me the lie of the riverbed as it passes here."

IN THE FOREST ON THE EASTERN BANK OF THE TRENT, Gerard Camville and his men waited. The sheriff was impatient; he had two of his archers stationed near the river's edge, staggered one behind the other, to relay to him what was passing at the spot where the Templar and Fulcher stood, but so far he had only been told of an exchange of words and the appearance of the boy and some of his captors on the far side of the water. Beside him, his son, Richard, felt his father's mood, but he knew his sire's temper. No matter how restless he seemed, he would wait until he gauged the moment right. It was one of Gerard Camville's greatest assets. The powerful coil of anger that seemed to be ever present in his personality was always in danger of erupting, and often did, but on the battlefield he controlled it, having an innate perception of timing and an almost eerie knowledge of the moment when an enemy was weakest.

Suddenly one of the bowmen from the riverbank appeared silently through the trees and made his way to the sheriff's horse. "My lord, the Templar is preparing to take the brigand across the water. He has lashed the outlaw's wrist to his saddlebow and is riding his horse down into the water."

"Hell's teeth," Camville swore under his breath. "Once

he is on the other side, we cannot reach him quickly. I told him to make them bring the boy to him."

"They would not, lord. I heard them refuse." The archer looked up, a slightly puzzled frown on his face. "Lord, I think the Templar must have a plan."

"Why do you think so, man? For the sake of Christ, spit it out." Camville's face had flushed a dangerous red.

The archer remained unperturbed at the harsh words, used as he was to the sheriff's temper. "Because he only made a pretense of tying the outlaw's wrist," he replied. "I could see clearly. He wrapped it, made as if tying a knot, but did not do so. Fulcher can slide himself free at any time."

"The bastard," Camville swore. "If he loses me my captive and does not recover the boy, I'll hang him instead, Templar or no."

"Easy, father," Richard counselled. "De Marins is not a foolish man, nor a cowardly one. We must see what it is he means to do, then assist when it is needed."

"Aye," the sheriff agreed, somewhat reluctantly. "We will wait, but not too long, and from a nearer perch than this." He urged the powerful stallion he rode nearer into the trees along the riverbank, and signalled Ernulf and the band of men-at-arms behind him to follow as quietly as they could. When the sheriff called a halt, they were near enough to the river for a quick charge to bring them through the trees and to the waterside in moments.

The other archer who had been watching at the river's edge came sliding back through the trees. "My lord sheriff, the Templar is well out into the river now. Almost halfway across."

"Then let us pray to God that my brother is there to help him when he reaches the other side, for our horses would need to sprout wings to come to his aid."

THE WATER WAS COLD AND WRITHED LIKE A SNAKE. Fulcher felt the shock of it, like red-hot iron on the welts and bruises on his body, as he slipped into the water at the Templar's side. He had felt the shudder that Bascot's mount had

given and the need for its rider to urge the horse forward
with a dig of spurs. On the other bank, the trio holding Gianni
watched intently, the boy seeming to shrink as he reached his
hands down between his knees and crouched, waiting. Other
shapes were appearing in the trees behind them, along with
the outlines of bows, held nocked and at the ready. Above,
the sky was darkening, seeming to lour in elemental disapproval. The rain continued to fall.

"How much farther?" Bascot asked Fulcher.

"Not yet. We must go just a few more paces." The outlaw
had to pull himself up out of the water to make himself
heard by the Templar. Once he had spoken, he dropped back
down, easing his shoulders.

They were in the middle of the river now. The water was
surging up around the chest of Bascot's horse, streaming
alongside in waves, soaking Bascot to the thighs and cresting
in Fulcher's face like the flap of a curtain. The brigand could
feel the slip of the rope at his wrist, the Templar's boot and
stirrup digging into his side, and the rough uneven bed of the
river as his feet touched it lightly and bounced away, letting
himself be carried forward by the horse's strength, not his
own.

Bascot's horse suddenly stumbled, its hooves hitting the
hard ridge of gravel that ran down the river just a little off
the middle of its course. The grey lifted one foreleg, then the
offside hind, as it prepared to scramble up the obstacle it
could only feel, not see. At that moment, Fulcher pulled on
the rope around his wrist, sliding it free, and said the one
word, "Now." Almost immediately he dove under the animal's belly, coming out on the other side. Bascot felt him
grab at his stirrup, the hand snake up his boot and grasp the
dagger, then Fulcher pushed away, sliding into the current
and cutting through the water with powerful strokes. Bascot
let out a shout, wheeled his horse in the water and drew his
sword. The outlaws on the bank ran forward, shouting at
each other and pointing to where Fulcher's dark head could
be seen just above the surface of the water as he cleaved a
path away from them.

Arrows erupted suddenly into the air as the bowmen in

the forest shot their missiles, not at Bascot, but at their supposed comrade. Bascot knew then that Fulcher had told him the truth. Frantically, he twisted his head, looking for Gianni. The boy was still there beside Edward but even as Bascot spied him, the lad, with a quick movement, bit the arm of his captor so that the reeve's nephew let out a yell and released him. Then Gianni shrugged, gathered his legs under him and ran, straight for the river. Bascot spurred his horse forward, towards the boy. The grey slipped at first, confused, then pushed with all its strength as his hind legs gained the top of the gravel ridge. Bascot guided him along it as Gianni, running like a deer, reached the bank and jumped as far as he could, legs flailing wildly to give him more distance. He landed with a splash in the water only a few yards from Bascot and, with one bound, the grey leaped forward and the Templar scooped the boy up from the roiling river, dragging him across the front of his saddle.

On the western bank all was confusion. The outlaw archers turned to aim their arrows at Bascot, and the Templar swung Gianni up behind him and pushed his shield over his shoulder so that the boy could huddle underneath its protection. He could feel the lad's hands clutching at the back of his surcoat, holding on like a leech. Then a shout of warning sounded from the woods behind the archers and from the screen of trees, William Camville burst, his two squires and Roget close behind, swords in hand. The terrified bowmen scattered towards the water but, from the eastern bank of the Trent, the sheriff now appeared, his mount at full gallop and a deadly mace swinging from his hand. The castle men-at-arms were fanned out on either side of him, short swords at the ready.

The battle was of brief duration. Apart from their bows, most of the outlaws had little in the way of weaponry—a few cudgels, some rusty knives, the crude blades of scythes. Some half dozen of the outlaw band were killed outright and almost twice that number captured. Only one of the sheriff's force sustained an injury; a man-at-arms had his wrist bone broken as one of the outlaws, more desperate than the rest, tried to wrest the soldier from his horse. The outlaw had died from a sword slash delivered by Richard Camville, the blow almost cleaving the man's torso from the lower part of his body.

The sheriff was well pleased with the outcome of the foray, although he showed some disappointment at the loss of Fulcher. "Still, de Marins, I agreed to exchange him for your servant and that is what we have done. These other miscreants will pay the price for his escape. And I will ensure that they pay dearly, not only for his loss but for that of my deer."

It was full dark by the time they reached the gates of Lincoln castle, with the captured outlaws, bound at the hands and to each other, stumbling between the men-at-arms guarding them on either side. Gerard and William Camville, along with Richard and the two squires, rode at the head of the procession, the sheriff for once in a jocular mood, while Roget and Ernulf passed a wineskin back and forth and exchanged jokes with the men of the garrison. More somber were the foresters, Tostig and Eadric. Bascot wondered if this was because they had not been able to capture Green Jack or whether it was because Fulcher, a poacher on the territory in their care, had escaped.

But the Templar gave the foresters, the outlaw leader and Fulcher no more than a passing thought. At his back Gianni was fast asleep, wrapped in one of the soldier's cloaks and with the cap that Ernulf had given him—rescued from the head of one of the captured outlaws—fastened securely on his head. To feel the boy's chest rise and fall in the soft rhythm of sleep and to know that he was safe, that was enough.

Twenty-five

◆—I—◆

FULCHER STRUGGLED AGAINST THE RIVER'S TOW AFTER he pulled away from the Templar's horse. Staying underwater, and close to the bank, he had surfaced only briefly to snatch a mouthful of air when it became necessary. The arrows loosed by the outlaws fell thick around him at first, pushing through the water near his head, shoulders and legs, finally losing their impetus as the current swept them away. When he judged it safe he let himself drift into a stand of osiers and, under their screen, came to a halt and cautiously put his head above the water and looked back. In the distance he could hear the sounds of fighting, like a buzzing of hornets, above the roar of the river but no one, neither soldier nor outlaw, came in pursuit of him.

Easing back into the river he swam, with the powerful strokes that seemed more natural to him than walking. He would put a good distance between himself and the warring factions downstream before coming out from under the protective blanket of the river. As he cleaved through the water, the sting of the contusions on his body eased, the deep ache of his bruises started to abate and he began to feel the life of the river around him; otters at play as they fed, trout darting between his legs, a heron prompted into hasty flight, startled by his sudden appearance. Clumps of reeds swept by on the periphery of his vision, then a willow with branches low from the heavy rain alongside clumpy fronds of sedge grass. How he had loved the river when he had, as a child, accompanied his father and uncle as they had gone out, in the early part of the evenings, to set snares for the eels that provided their livelihood. He had loved it all, even weaving osiers to make traps or, in winter, fashioning nets from hemp that his mother had made from nettles gathered in the summer and then pulped and spun, just like wool. He had proved himself even better than his kinfolk at discovering the secret places where the snake-like fish loved to gather, especially in winter when, with only instinct to guide him, he would creep quietly into the mud and unerringly find their nests.

His family had been poor, but he had never lacked a full belly—most often eel stew thickened with barley—or wished for a home within the protective walls of a nearby village. Their shack on the water's edge was always damp, but it had been clean and they had been free of a lord's demands, for his father's family had long before been granted their plot of ground on the riverbank and held their status as free men. He had been happy then and had expected to continue so. And perhaps he would have, except for his sister, a young girl who, although barely nubile, was possessed of a shape that belonged to a girl of far older years but had retained the mind of a child.

His mother had tried to keep her daughter by her side, but often the girl would wander off to pick the wild flowers that grew in the grass alongside the riverbank or to sit in a shallow pool, unaware of the wetness of her clothing, as she laughed with glee at the little fish come to nibble her toes. She had been doing just that on the day a lone man-at-arms from the garrison at nearby York castle had ridden past the spot where she was sitting. Fulcher knew she would have felt no fear of the man as he approached her, for she had never been treated with other than kindness by her kin or the villagers. No inkling of the dangerous lust her ripe breasts and

shapely bare legs could incite in the stranger would have occurred to her.

Fulcher had been on his own with her that day, his mother
gone to trade eels for flour from the miller on the far side of
the village. So engrossed had he been in making himself a
new belt fashioned from dried eel skins that he had not paid
enough attention to his sister, and had not noticed when she
strayed from the spot where he had left her playing with
shiny stones collected from the riverbed.

It had been her screams that had alerted him to her absence and he had leaped up, fear pounding in his throat as he
dropped the belt and ran towards the noise. The pool where
she was wont to sit was not far from their hut, in the shade of
a stand of elder and oak, and it was from that direction that
her howls of terror were coming. As he ran, Fulcher could
hear the harsh threatening tones of a man's voice mingled
with his sister's, then suddenly her shrieks had stilled, and
when he came to the place where she had been sitting he saw
her body sprawled half in, half out of the water, her head
with its long fair tresses lolling on a tuft of grass, and her
legs splayed wide apart. The water beneath her buttocks was
tinged pink and he could see her maiden blood smeared on
her thighs. Beside her stood the soldier, still pulling up his
hose, looking down at her with disgust on his face. The man
spun around when he heard the sound of Fulcher's approach,
his hand going to the dagger at his belt, but he was not fast
enough to stop the boy's wild rush.

Fulcher never knew afterwards where he found the
strength to kill the man-at-arms. He had been only fifteen,
albeit tall and with shoulders well muscled from constant
swimming. But the soldier had been a man in his prime,
hardened from practice with sword and lance, and should
not have needed to expend much effort to defend himself
against a lad with little experience of fighting apart from
friendly brawls with village boys his own age. It must have
been that Fulcher's headlong charge at the soldier had taken
him by surprise, for the man-at-arms fell backwards into the
shallow water and had no time to recover before Fulcher fell
on top of him and was smashing at his face with a large

stone picked up from the bottom of the pool. On and on Fulcher had pounded, aiming below the protection of the leather cap the man wore strapped to his head, crushing nose and cheekbone until the face was no more than a bloody pulp and the water around the two struggling figures streamed with gore.

Whether one of the blows killed him, or if the soldier drowned in his own blood, Fulcher did not know, but suddenly he had become aware that the man was dead. Only then had he turned to see to his sister. She still lay as she had when he had first come upon them, sprawled as though in careless sleep, but with eyes wide open and sightless. Gently Fulcher had picked her up and cradled her in his arms, but the unnatural tilt of her head to one side told him that her neck was broken. He had carried her back to his family's one-room shanty and had sat, cradling her in his arms, until his mother returned.

After that, events passed in a blur. His mother had gone to fetch his father and her brother from where they had been setting out traps for that night's catch. Haltingly, through his tears, Fulcher told them what had happened. His mother had hastily packed a small sack with some hard bread, a few onions and some eels pickled in their own brine in a little mud-and-clay jar. She had added a small stopped pottle of ale before his father and uncle had hurried him from the shack to where a small coracle, one of the two boats they owned, was fastened to a stake in the riverbank.

"You must run, son, and hide. Once the soldier's body is found there'll be a hue and cry for him who did it. For all the whoreson's evil act was deserving of death, his lord will still hang you for killing one of his men. Go far and go fast. And may God protect you."

Fulcher had never forgotten the last look he had of his family. His father, tears creasing the deep folds of his face as he spoke; his uncle pressing the knife he had always prized into his nephew's hand before clasping him with rough tenderness about the shoulders; his mother, face white with strain, wrapping him in her arms and murmuring a prayer as she kissed his cheek. Still dazed with shock, he had done as they instructed and lowered himself into the little boat. Only once had he looked back as he worked the paddle that skittered the tiny craft over the water. The remnants of his family had stood as though in a tableau like those painted on the walls of the village church, frozen stark against the sun-washed blue of the sky and the green trees of the forest at their back. It was the last time he was to see them, or they him.

Although that had been many years ago, Fulcher had always kept them in his mind's eye and in his heart, through the days that followed when he had been fearful of capture and during the months afterwards as he had foraged for food and shelter. He had kept clear of towns, working when he could for cottars glad to exchange a bowl of food for a helping hand, stealing when there was no employment to be had. Even through one terrible snowbound winter when he had been forced to poach the king's deer to stay alive, he had never forgotten his family.

Many years had passed before he had finally come to Sherwood and had crossed the path of Green Jack. In all that time he had never slain another man. He had promised the Templar that he would kill Jack if he had the chance. Would he? The sounds of fighting behind him after he had swum away from the Templar's horse did not bode well for Jack's band of outlaws, or for their leader if he had been captured. The sheriff was not a man known for his clemency. It could be that Camville had taken Fulcher's revenge for him, or perhaps the Templar had, especially if his young servant had been harmed.

Fulcher knew that his best course would be to continue his flight southward, follow the Trent's course and put as much territory between himself and Lincoln as he could, past Nottingham perhaps, south to a part of England he had never been before. He had only to lay up somewhere and get himself dry, beg or steal some clothing that was warmer than the rags he had on, and then keep going. But if he did, he knew that the memory of Green Jack would follow him, haunt him; that if he did not find out whether his old adversary had escaped or been captured and hanged, he would never rest. Whatever patch of the greenwood in whatever part of England he stepped into, he would be looking for Jack behind every tree trunk, in every dark copse in the midst of winter. No, he had to go back, back to the camp and see if he could find out what had happened. If he came upon a victorious Jack with the Templar in his clutches, Fulcher would challenge him, and in doing so, probably die. But if Jack's plan had not worked, if he had been taken, then he could safely leave the fate of the treacherous outlaw leader to the sheriff. Either way, Fulcher would be satisfied that their old score was settled.

GREEN JACK WAS SITTING SNUG UNDER THE ALL-embracing arms of an oak tree a good few miles from where the rout of his plan had taken place when Camville's soldiers had attacked. He had stayed in his perch high above the riverbank only long enough to watch as first Fulcher had escaped from the Templar, and then that damned mute servant had freed himself and leaped into the river. As soon as the men of the castle garrison had erupted from the forest on both sides of the river, Jack had made his escape, and quickly, calling to the two men he had kept by him to follow.

They had not made their way back to the camp where the women and children of the band were waiting for their return. If any of the men that had been captured had let loose their tongues, that would be the first place the sheriff would look for him. No, Jack had never been known as a stupid man, and he was not going to spoil that reputation now. The women would have to look after themselves, or starve. He had given them no more than a passing thought before he and his two cohorts had gone south, towards Nottingham. He led them to a billet he had made safe from all eyes but his own, a snug little glade in the middle of a thick ring of trees and a hedge of bramble, penetration of which was impossible unless you knew the secret of a narrow opening at the base of the prickly growth, and Jack had made sure he was the only one who did by covering it cunningly with vines very much like the ones he wore twisted about his person.

Now he was forced to share this secret with the two out-laws who had accompanied him. They were both men who had been with him a long time, good bowmen who would be loyal as long as he kept them free of the sheriff's clutches and provided them with a hefty share of the rich pickings gleaned from robbing any travellers they came across.

For now, he sat alone, having sent his men off to forage for game. He needed time to think. They would have to stay hidden for a while, he ruminated, and, as he thought of the problems that faced him, the scene on the riverbank once more played through his mind. Damn the Templar! And damn Fulcher! He had known the risk involved in pretend-ing to exchange the Templar's brat of a servant for the out-law, but the lure of having one of the hated monks and his old adversary both within his grasp had been too powerful. And it would have worked, should have worked, if Fulcher hadn't made his successful grab for freedom. Jack had known the sheriff's men would be waiting within the screen of bushes; what he hadn't bargained for was that they would also be on the Sherwood side of the river. A mistake in his own judgement, he had to admit, but he had gambled that Camville's foresters would not know of the one and only track that led to where his men lay in wait. But even so, if Fulcher had not broken free when he did, there might still have been time to take the Templar. . . .

Jack let his heart fill with the deep anger he had felt the first time he had laid eyes on Fulcher. He was of a type, was the eeler, one of a sanctimonious breed reminiscent of the Templar monks. Always bleating about feeding the women and children first, wanting to share whatever meagre pick-ings there were with the others, as if he were God and Jesus all rolled into one. Jack had known he was a threat to his leadership right from the moment they met and he had not been wrong. Only two days in Jack's camp and Fulcher was objecting to the order Jack had given for one of the women to be flogged because she had taken a knife to a bowman who had been trying to bed her. Cut the man's arm, she had, plunged it right into the muscle of his bicep. He would not be able to pull a bow until it was healed. Her punishment had been justified. Did she have the ability to take the bowman's place until he was fit again? No, but she would most likely be one of the first to complain when there was less food to be shared for lack of his skill. But Fulcher had not seen it that way, and he and Jack had argued, an argument that had culminated in a fight with Jack getting the worst of it before his men had pulled Fulcher off. Later that day Fulcher had left the camp, taking Berdo, Talli and their womenfolk with him. Jack knew then that he would have to get rid of Fulcher. He had seen the admiration in the eyes of some of his own men for Fulcher's strength, and for his open disdain of Jack's leadership. And by ordering some of his more trusted men to keep the little renegade band from food, he had nearly managed to destroy the danger that Fulcher represented. When Fulcher had been taken into custody, with Copley's connivance, by Camville's men-at-arms, how Jack had rejoiced to know that Fulcher was in the clutches of the sheriff. And that would have been the end of it, with Fulcher dangling from the end of a rope, had Edward not come carrying the Templar's servant. The temptation to have Fulcher at his mercy, to humiliate him and see his arrogance humbled had been too great to resist. And his indulgence had been his undoing.

For a moment Jack almost let self-pity engulf him, the feeling that fate had once again played him false, mischievously letting the double prize come so close to being in his grasp before snatching it away, but he shook his head and forced himself to control his despair. For now, he was safe, as was his cache of silver. He had built up a band before; he would do it again. Time enough when the winter was over. Until then he and his two men would be snug enough here. Yes, when spring came, all would be well once more.

His thoughts were interrupted by the return of his companions. Later Jack realised that he should have known something was amiss by the way they came in almost silently, with not a word of greeting or a look at each other. But, at the time, his thoughts were elsewhere and only the game they had brought in—two small hares, a hedgehog and a badger—caught his notice briefly. Nor did he pay much attention when they started a small fire and damped it down with turf after burying the game, wrapped in leaves, beneath the flames. It wasn't until the food was done, barely cooked but edible, that he observed there was something shifty about the way his two cohorts were eyeing him across the fire.

"What's up?" he asked, his hand straying stealthily to the dagger at his belt.

"Nothin', Jack," replied Warin, the older of the two, a tall thickset man with a nose that had been slit for stealing. "We were just wondering what you reckon on doin' now."

"What need is there to do anything?" Jack responded. "We're safe enough here and there'll be plenty of game in the woods to do us through the winter. What do we lack with food in our bellies and a dry spot to lay our heads?"

"There are other bands in Sherwood," put in the other bowman eagerly, a youngster named Geraint, who had escaped into Sherwood when the hue and cry had been set after him in Nottingham after he had killed a man in a drunken brawl. "In the southwest; we could join one of them. Short Shank's maybe. He's always looking for men that are good with a bow."

"Aye," said Jack. "That's because he can't pull one himself."

The jest did not produce a smile on the faces of the two men. They looked first at each other, then at him. Finally Warin said, "We're not of a mind to stay here, Jack, not all winter long. Aye, it's snug enough, but there's no ale, and there's no women." He shrugged his broad shoulders. "For a week or two, maybe, but not for the long months 'til spring. We've decided, Geraint and me, that we'll head south. Join another band, or forage on our own, if need be. We'll not spend the winter pent up in here like monks in their cubbyholes."

Jack stood up. "Well, you'd best go then. I'll not deny I'd expected more loyalty from you, but ale and women are as powerful a lure as any to a man. I wish you good fortune."

Still the two men stood there and the tenseness in their stance made the hackles rise on the back of Jack's neck. His hand found his dagger and he pulled it free, but his movement was not quick enough. Both Geraint and Warin had arrows nocked to their bows, the barbed tips pointing at his chest.

"We've no wish to harm you, Jack," Warin said, "but we'll need a little silver to pay our way until we've earned some of our own. Ale does not come cheap even if women do, and I doubt whether Short Shanks will provide us with either unless he sees we have something to share that will prove our good faith." He motioned with his head and Geraint moved a little to one side. "Now, we knows that you has silver here, for you would not have left it behind at our old camp if you had stowed it there, so here it must be. And we wants it."

"What makes you think I have any silver at all?" Jack asked, trying not to sound intimidated. "The pickings have been lean these last months."

Warin laughed, a dry hacking sound. "If you hasn't any, then that's your misfortune, for if you come up with nowt, then I reckon as how we'll have to kill you. All we're asking of you is what we ask of any we rob—pay up or give us your life. Now that's fair, ain't it, Jack?"

As Geraint took another step, Jack took his chance and threw his knife at Warin, diving to one side as he did so. As he rolled he snatched at a thick length of tree branch, hearing an arrow thud into the log on which he had been sitting moments before. Straightening, he saw that Warin had fallen face-first across the fire and Geraint, white with fear, was in the act of fitting another arrow to his bow. Jack swung the branch, loosing it as it reached the apex of its arc and it slammed into Geraint's left arm, knocking him backwards into a stumble so that his arrow misfired and flew low, piercing the meaty part of Jack's thigh. Ignoring the pain, Jack was on the bowman in a trice, knocking him to the ground and pushing the tree branch across the young man's neck. It took only a few moments' struggle before he ceased to move, his windpipe crushed.

As quickly as he could, Jack rolled, cursing the stab of pain that shot up into his groin as he did so, to see if Warin had recovered. It was with a sigh of relief that Jack realised the older archer had not moved. Already an acrid stink was beginning to fill the air from the scorching of his flesh and clothes. Jack pushed him off the burning embers and turned him over. The dagger had taken him clean in the heart. He was as dead as Geraint.

WHEN FULCHER PULLED HIMSELF FROM THE RIVERBANK he travelled quickly and quietly back to the place where Green Jack had been making his camp on the day that Fulcher and the others had left the band, praying it had not been moved in the interim. It was full dark now and the wet rags he wore clung to him like freezing fingers of river weed, bringing shivers to his body whenever he paused to catch his breath and bearings. He kept the Templar's dagger in his hand, wary not only of being discovered by Jack's men, but of wolves. Once or twice he glimpsed a shadowy shape moving amongst the trees, but they drifted away at his approach, proving to be only small animals as fearful as himself. Above him a nearly full moon shone a silver light through the bare branches of the trees, showing him the path he sought clear like a snail's track through the forest. The rain had ceased but it had grown colder, and there would be frost before morning. He hoped he was either warm or dead by then. He might be both, perhaps. The teachings of the church warned that the flames of hell were as hot as the heart of the sun.

When he came to the dell where the camp had been situated, he took care not to let his presence be known until, by peering through the surrounding foliage, he could see a few people were still gathered there. Only women and children seemed to be huddled in the small glow of a dying fire, but then he noticed that on the periphery of the dim circle of light were two of the younger men of the band, sitting hunched over on the ground and staring into the dark. All looked forlorn and miserable, and there was no sign of Jack or any of his bowmen.

Fulcher straightened and walked into the enclosure. At the noise of his approach, a few of the women started up in fear, clutching their children to them, while the two men bolted upright, one clutching a stout wooden club in one hand while the other brandished a piece of rusted iron that had once protected the wheel of a cart.

"Peace," Fulcher said as he went up to them, mindful of their nervous glances at the dagger in his hand and of the fear on the faces of the two boys, as well as the countenances of the women.

"We didn't know the bowmen were going to shoot at you, Fulcher," one of the young men blurted out, the one with the old shard of wheel rim clutched in his fist. "Jack only told us we was to lure the Templar to our side of the river and then we'd get to hold him for ransom as well as loose you from Sheriff Camville. 'Twould be a double victory, he said, with plenty of silver paid as ransom for the Templar. I swear, he never said aught of playing you false. . . ."

"He's telling the truth, Fulcher, 'though I don't suppose you'll believe me," one of the women interjected. She had most likely once been very pretty, but now weeping sores covered her face and neck, and her hair, a matted tangle of grime, hung lank around her shoulders. "Jack told us just what Will said—the women and those of the lads who weren't one of his trusted bowmen, that is. Said it would be a great victory over the sheriff to get you out of his clutches and hold the Templar for ransom besides. Black-hearted liar that he is, we believed him. Even cheered him for being so bold on behalf of you, an old enemy. Well, do to us what you will, Fulcher. Our men are gone, all except for Will and young Thomas here. There's no one to hunt, or keep us safe. We've naught to face but starvation or being eaten by wolves. If you've a mind to kill us, at least it'll be a quick death."

Some of the children started crying at her words, burying their faces in their mothers' bosoms. Fulcher hunkered down by the fire, laying his knife between his feet. "I've no mind to hurt any of you," he said. "Tell me what happened at the riverbank. Were all the men taken by the sheriff? Where is Green Jack?" As he spoke he reached out to the warmth of the fire, holding his hands in plain sight.

Reassured by his manner, a babble of voices broke out as

they explained what had happened, how the sheriff and his soldiers had burst from the wood and captured or killed most of the men, and how the Templar had retrieved his servant and got away.

"Me and Thomas only escaped because we were at the back, hidden in the bushes," Will said. "When the horsemen rode out from the north, on our side of the river, they had swords and maces. Dropped our men like they was a rack of skittles at a village fair." He looked down, shamefaced. "We ran. I had only this"—he lifted up the club, which he had laid across his knees—"and Thomas's weapon was not much better. We just ran and kept going until we couldn't hear the fighting anymore. Then we made our way back here."

"And Jack? Do you know if he was taken with the others?" Fulcher asked.

Another woman spoke. Heavily pregnant, she was sitting on the ground near the fire, an old rag drawn around her head and shoulders for a shawl. Her eyes were dull, uncaring. Fulcher remembered that she had once been Jack's doxy. "Not him," she said. "Not Green Jack. Never even came near the fight, just stayed back and let the others carry out the devil's plan he had made."

"How do you know that?" Fulcher asked, nodding with thanks as one of the other women passed him a rough wooden mug filled with watered ale heated over the fire. Talli's sister, he noted; Talli and Berdo must have been among those taken by the sheriff.

"Followed him, didn't we?" Now it was the first woman who had spoken that piped up. "Well, I did, anyway. Mary, here, she couldn't keep up, what with her belly being so big."

"Followed him to where?"

"When all the men left, with the boy, to where they was to meet the Templar, I saw Jack go off in a different direction, with Warin and Geraint. I heard him tell the others that he would meet them in a little while, that he was going to make sure the sheriff's men had not got onto our side of the river."

She stopped and picked at one of the sores on her chin, then continued, "Me and Mary thought it was strange, for he went *upstream*, not down, and there's no ford there for the soldiers to cross, not without making a commotion. So we went after them. I saw Jack climb up into a tree, high, the way he does, and thought at first that maybe he was doing what he said and could see better from up there. But he didn't come down. And Warin and Geraint waited at the bottom. Never stirred towards where the other men were."

"Then the noise of fighting at the riverbank started." Mary took up the tale, her voice still listless. "I was scared, but I waited until Leila came back, and then we ran here as fast as we could. Then Will and Thomas turned up." She nodded in the boys' direction. "We all just stayed here. We didn't know what else to do. We couldn't run, not with the children. Besides, where would we go? We thought that if the soldiers came and found us, it'd be no worse a fate than being a meal for the wolves."

"So you don't know where Jack is?" Fulcher asked, his anger at the outlaw leader beginning to burn bright again.

"Only that he probably made his way south," Leila said. "Wouldn't go north, would he? Sherwood's trees peter out a few leagues that way and he'd be in open country. He likes to be deep in the greenwood, does Jack."

"In the morning, will you show me the tree that he climbed?" Fulcher asked Leila.

She nodded, puzzlement on her face. "I will, but I doubt you'll track him. He's too canny, and too much of a coward, to be caught."

"That's exactly what I'm hoping he'll think, Leila," Fulcher replied.

Twenty-six

✛

THE NEXT MORNING, NICOLAA WAS UP LONG BEFORE dawn, working. In front of her lay neat piles of parchment containing lists of stores, tallies of candles and bed linen, countings of cups and tableware. All of these she was checking and rechecking. This was her forte; here she knew her work and knew it well. All was prepared for the king's visit and for his meeting with William of Scotland. In and out of her room the castle staff came and went—steward, wardrobe keeper, butler, laundress—from the highest servant to the lowest, as she heard from each the progress of their duties. Every one of her servants knew they would feel her displeasure if they were lax. Unlike Gerard, Nicolaa's disapproval was icy and spare of words, but final. If any were indolent, or lied, never again would they have a place in her retinue, nor a good word said for them in Lincoln town.

In a separate pile of parchment lay the messages she had received from King John. Alongside it was notification from the abbot at Torksey of the Scottish monarch's safe arrival, which included a separate list of the names of the lords in his retinue and the number of his retainers. There was also a letter from the Templar preceptor in London, telling her that Bishop Hugh was *in extremis* and was not expected to retain his life for as long as it would take the letter to reach her. In a corner behind her, at a small lectern, one of her clerks was penning a fair copy of the replies she was sending to both men. The guard on the gate tower had been instructed that she was to be informed immediately the king's entourage was sighted on the approach to Lincoln, and she had runners waiting on the road from Nottingham to let her know of John's progress from that city. She could find nothing she had forgotten. All was in readiness, yet still a throbbing kept on at her temples, like a small drum, banging as though to draw her attention to some detail she had forgotten. She thought she knew what it was, this nagging warning of dereliction, yet it was something that all her care and efficiency could not remedy. It was the unresolved matter of the squire's death.

How soon would some courtier, looking for advancement, or to displace her and her family from favour, whisper in John's ear of the rumour that surrounded Hubert's hanging? She had known John since he was just a child, with herself only a few span of years older. She knew how suspicious he was, how he saw devils in every corner, treachery in a glance or a carelessly spoken word. And she had seen him take his revenge, not boldly like his brother Richard, or with measured justice like his father, but with a sly quietness, feigning naivety and friendship, then thrusting retribution when it was least expected. For all that John valued her, and she him, he would strike without compunction at Gerard or, heaven forfend, her son.

She wished desperately that there was some way she could quash this rumour about Hubert, but without proof of the identity of his murderer, and the reason for it, gossip would run rampant. Blaming outlaws would be seen by John for the lame excuse it was and dismissed. As would the possibility that the villagers had killed him for attempting to defile one of their womenfolk. She shook her head to clear it. Ruminating thus would bring no profit and would only encourage the ache in her head to strengthen.

She had been meaning to look into the matter that Ernulf had mentioned to her about Copley. She had already had her clerk bring the relevant documents to her chamber and had asked her bailiff to speak to the regarder for the area, a local knight whose task it was to inspect the royal forest for infringements. The bailiff had reported his findings to her steward that morning. Now, she called to her clerk to bring the letters he had completed along with all the other papers, and to light another candle. Hard work had always given her comfort in times of trial. It was a medication she would apply now.

IN ERNULF'S CHAMBER IN THE BARRACKS BASCOT AND Gianni were breaking their fast. Both master and servant had missed the morning service of Mass, Bascot deciding that the boy needed sleep more than anything else after his ordeal and, reluctant to leave the lad's side, he had said his own prayers, including one of fervent thanksgiving for the boy's safe recovery, while quietly kneeling by his pallet. When Gianni had awoken, Bascot had given him a few strips of salted beef left in the chamber from the day before, along with some ale to wash it down. For himself, Bascot made do with coarse bread and a piece of goat's cheese from Ernulf's private store.

"Are you recovered enough now, Gianni, to tell me why you were out in the forest on your own?" Bascot asked, trying to sound stern. He knew he should berate the lad, but having so recently come near to losing him, he could not find it in his heart to be angry.

Gianni looked down, his jaws almost ceasing their avid chewing of the meat. "I know you must have had a good reason for leaving the castle without telling anyone where you were going," Bascot continued, "but I still must know what it was."

Gianni looked up at his master, tears forming at the corners of his eyes. With a sigh he reached for the small casket that contained the writing materials on which he practiced his letters. Slowly, and with great care, he wrote a few lines, then gave the scrap of parchment to the Templar to read.

JUST AS DAWN ANNOUNCED ITSELF BY A SLIGHT LIGHT-ening in the heavy sky, Godfroi de Tournay was spurring his mount towards Nottingham. He had spent a sleepless night tossing his worries about Hubert's death to and fro, and had come to no resolution. Finally he had decided that he could not, would not, wait for the accusation of treason to be levelled at his family. He would go to see King John, not to confess, but rather to express his outrage at the rumour that was being bruited abroad. For the moment, he had the king's favour; if he could couch his anger in convincing enough tones he was sure John would believe him. To wait for another to level the allegation would be folly; far better to bring it out into the open himself, and pray the king did not see through his ruse. He wished he had time to find his brother and consult with him, but he did not. Ralph had been away from home inspecting a property many miles away that included buildings in dire need of repair when he and Richard had gone to Boston. It was unlikely he had yet returned. By the time he found Ralph, the king would be in Lincoln and the de Tournay cause lost. He would have to act as he thought best and hope that God would show him mercy and, at the same time, protect him.

IN THE WARD OF LINCOLN CASTLE, WILLIAM CAMVILLE and Richard de Humez stood beside the sheriff and watched the shuffling row of outlaws, the reeve's nephew amongst them, being shepherded towards the south wall of the castle by Ernulf and a contingent of his men-at-arms. At Gerard's feet two of the castle dogs, large boarhounds, sat alertly watching the prisoners. They resembled their master, broad of chest and heavy of jaw, and looked up at him from time to time as though waiting for his command to attack.

"Stretch their necks on long ropes, Ernulf, so they dangle

well over the battlements," Gerard commanded. "I would have their bodies in plain view of the king when he arrives. He will then know that I keep the peace in Lincoln and keep it well."

"Are you sure this is wise, Gerard?" William asked. "Would it not be better to wring a confession to Hubert's murder out of one of them before they are despatched? You still need an answer for the boy's death to give to the king, as it is certain he will ask for one."

De Humez shuffled restlessly as William waited for his brother's answer. This matter of the squire's murder and Nicolaa's questioning of his own culpability was making him uneasy.

"If I did that, William," the sheriff said to his brother, "it would seem I had need to find a scapegoat, one that was conveniently dead."

"There is another side to that argument," William declared. "It might be said that one of these men was paid by you to kill the boy and, by hanging him so summarily, you sought to guarantee his silence."

Gerard turned and glowered at his brother. "Whatever is said will be said. I am tired of plots and manoeuvres to gain royal favour, or to dispel distrust. I am sheriff. These men are outlaws. It is my duty to hang them, and hang them I will."

William knew better than to push his brother further. He stood silently by as, one after another, the brigands had a noose placed around their necks and were thrown over the castle wall.

As THE CHURCH BELLS RANG OUT THE HOUR OF TIERCE, Melisande Fleming was giving her daughter a thrashing. The girl whimpered as the thin rod struck her back and buttocks, but she did not cry out.

"You will tell me why you were at the castle yesterday. And you will tell me who you went there to meet."

Still the girl remained silent and Melisande signalled to the two female servants holding her daughter to stretch her out farther. Again the rod fell, this time catching her shoulder and biting through the thin material of the only garment she wore, a shift of fine linen.

"Joanna," her mother said, her bosom heaving from her efforts, "I will beat you senseless if I have to, you know that. Tell me his name."

The girl lifted her head from where it had drooped between her shoulders. "Then beat me senseless you will have to, Mother. Or kill me, I care not. For I will not tell you."

JUST A LITTLE BEFORE SEXT, UNDER A LOWERING SKY, Bascot and Gianni were approaching the village where Edward's uncle was reeve. The gateward, a small skinny youngster with a pimple-scarred face, gave them admittance. Inside the enclave all was still, and the sound of women sobbing could be clearly heard. No one came to greet the Templar and Bascot sent a boy who was tending a flock of geese to fetch Father Samson. When the old man came up the path from the church his steps were slow, and his face wet with tears.

"Greetings, Sir Bascot," he said unsteadily. "You must excuse myself and the villagers if we seem discourteous today. We have been told of Edward and his involvement with the outlaws, and that he is being punished for his crimes at this very hour. His family is sorely grieved. None of us had any knowledge that he was party to such deviltry."

"You may not have been privy to it, Father, but his family surely was."

The old man lifted his rheumy eyes to Bascot. "Oh no, my lord. They were not. Of that I am certain."

Bascot got down from his horse and went up to the elderly priest. "Father, your duty to God binds you to see the good in men. Yet where there is good, there can also be evil. Believe me when I say that Edward was not the only man of this village to consort with the outlaws, even if the others did so unwillingly. I will have the truth from them, and if I do not, I will let the sheriff extract it by force."

Samson's mouth fell open at Bascot's words, then he

clamped it shut along with his eyes and mumbled a prayer under his breath, fingering the plain wooden cross that hung from a leather thong around his neck. "May God forgive them if you speak true, Sir Bascot. And me also, for I have failed in my duty as shepherd of this small flock."

"Bring all the men into the church, Father, and the milk-maid, Bettina," Bascot said kindly to the distressed priest. "And there you and I will together hope that your errant parishioners will finally give truthful answers to my questions."

Twenty-seven

LATE THAT NIGHT, ERNULF, ROGET AND BASCOT WERE
sitting in Ernulf's quarters in the barracks, sharing a jug of
wine and the warmth of a glowing brazier. At intervals, as
they replenished their cups, Ernulf took a short poker from
where it rested amidst the red-hot embers of the brazier and
plunged its tip into the wine. The sizzling sound and smell
enhanced the taste.

Outside it was cold, with an icy rain falling that was mixed
with snow. In a corner Gianni sat, alongside another, smaller,
brazier, wrapped in an old blanket and with Ernulf's cap
pulled firmly down around his ears. He was dozing lightly.

Bascot regarded him with affection and felt a renewal of
the relief he had felt when he had hauled the boy up onto his
horse in the middle of the river. He was now reluctant to let
the lad out of his sight, even if it was only to a pallet outside
Ernulf's chamber in the larger common room of the barracks.

"So, *mon ami*," Roget said, the brass rings that were
threaded through his beard throwing off sparks of light as
the movement of his lips set them dancing, "are you going to
tell us what you have discovered?"

"It was what Gianni discovered, really, Roget," Bascot replied. "If he had come to me about what he had overheard in the hall instead of trying to play the hero himself, we would have been spared our trudge through the forest to rescue him."

"True," the former mercenary replied, "but then we would not have captured all those brigands, my friend. That alone made the effort worthwhile. Although," he added, with a glance towards the sleeping figure of Gianni, "I would as lief the boy had not been put into such danger."

"Nor I," Ernulf agreed, refilling his cup, then raising it to the captain. "This is a good vintage, Roget," he said. "I thank you for it."

"Ha! Enjoy it well. That is the last jug from my store. I do not know how soon I can get more." The captain made a mock expression of such ruefulness that Bascot burst out laughing.

"He was tumbling a wine merchant's daughter," Ernulf explained to the Templar. "The father gave him a dozen jugs of this"—he raised the cup high—"for a promise to leave the girl alone."

"I was tiring of her in any case," Roget commented, shaking his head. "I never like to spend too long with one woman. They get ideas that are dangerous."

Ernulf leaned towards Bascot. "But tell us, what was it Gianni overheard, and what did you find out in the village?"

Both the sergeant and Roget listened silently as Bascot told them his tale. Then Ernulf refilled all their wine cups and said, "So you have discovered who murdered Hubert and the charcoal burner and his sons."

"Yes," Bascot agreed. "But I cannot prove it."

"*Ma foi*, does it matter?" Roget asked. "The sheriff will not care for such a nicety."

Bascot shook his head, but it was Ernulf who answered Roget's question. "The sheriff may not, but the king will."

"The king?" Roget protested. "Why should it worry him? The boy was of no importance, not to King John anyway, and I do not think that our new monarch will care overmuch about the fate of Chard and his family."

"You are right, Roget," Bascot replied, "but he *will* care

about the rumour of treason. Proof of the motive for Hubert's murder, and of who committed it, must be given to him."

"Have you thought of a way to get such proof?" Ernulf asked.

"I think so," Bascot said. "I have discussed the matter with Lady Nicolaa, who has, by the way, discovered another, and separate, transgression against the king's justice. We have devised a plan, which, if it succeeds, will bring all these matters to light in front of witnesses and thus resolve them. She has instructed me to explain your part in the ruse we propose to play."

Roget chuckled deep in his beard and Ernulf grinned. "Just tell us what it is that we are to do, de Marins," the serjeant said. "We both have much relish to hear of it."

I⸻T WAS EARLY THE NEXT MORNING THAT MELISANDE Fleming received a request from Nicolaa de la Haye to attend a meeting at the sheriff's hunting lodge for a discussion of the preparations necessary for a hunt planned for the king during his stay in Lincoln. Melisande was in her gold manufactory when the messenger arrived. The workshop was housed in a building adjacent to her house on Mikelgate, and she always enjoyed being in its confines. The sight of the master goldsmith at work on his small anvil, his tiny hammer and tongs stretching and tapping the gleaming yellow metal, always soothed her, and she often herself performed the task of polishing a finished piece with the fine soft fur of a rabbit's foot.

It had been decided by the goldsmith's guild that King John would be presented with three gifts from the workshops of Lincoln. Melisande's manufactory had been allotted the making of a hanap—a large cup—which was to have a cover and footed base and be encased in a wooden box inlaid with silver decoration. The cup was now finished, and Melisande was holding it in her hands, admiring the workmanship of her staff when the messenger came to the door.

The goldsmith's widow was annoyed at Nicolaa's request. She knew that John was now at Southwell, having travelled there from Nottingham, a distance of fourteen miles, the previous day. From Southwell he would come the final twenty-three miles to Lincoln and was expected to arrive the following afternoon. She had intended to spend the day preparing for the monarch's arrival at the castle. There was much to do; the hanap and box must be enclosed in a bag of soft velvet for its presentation, there was her gown to inspect and the choosing of the jewellery she would wear and, most vexing of all, she still had the rebellion of Joanna to contend with.

Impatiently, she threw the short note from Nicolaa onto the floor. She would have to go, like it or not. Even though she held the office of chief forester and, as such, received her salary directly from the crown, it would be unwise to irritate the castellan by a refusal. Nicolaa was well thought of by King John and any commissions the goldsmiths of Lincoln hoped to receive from him could easily be withdrawn if she chose not to recommend them. Angrily Melisande called for one of her servants to saddle the palfrey she kept in a stable behind the house, and for another to bring her a warm cloak. Before reluctantly leaving the manufactory, she sent an urgent message to Copley instructing him to attend her at the lodge for her meeting with Lady Nicolaa. Still in a fury, she left the warm glow of the manufactory's small furnace and, with a groom to accompany her, rode towards the western gate of the city.

In the chamber that had been allotted to Baldwin high in the top of the keep, Alys and Alinor kept the sick boy company. His excitement at the imminent arrival of the king had brought on another of his spells of breathlessness and the castle physician had recommended he rest until it should be time for him to be presented.

"I must be well enough to see King John, Alys, I must," he said tremulously as she held out a cup of heated wine for him to sip.

"If you don't stop fretting, little brother, you most assuredly will not be," his sister said tartly.

"I have sent Osbert for his lute," Alys told him. "He plays passably well and a little soft music may soothe you and allow you to rest. Now come, lie back and drink your wine. It has a generous dollop of honey in it."

Baldwin, his face flushed from his recent exertions of struggling for breath, did as he was told and, when Osbert arrived, was lying comfortably and breathing easier.

The page took a seat in the far corner of the room and strummed his instrument quietly. His young fingers were nimble on the strings and his high clear voice carried gently to where Baldwin lay as he sang the opening lines of a ballad about two young lovers travelling together on a pilgrimage to the Holy Land. Soon Baldwin was asleep and Alinor motioned to Alys that she would leave her brother in her friend's care, and quietly left the room.

Outside she tripped lightly down the circular stone steps to the hall, looking for Alain and Renault. They were receiving instructions from the Haye steward, Eudo, along with Hugo and a few other squires and pages, on the correct etiquette to be observed when it came their turn to serve at King John's table. Alinor waited with little patience until Eudo finished his lecture, and then called urgently to the pair to join her in a corner of the hall. Hugo came trailing a few steps behind.

"I think something is afoot to do with Hubert's murder," she said to them conspiratorially. "I heard my aunt say that she would be going to my uncle's hunting lodge later today and that she intended to take Ernulf and some men-at-arms with her."

The two squires looked at her in bafflement. "Why should you believe that any such excursion would be concerned with who killed Hubert?" Renault asked.

"It is only a feeling I have," Alinor admitted, "perhaps because earlier the Templar went to speak to my aunt privately. He was in her chamber for a long time and when he came out she sent a servant to fetch my father and Uncle William."

"I still don't see why you think these conversations, or Lady Nicolaa going into the forest with a guard, should have anything to do with who killed Hubert," Renault objected.

"It was something my father said when he came from seeing my aunt," Alinor confessed.

"And what was that?" Alain asked.

"That he hoped I had learned the folly of meddling in affairs of which I knew nothing," Alinor replied, a frown creasing her brows. "He said the next time I was tempted to eavesdrop on a conversation, I would be well-advised to stop up my ears with my fingers. He was very angry."

As she was saying this, Osbert appeared, carrying his lute. "Your brother is sleeping soundly, Alinor," he said. "Alys will stay with him until he wakes."

Alinor nodded absently and Osbert asked what was troubling her. When Alain, in a scoffing manner, told him what she had said, Osbert shook his head.

"She may not be wrong," the page remarked gravely. "I, too, saw the Templar go into Lady Nicolaa's chamber. He looked even more determined than usual. Perhaps he has found some new trace of who killed Hubert."

Hugo had been listening to the conversation with growing agitation. "Oh, Alain," he burst out, "it wasn't you who murdered him, was it?"

Alain looked at his cousin in surprise, then reached out a hand and ruffled the boy's close-cropped hair. "Of course not, you donkey. I told you, I did not find Hubert that night. And even if I had, I had no intention of killing him. I was only going to give him a good thrashing."

Alinor looked round at them all. "This murder has set us all one against another with suspicion and distrust. It seems as though Hubert, even after death, still possesses the ability to cause us as much distress as he did when alive. How amused he would be if he could see us now."

IN THE VILLAGE AT THE EDGE OF THE SHERIFF'S CHASE, the inhabitants were all gathered in the church. Alwin, the reeve, and his son, Leofric, stood at the head of them, listening intently as Father Samson finished serving Mass and turned to speak to them. The feeling of grief was strong. Edward had been foolish, but he was one of their own. At the

back of the tiny church, the women stood sniffling with
tears, all except Bettina. Her face was unnaturally white and
her hands were clenched in front of her. She mourned her
cousin's death, but was frightened of what was to come.

"You must all do exactly as Sir Bascot has instructed,"
Samson was saying. "If you do, he has promised to speak to
the sheriff on your behalf. If you do not, neither he nor I can
help you." The old priest's face was sad. He had failed his
parishioners. If they had only trusted him enough to come
and tell him what was happening, Edward and the murdered
squire might still be alive. He raised his hand in a benedic-
tion. "Those of you who are involved in the Templar's plan
must go now. The rest of us will stay here and pray for you."

Bettina, Edwin and Leofric left the hall and, as they did
so, a collective sigh rose from the rest of the villagers, bolstered by a great sob from Edwin's wife. Then they all bent
their heads in prayer as Father Samson began to intone a *Pa-
ter Noster.*

Twenty-eight

✦✦✦

MELISANDE ARRIVED AT THE HUNTING LODGE JUST past the midday hour. Copley met her on the track that approached the building with three of the bowmen that worked under him, and was standing respectfully beside his horse as his mistress approached.

Copley looked nervous. He had fortified himself with a small measure of wine when he had received Melisande's message, but had dared take no more for fear of a reprimand from his cousin. "Good morrow, mistress," he greeted Melisande obsequiously. "I believe Lady Nicolaa is already within the lodge. There are horses outside."

Melisande dismounted impatiently. "I have eyes to see, Copley," she said brusquely. "Let us go in and find out what it is that Lady Nicolaa wants of me. If King John is to have a hunt on Camville land, I cannot see how I am involved, but if my assistance is needed I would prefer to deal with it quickly. I have much to do before the king arrives."

Inside the lodge, Nicolaa sat on the chair used by her husband when he stayed at the lodge. It was of oak, with broad comfortable arms and a padded seat. Beside her, her son,

Richard, who had been standing at the entrance to the lodge, was now sprawled on a bench and, at her back, stood Ernulf and two of his men-at-arms. In a corner of the large chamber, Tostig, Eadric and a couple of the Camville huntsmen waited and watched as a pair of servants from the castle set wine and cups on a table. In the hearth a fire blazed. As Nicolaa waited for the goldsmith's widow she ran an examining eye over the preparations made for the king in case he should decide to indulge in a foray after deer or boar during his stay in Lincoln.

The lodge was a capacious structure, built of timber, with a cavernous fireplace on one side and an ample scattering of rugs made from wolf hides on the floor. In one corner was a space concealed by a curtain that was fitted with a comfortable mattress and blankets. Although this was for Gerard's convenience, it had been freshly made with washed linen and a newly covered bolster, in expectant readiness for the king.

Other preparations had also been made. Bottles of wine lay in caskets filled with straw alongside an assortment of cheeses, including the soft white one that John preferred. There were piles of linen napkins and small sealed earthenware jars of fruit preserves and pots of honey. Nicolaa was well aware of her monarch's penchant for sweetmeats.

On the walls hung coils of rope, snaring nets and leather cases filled with arrows. Wooden chests filled with leather harnesses, fletching knives and candles were set against the walls and near the bed-space straw sleeping pallets for the king's servants were neatly piled.

The noise of arriving horses distracted Nicolaa from her mental inventory and she looked towards the door as the goldsmith's widow entered.

"Greetings, Mistress Fleming," she said in an even tone. "It is a cold day outside. Shed your cloak and have a cup of wine to warm you."

Melisande nodded her acceptance and came forward to sit on a settle placed near the fire, handing her cloak to the servant who proffered her the wine, looking about her as she did so.

"You come well escorted today, lady, for just a parlay about planning the king's hunt," she said to Nicolaa.

"My son thought it wise, with so many recent trespasses by outlaws into our chase, to have me protected by my serjeant and his men as well as his own sword."

Melisande looked at Richard. He was regarding her with what seemed like amusement, the red Haye hair glinting in the light from the fire as he lifted his wine cup to his lips and drank. "Did you have no fear for your own safety, Mistress Fleming, to come with only a groom into the forest?" he asked languidly.

Melisande flicked a glance at her agister. Copley was nervous, licking his lips and staring longingly at the wine cups laid out on the table. "I knew my agister would meet me along the way," Melisande replied. "And I was in a hurry."

She felt as though the sheriff's son was baiting her and decided to try to take control of the conversation. "Although I do not understand the reason for this meeting, lady," she said, addressing Nicolaa. "If a hunt is planned for the king in your husband's chase, there is not likely to be much infringement into the part of the woodland that my deputy patrols."

Nicolaa rose from her chair and walked slowly to where Melisande sat. Her short, plump figure seemed dowdily dressed beside the rich finery of the other woman, but her stance, and the calmness of her face beneath the plain white coif, would have given any observer not familiar with her status no doubt that she had authority, and knew how to use it.

"It has come to my notice that there is more infringement, as you call it, in the forest than is at first apparent," she said.

Melisande's head came up. She regarded the castellan with an intense stare. "What do you mean, lady?" she asked.

"I mean, Mistress Fleming, that serious crimes have been discovered. Crimes committed against the very warrant that you are sworn to uphold."

Melisande stood, placing her wine cup on the settle as she did so. "Are you accusing me of dereliction in carrying out the duties of my office, Lady Nicolaa? If so, I would know the charges, and then will answer for them to the chief justice at the forest eyre court, not to you."

"Sit down, mistress," Nicolaa commanded abruptly. "You will listen to me, and listen well. If you do not, you will be taken back to Lincoln and held confined until the king arrives. On the authority of my husband, the sheriff." To reinforce her threat, Nicolaa withdrew from the pouch at her belt a small rolled parchment, from which a seal dangled. On it, the imprint of the Camville emblem of two lions passant could clearly be seen.

Shocked by the sight of the warrant, Melisande did as she was bid, reseating herself unsteadily on the settle. Nicolaa turned away and walked back to her chair. There she turned, and said, "My bailiff has conferred with the regarder for the royal chase over which you hold your post as chief forester. Also, an inspection has been made of the statement of revenues for the area. It would appear that these incomes have not been truthfully reported."

"I have no knowledge of such—" Melisande began.

"Be quiet, mistress, and do as my mother has bid you. Listen." Richard's words cut effectively through what she had been about to say and, with an effort, Melisande swallowed her protest.

"As I said, Mistress Fleming," Nicolaa continued, "the statement of revenues—which you submitted—is not a true one. For example, they do not include the income from the deforestation of two fine stands of oak, the timber from which was sold, purportedly on behalf of the king. It also seems the fees collected for pasture and pannage have been grossly understated, as have those the peasants pay for the right of estover so they can gather wood." Nicolaa sat down in her chair and motioned for a servant to refill her wine cup before she continued. "How do you explain these irregularities, mistress?"

Melisande's face was ashen. Her hands, of which she was so vain, were clenched together with such intensity that the knuckles were like raw red spots against the whiteness of the tendons. She made no response.

"You cannot, can you?" Nicolaa said quietly. "Yet you are pledged to preserve the rights of the king in the venison and vert of his forest, not abuse them."

Nicolaa made a signal to Ernulf and the men-at-arms came to stand beside Copley and the other woodsmen in Melisande's employ, all of whom had begun to shuffle uncomfortably towards the door.

"Well, mistress?" Nicolaa prompted. "Have you no answer to these charges?"

Melisande sat silent, only the shaking of her head in a small tight gesture indicated that she had heard.

"There is another matter, as well, Mistress Fleming," Richard Camville said. Slowly Melisande looked up, eyes glazed with fear.

"What is that, my lord?" she asked in a voice hardly louder than a whisper.

"The death of my uncle's squire, Hubert de Tournay."

"No!" The denial shot from Melisande's mouth with vehemence. "Of that I know nothing, I swear. Why would I have had any hand in his death? I did not even know of his existence until the townspeople began talking of his murder."

Richard's response was quick and harsh. "It is believed he was killed by outlaws, poachers in my father's chase. And you, mistress, have consort with outlaws, do you not?"

Melisande's face, through her fear, began to blaze with anger. "I know nothing of these matters. Nor do I have brigands in my household."

"Not in your household, perhaps," Nicolaa said, "but most certainly on the roll of those you pay to assist you in committing your crimes against the crown."

"It is a lie," Melisande burst out. "I tell you, I know nothing of this."

Richard spoke quietly into the widow's outburst. "It seems strange that you do not, when your agister most certainly does."

He looked expectantly at Copley, who was visibly trembling. "You have an arrangement with the outlaws in Sherwood, don't you, Copley? For a few of the king's deer you trade with brigands for loot they gain from preying on honest travellers through the forest. And Hubert de Tournay found out about your arrangements, didn't he? He was an unlikeable little turd, but he had a gift for ferreting out secrets. And he found out yours and threatened to report you unless you gave him what he wanted. What did he ask for—one of the village girls for his bed, perhaps, or maybe a piece of jewellery from your mistress's wares?"

Copley was shaking his head violently from side to side in negation as Richard relentlessly continued, "But you couldn't take the chance that the squire would betray you, so you killed him. You are often in the forest; it would be an easy matter for you to lure Hubert there by the promise of payment for his demands and then, with the help of a couple of your outlaw cohorts, take him by surprise and string him up from the oak. But you didn't expect there would be such a hue and cry after the murderer, did you? Or that the Templar would be set on your trail. When Sir Bascot started to come too close to the truth of the matter you decided a scapegoat was needed, so you provided us with one—Fulcher."

Richard leaned forward now, his resemblance to his father apparent as anger hardened his jaw. "You are the confidant of brigands, Copley. We have witnesses to that fact. It was a simple matter to get one of his own kind to betray Fulcher, and that is how you came to be so fortuitously on hand to capture him. And why you brought him so joyfully to my father—so that we would be led away from discovering the identity of the real murderer of Hubert de Tournay—and that murderer is you, Copley."

The agister's face was ashen by the time Richard Camville had finished speaking. Falling to his knees before the sheriff's son, he sobbed as he proclaimed his innocence. "No, no, my lord, I swear by all that is holy that I had nothing to do with the death of the squire," he said earnestly. "As God is my witness, Sir Richard, I am innocent of murder."

Nicolaa rose from her chair, her gaze flicking with disgust over the man cowering at her son's feet and the stricken expression on the face of Melisande. She called to Ernulf. "Take Mistress Fleming and her deputy to Lincoln. And their bowmen as well. Tostig will aid in the escort with our own woodsmen."

ON A SMALL SLOPE AT THE BOTTOM OF THE HILL ON which Lincoln castle stood, Bascot met with the three villagers. "You are clear in what you are to do?" he asked. "Remember that your own reprieve from punishment depends on carrying this task out well."

"Yes, my lord, we know. We will do it," Bettina replied and looked to her uncle and cousin. They nodded in turn.

"Then follow me into the bail and we will wait there," Bascot said.

WHEN NICOLAA AND RICHARD ARRIVED AT THE CAStle gate with their prisoners firmly under guard, the bailey was crowded. The news of the arrest of the chief forester and her deputy had flown ahead like wildfire and not only were Gerard Camville and his brother on hand to meet them with their retinues, but most of the castle staff as well, while Richard de Humez and his daughter, Alinor, surveyed the scene from the steps that led up to the new keep. A little distance into the crowd was Joanna Fleming, brought to the castle ward just moments before by Roget, who, following Nicolaa de la Haye's direction, had not only escorted her from her home, but was keeping her under close surveillance. She watched the little cavalcade enter the bail with anxious eyes, glancing up at the mercenary captain from time to time with fear on her face. Bascot, clad in mail and his Templar surcoat, waited a small distance from the gate, ensuring that he could keep Gianni, safe in the shelter of the door to the barracks, within his view.

The sky was beginning to darken as evening approached and, although the sleety rain had ceased to fall, it was still very cold, with the occasional tiny flake of snow drifting down on the waiting throng. But no one seemed to heed the discomfort of the weather, for the gaze of all gathered there was concentrated on catching sight of Melisande and her agister being brought into custody.

As Richard led his mother in through the gate, Bettina, standing just inside its arch with her relatives beside her, stepped forward and sketched a brief curtsey.

"Lady Nicolaa," she said in a voice that was hesitant, "may I have speech with you?"

Nicolaa looked down on the milkmaid, and checked her horse. "Can it not wait, girl? As you can see, I have much to attend to."

"It is important, my lady, and cannot be delayed."

Nicolaa gave her a brief nod. "Get on with it then," she said.

Bettina raised up her courage and spoke clearly. "It is said you have taken Mistress Fleming and her agister in charge for murdering Sir William's squire, but it is not so, my lady. They did not do it."

A stirring of voices rumbled through the crowd, ending in a sigh as they all fell silent to hear what came next.

"How do you know this, Bettina?" Nicolaa asked.

"Because all of us in the village know who it was that murdered the squire, and it was not the goldsmith's widow or her deputy."

Bettina's voice had begun to weaken, but it grew stronger as she caught Lady Nicolaa's glance. Awareness that the castellan knew what she had been primed to say gave her the temerity to continue. "The man who committed the murder told us to stay within the compound and not go out into the forest while he dealt with the squire. And he told the Chards to do the same."

"Why did John Chard, and you, not give this evidence when asked by my husband and Sir Bascot?" Lady Nicolaa asked, her voice stern.

"We were frightened, my lady. We had been ordered not to speak of what we knew. Then, when the charcoal burner and his family were killed, all of us in the village thought it right to be fearful, and so we did not speak for dread of our own deaths."

Nicolaa leaned down in the saddle, but her voice still carried out over the crowd. "Then why have you come forward now?"

"Because our priest, Father Samson, found out our secret and said that if we did not tell of it, we would be committing a sin, a grievous sin, by letting innocent people be charged with a crime they did not commit."

Nicolaa looked out over the crowd. They stood with bated breath, avid for more revelations concerning the murder of Hubert de Tournay. At the back of the group of prisoners behind her she could hear a stir of feet as Ernulf positioned his men across the open gate. There was in the air a taint of apprehension, and, from Melisande Fleming, an audible gasp of hope.

Nicolaa regarded the milkmaid, admiring the girl's courage. Behind Bettina her kinsmen stood with uncertain looks on their faces, glancing apprehensively at the soldiers around them, but they kept resolutely to their places.

Finally Nicolaa spoke. "Then, Bettina, you had best tell me who it was that murdered Hubert de Tournay."

Bettina swept her gaze slowly over all the company assembled there, taking her time, as she had been told to do, so that there should be no mistake as to the identity of the man she pointed out. Passing over the barons and squires gathered on the edge of the crowd she finally turned toward the line of men behind Nicolaa and Richard. Holding up her hand, she raised a forefinger and pointed it in steady accusation. "It was him. Sir Gerard's forester, Tostig."

As she called out his name, Tostig kicked his heels viciously into the sides of his mount so that it bolted and shot free of the press of prisoners and men-at-arms that surrounded him. With a curse, the forester drew the wicked blade of his hunting knife from his belt, and swerved the horse straight at Bascot.

The animal, wild-eyed and snorting, thundered across the bail. Bascot was well aware that the only chance a man on foot had to escape the flying hooves of an adversary's mount was to wait until the last possible moment before stepping aside. If he could do that, others would bring the woodsman down. Murmuring a prayer, Bascot kept still, bracing himself to wait, focussing the vision in his sighted eye so completely on the hurtling animal that the people, the bailey, and even the sky, faded from his perception.

Just as it seemed that he could allow the iron-shod hooves to come no closer, a darkness, like a sudden cloud, flew between Bascot and the horse. Renault, who had been standing within the fringe of people closest to Bascot, had swirled the loosely draped cloak he had been wearing up into the air and over the horse's head. The animal, already frightened, reared in alarm, sliding on its hind legs as it tried to stem its headlong flight. With an equine squeal, it lost balance, toppling over as Tostig frantically pulled on the reins in a futile attempt to control his mount. With a crash, and a pitiful whinny from the horse, it fell, pinning Tostig underneath.

For one brief moment there was silence, then Renault leaped forward and snatched up the knife that had fallen from Tostig's hand. Breathing heavily, the horse shook its head free of the cloth that had blinded it and struggled to its feet. With quivering legs, it stood for a space before trotting away, head tossing and tail swishing.

Tostig lay still on the ground, his legs bent at an unnatural angle. His eyes, like the horse's, were rolling, and sweat beaded his brow as he tried to lift himself, then fell back. A slow trickle of blood began to form at the corner of his mouth. The crowd in the bailey started to surge forward, but a voice that carried with a loud resonance gave a sharp command for them to keep back. Through the press Gerard Camville stepped and made his way to where the stricken forester lay.

Before he could reach Tostig, another figure streaked through the shocked throng. It was Joanna. She ran to Tostig and knelt by his side, tears streaming down her cheeks. Bascot moved to stand at Tostig's feet. It was plain the forester was mortally hurt. There would be no recovery from such an injury.

Tostig had closed his eyes, but he opened them as he heard Joanna call his name. His gaze fell on Bascot. "Damn your heart, Templar. If it had not been for you, I would not have been found out."

Joanna shook her head and, with one long slim hand, she smoothed the hair back from the forester's brow. "No, my love," she said quietly. "It is not the Templar you should damn, but my mother. May she be consigned to hell for this day's work."

The girl looked up to where Melisande still sat captive on her horse, frozen into place as she watched her daughter cry over the woodsman.

"It was you, Mother, who caused all this. You, and your love of gold and position." Joanna threw back her head and laughed, a bitter sound that died in her throat and became a sob. "It would not have been seemly, would it Mother, for your daughter to marry a common woodsman? You wanted a rich merchant, at the very least. And all the while you were more base than the lowest serf, stealing the very revenues that the king pays you to protect. Well, Mother, now you shall have a just reward for your treachery, and so shall I. But I, at least, shall feel that my pain was worth it. Will yours be?"

The sheriff had reached Tostig as Joanna was speaking and, calling for a measure of wine, he knelt beside the dying man and held the cup to his lips. Tostig tried to drink, but it ran out of the corner of his mouth, mixing with the blood that had begun to flow in a heavy stream. He coughed, and looked up at Gerard. "I am sorry, my lord, for failing you."

"You did not fail me, Tostig," Gerard Camville said gently, and Bascot was surprised to hear the compassion in his tone. "You have served me well and faithfully all these years. I will not forget that."

"Thank you, my lord." The words came with effort from Tostig's lips as, with a shudder and a great outpouring of blood from his mouth, he died.

Twenty-nine

✛

Bascot FELT THE TIREDNESS IN HIS BONES AS HE MADE his way up the stairs to Nicolaa's chamber. It had been a long day, and an even longer evening. It was an hour past Compline and he had yet to give his report to the castellan. After sending Gianni to bed in the barracks, he and Ernulf had taken Joanna to a room off the armoury and questioned her. Anger had pushed through her tears as she had told them all of the tale, of her mother's cupidity and intransigence, of Hubert's demands and, finally, of her love for Tostig.

"We knew it was only a matter of time before my mother found out about us, Tostig and me," she had said, her mouth quivering as she fought the urge to sob, "but we had thought to force her acceptance of our union. Tostig knew of her theft of the king's revenues and of Copley's traffic with the outlaws. He was going to threaten to reveal it to Sir Gerard unless she gave us her blessing."

Joanna shook her head and then bowed it in her hands. When she lifted it her face was full of misery. "We needed only a few days, until King John should be here. Tostig said that would be the best time to do it, for my mother was all agog to please the king. She would have been too fearful of his displeasure to have done other than as we asked."

"And Hubert found out about you and Tostig before you could carry out your plan?" Bascot had prompted.

"That maggot!" Joanna's vehemence was plain. "We made certain he would regain his senses before we hanged him," she said with bitter satisfaction, "and know the fate that awaited him. I watched Tostig kill him with pleasure."

"And the charcoal burner and his family, did you watch their deaths with pleasure, too?" Bascot could not hide his anger.

Joanna's shoulders slumped. "No," she whispered. "Neither Tostig nor I had any joy in that." She had lifted her head defiantly. "But that was *your* fault, Templar. If you had left well enough alone and not gone chasing into the forest with your questions . . ."

These last words kept ringing in Bascot's mind as he reached the top of the stairs and tapped lightly on the door of Nicolaa's chamber. When he went in he found the castellan seated, as usual, at her desk, and Gerard's brother, William, standing by the fireplace with a cup of wine. Two torches flared in wall sconces, giving the room a bright illumination.

"My husband has gone to keep vigil at Tostig's bier," Nicolaa said by way of explaining the sheriff's absence. Bascot nodded. He was not surprised. The evidence that Gerard Camville felt genuine grief for the death of his servant had been plain when he had overridden the castle priest's protests and ordered that the body of the dead forester be placed in the castle chapel to await burial. "He may be a murderer," he had said to the shocked cleric, "but he was my loyal servant. If I show God how much I valued him in life then perhaps our Good Lord will be compassionate when Tostig stands before him at death. Now, get out of my way, priest."

William offered Bascot the wine jug as Nicolaa invited him to be seated. "I gave orders for Melisande and Copley to be detained at her home under guard until I should know the king's pleasure in the matter," she said. "You have left Joanna under lock and key?"

Bascot nodded. "Ernulf has her secured."

Nicolaa stood up from her seat but motioned for Bascot to keep to his when he would have risen. "I need to move," she said with a small smile. "My limbs are so weary that if I do not stir them, my feet will take root in the floorboards."

She took a few steps to the end of the room, then paced back. "What did the girl Joanna tell you, de Marins? Did she confirm the dairymaid's tale?"

"For the most part. Hubert did proposition Bettina and threaten her with ravishment if she did not comply. . . ."

"So the little maker of buttermilk was telling the truth?" William said.

"Yes, she was," Bascot replied, "except she, and the other villagers, omitted to tell us that it was two nights *before* Hubert was killed that he first demanded she meet him."

At William's look of confusion, Nicolaa interrupted. "I have not told William all of the tangle, de Marins. I thought it best to wait until it was confirmed by Tostig's paramour. He does not yet know how all of this began."

Bascot took a sip of his wine and spoke directly to the sheriff's brother. "According to Joanna, she and the forester took advantage of any occasion that Melisande was absent from her home or early abed to spend the night together in the hunting lodge. On the night that Hubert waited in vain for the dairymaid, he saw them together in the forest. The next day he got Bettina alone in one of the castle cowsheds and berated her for not coming to meet him, demanding that she turn up the next night or he would take her then and there on the bare boards of the floor. Frightened, she promised she would do as he asked. Then Hubert asked her the identity of the girl he had seen with Tostig the night before and Bettina told him she was the daughter of a wealthy widow in Lincoln. Hubert laughed and said she was a toothsome piece and he had a fancy to have a turn with her himself. He told Bettina to tell Tostig of his desire and, if the forester proved unwilling to share his bawd, then he, Hubert, would apprise the sheriff of the use to which his servant was putting the hunting lodge."

Bascot shrugged. "Whether the squire was serious about

carrying out his threat we will never know, but both Bettina and Tostig had no cause to doubt it, if only because Hubert had shown himself relentless in his pursuit of the dairy-maid."

"I knew he was a singularly unpleasant boy, but I never suspected he was capable of such villainy," William said.

Bascot nodded. "He was sly enough not to reveal his true nature to his elders, but your other squires and pages knew of it and had good reason to hate him. He seems to have been a boy who had never learned to keep his appetites un-der control. And he had become so accustomed to exploiting any weakness he found in others, or in gaining an advantage by threatening to reveal a secret they nurtured, that he had come to believe that he would never come to any harm by doing so. And that is why he failed to recognize the danger of trying to use Tostig in such a manner."

"What happened when Bettina gave the forester Hubert's message?" William asked. "Did Tostig and the dairymaid devise the plan to kill him?"

The Templar shook his head. "No. When Bettina told the forester of her conversation with the squire, Tostig was un-derstandably furious. He told Bettina that she was, on the following night, to do as she had done before, stay in the vil-lage and tell her uncle to again close the gates and guard them against intrusion. If asked, they were to deny any knowledge of the matter. And they did as they were told. But they did not realise that Tostig was going to kill Hubert; they thought he meant only to give him a beating or perhaps threaten to expose the squire to his lord. When they learned what the forester had done, they feared to be punished for their own involvement.

"Joanna told me that she waited with Tostig for Hubert to arrive at the old hunting lodge where he expected to find a thoroughly cowed Bettina. The squire knew the area well, ap-parently, from previous visits to Lincoln and accompanying you, Sir William, on numerous hunts. It is possible he may have used the old lodge for dalliance before. When Hubert arrived, he found Joanna in the dairymaid's stead. While she pretended acquiescence to his lust, Tostig came up behind and rendered him speechless—and senseless—by half-strangling him with a thin cord."

Bascot took a swallow of wine before he continued. "Although it was their intent to kill him, they did not want to leave his body there; it was too close to the new hunting lodge where Tostig had his bed and belongings. So they trussed Hubert's hands and took him away from the area, to the oak where they hanged him, because it grew by one of the main tracks through the forest. Tostig wanted it to appear that the murder had been carried out by someone from the town, not anyone associated with the forest and its inhabitants. It was common knowledge among the castle servants that Hubert was held in extreme dislike by his peers, and even with hatred by some of them. Tostig wanted the hunt for the murderer to be behind the city walls, not in the woodland where he lived and worked."

"That was why the boy's body was left clothed, and his dagger in his belt," Nicolaa interjected. "To make it appear that Hubert had been killed over some private quarrel with a person of his acquaintance, and not for profit by someone in the forest."

"In retrospect," Bascot added, "it was a simple plan and should have worked. But things began to go wrong for Tostig almost from the start."

"The poachers, you mean?" said William.

"That was the first problem to plague him, yes, but it was not an insurmountable one," said Bascot. "When he came to 'discover' the body the following morning and found the slaughtered deer, Joanna said he considered cutting Hubert down and stripping him to make it look as though the poachers had killed the squire, but he feared that to do so would bring the very thing he didn't want, an active search throughout the woodland, so the forester left the squire's body as it was in the hope that his original plan would still work. And it might have, for it seemed unlikely that outlaws would have left such valuables as his clothes and dagger behind if they had killed the boy. But it was after he had dealt with the matter of the poachers that a much greater difficulty arose."

"Something to do with Bettina, I presume?" William said.

"Yes. Tostig had neglected to tell the villagers— including Bettina—that he had moved the boy and hanged him near the track, not at the old hunting lodge. And when you and your brother went to question the villagers about Hubert's death, you did not mention where it was that he had been found, did you?"

William thought for a moment. "No, we did not."

"So, when I went to the village the following morning they believed that the boy had been hanged at the place where he had ordered the dairymaid to meet him. When Gianni found Bettina hiding—and she had concealed herself for fear of being recognised and perhaps remembered as seen in conversation with Hubert—she blurted out the tale that she told to protect herself and the villagers. But it led me to search where Tostig did not want me to go—the grounds of the old hunting lodge."

"So it was he that fired the arrow at you on the day of the hunt?"

"It was. He had heard Alain and Renault speak of seeing me ahead of them that morning and he tracked me. When he saw me kneel to look at the marks Hubert's boots had made on the ground he was worried about what implications I might draw from them, and so he fired the shaft. He didn't mean to miss. If I had been killed it would have been assumed that a stray arrow meant for the deer had caused it. I was too close to where he had apprehended the boy, you see. And I kept on asking questions. He was worried that, in the end, I might get answers."

"And the charcoal burner and his family—what part did they play in all of this?"

Here Bascot gave a deep sigh and put his wine cup down. "Their deaths might have been avoided if I had brought the burner into the castle for questioning on the day that I went to see him. The fact that I did not consigned them to their fate."

"How so?" William asked.

"Tostig followed me when I went to the burner's mounds. Everyone in the forest knew of his liaison with Joanna, including Chard and his sons. It would have been impossible for the pair to keep their meetings secret from people who live in the forest and know and use all of its byways. But Chard was a truculent man and, unlike the villagers, had nothing to fear from the sheriff. While he may only have guessed that Tostig had murdered the squire, he had sure knowledge of the extra purpose to which the forester put the hunting lodge. Tostig told him to say nothing of Joanna if he was asked and the charcoal burner agreed, but when I threatened Chard with the sheriff's authority, the forester was worried that if I returned, the charcoal burner would tell what he knew. Especially since Adam, in an attempt to forestall me from further questioning of his father, told me the partial truth of seeing a man and a woman on a forest track. I had assumed the pair to be Hubert and a woman he had an assignation with, but Tostig did not know that, and feared Chard would reveal that it was himself and Joanna."

"So the forester killed them all, including the youngest son, who was only a small boy." William's voice was heavy.

"Yes, he did," Bascot replied.

"I cannot say that I feel much sympathy for my squire," William said. "It would appear that the forester had a great love for his paramour and that he also put much value on his post as my brother's servant. By threatening to defile the girl and jeopardise Tostig's position, Hubert provoked his own death, grievous as that may be. But the burner and his sons— that is different. They were the innocents in all of this."

They all fell silent at his words and stayed so until Nicolaa rose and poured them all more wine.

"The day that you went to rescue your servant," William said heavily, "and Tostig denied knowledge of a track that would lead me to your aid—then, too, he must have been lying, in the hopes of provoking your death at the hands of the outlaws."

"I do not know for certain, my lord, but it is possible, even probable. He was not aware of the information that Gianni possessed, but since I would have gone on investigating the murder of your squire if I survived the confrontation with the brigands, it is most likely he would have welcomed

my capture, or death, at their hands. If he had been successful in keeping you from assisting me, that is most likely
what would have happened."

"Thanks be to God that Eadric decided to speak up, then,"
William said fervently. "Was he not privy to Tostig's culpability?"

"No," Nicolaa replied. "He knew of Copley and his
arrangements with the brigands, but he also knew that Tostig
had warned the agister that he would not betray him as long
as he kept his unlawful activities out of Gerard's chase. Of
Tostig's liaison with Joanna, and the killing of the squire,
Eadric knew nothing. He was most often away from the
area, in the southern part of the bailiwick, and did not keep
company with the villagers in the north."

William turned to Bascot. "But you weren't aware of any
of this at the time, de Marins. How did you discover that it
was Tostig that had murdered Hubert?"

"Something my young servant, Gianni, overheard. One
day in the hall he heard two merchants talking about Tostig
and 'his pretty town piece.' One of the men said that it was
only a matter of time before the forester's lechery was discovered and that would put an end to his trysts in 'the bower
in the greenwood.' It was also said that if the forester had
been riding his horse instead of his leman on the night the
squire was killed, it might have been him that caught Fulcher
instead of Copley. Gianni remembered that Tostig had told
me that he had not been in the area where Hubert was killed
at the time the squire met his death, saying he had gone to
the southern part of the chase and, due to his horse throwing
a shoe, had not arrived back at the lodge until well past the
middle of the night. Why had he lied? It could have been
merely to cover up his relationship with a woman, but could
it have been more than that? Was he hiding something else,
something that might be connected to the deaths of Hubert
and the charcoal burner's family? Gianni decided it was
worthwhile to try and find out.

"So he set out to go to the village and ask them the name
of the forester's paramour. Gianni reasoned that the villagers
must know who the girl was and he could, through written

questions to the village priest, get them to reveal her name. Once he knew her identity she could then be questioned about Tostig's whereabouts on the night of the killing. He should not have gone alone, I know, and should have told me instead, but like many a young lad, he envisioned himself being lauded as a hero and impressing everyone with his cleverness."

Bascot paused as he remembered the fear that had snatched at his heart the day Gianni had gone missing. "He became frightened, however, once he was out in the forest on his own and decided to turn back. That was when Edward snatched him and took him to the outlaw called Green Jack."

"So Tostig had nothing to do with that?"

"No, it was pure accident. Edward just happened to come along as Gianni was trying to find his way back to Lincoln and he grabbed the boy, thinking he would fetch a goodly ransom for Jack's band.

"When Gianni was safe and told me what he had heard I went to see the villagers. They were still fearful of Tostig, but were now even more frightened of the sheriff, since one of their own had been hanged just that day. I had thought to overcome any reluctance they might have had in telling me Joanna's name by reminding them of their knowledge of Edward's complicity with the outlaws. But I had no need to take such a precaution. As soon as I mentioned Tostig they blurted out, without further prompting, what had really happened on the night Hubert met his death."

William Camville got up and threw another log on the fire, mulling over what he had heard before saying, "And then the two of you concocted this scheme to get Tostig to reveal himself?"

"It was the only way, William," Nicolaa said. "We had enough proof to satisfy us that the forester was the murderer and, if it hadn't been for all this talk of Hubert being privy to plots hatched against the king, he could just have been arrested and stood trial. But the rumours had to be proved to be unfounded as a reason for the killing, since they were becoming generally accepted as a motive, so we used Melisande Fleming and her crimes against the crown to provide an excuse to provoke Tostig into revealing his guilt, and the real reason for Hubert's death."

William took a sip of his wine. "And the forester's crimes were all for naught. If your servant overheard two townsmen speaking so openly about him and Fleming's daughter, it is more than likely their liaison would soon have become common knowledge. It does not take long for such gossip to spread. Hubert's murder brought the forester and his paramour little gain. And the Chard family none at all."

Bascot nodded in agreement, as did Nicolaa, but she added, "But are not all murders profitless in the end, *messires*, when at our own death we stand in judgement before the highest lord of all?"

Fulcher found Green Jack by accident. He had been able to track him south from the tree which Leila said the outlaw chief had climbed on the day Fulcher had crossed the river with the Templar, but he was not completely sure if he was headed in the right direction. He had found old trails that looked as though they had been recently used; a few broken twigs and branches that seemed to have been snapped by recent passage and one spot that looked, and smelled, as though it had been soiled by human excrement and urine. What he could not determine with any certainty was whether any of the signs were of recent origin, or if they had been made by men and not animals. The trail had stayed close to the course of the river.

Just as he was near to a reluctant decision to abandon the hunt for his enemy, he spied a vixen creeping from a hole in what he took to be the edge of a bramble-covered bank. In front of the bank a small trickle of a stream meandered its way to the river. He dropped behind a fallen log and watched her. His stomach was rebelling against the raw fish he had been taking from the river to sustain him. If he was canny, he might have red meat to eat tonight. Wrapped about his shoulders was a rope made of braided river weed that he had fashioned just like those he had done as a child so long ago. It would make a good snare to catch the fox.

The vixen did not venture far, however. Nose thrusting, she crept to the edge of the stream, lapped a few mouthfuls of water, then turned tail and ran back into the hole. Fulcher crept forward and, with care, lay flat on the ground to spy through the opening and see if he could locate her nest, thinking it would be a burrow in the base of the bank. What he saw, however, surprised him, for there, instead of a lair in the dank earth, was a dark tunnel and, at the end of it, daylight could be seen. Fulcher straightened and made a further inspection of the opening into the tunnel. Now he could see that it was man-made, with twigs and ivy artfully plaited together to hide the larger space behind.

Retracing his steps to where he had hidden to watch the fox, Fulcher climbed a tree. From the top of it he could see over what he had taken to be the tussocky swell of a hummock in the earth, and could make out that there was indeed a clearing beyond. He could not see into it, but the sparseness of the treetops indicated that there was nothing but low growth inside the circle of the prickly hedge.

It was then that he caught a whiff of wood-smoke. Faint, but unmistakable, and with it the scent of charred flesh. Quickly he returned to his hiding place. Someone was on the other side of the tunnel. Straining his ears, he could not make out any sound, but he settled himself down to wait.

Light was just beginning to glimmer in an overcast sky when there was a movement at the aperture in the bottom of the hedge. Fulcher, tired but still awake, watched as a man wriggled through the cleft then heaved himself upright, pulling a long stout stick behind him. After propping himself up on its length, the man slowly moved towards the stream, appearing to be in some pain from his left leg, which he was dragging behind him. There could be no mistaking the identity of the figure. Tendrils of dead ivy were wound about the arms and shoulders of the man, and the dirty gold colour of his beard glistened with dew. It was Green Jack. Fulcher smiled. The rope of river weed would make a snare that would catch a man just as easily as a fox.

Thirty

❖—I—❖

KING JOHN'S ENTRY INTO LINCOLN WAS TRIUMPHAL, despite the intermittent sleeting rain and biting cold, and the warnings of the old legend that said calamity would befall any king who entered the city. The people of the town lined the streets to watch as their monarch passed before them, his figure resplendent in purple and gilt, astride a snow-white charger caparisoned in the same colours. He waved and smiled at his subjects from the warmth of a fur-lined cloak and hat, leading a procession of knights, squires and pages. Beside him, his new young wife, Isabelle, barely thirteen years of age, peeped out at the throng from the depths of her hood and smiled in her turn, albeit tremulously. Every time she did so, the crowd redoubled its shouts of welcome, strewing garlands woven of winter leaves and berries in front of the procession to proclaim their joy.

Lincoln castle's reception was no less warm. Ernulf and his men-at-arms lined the inner side of the huge eastern gate into the bail, all at attention. The metal of their caps was polished bright as a summer sun and the Haye badge of a twelve-pointed star of red glowed proudly against its silver background on the breast of their tunics.

At the entrance to the new keep, Gerard and Nicolaa awaited the monarch and his queen. Beside them stood their son, Richard, and down the stairs on either side were ranged the barons and knights that had come to do the king honour and stand witness to Scotland's pledge of fealty. John, greeting all affably, led his young wife up the stairs and into the hall, where a feast of no less than ten courses was laid out for the company.

Bascot stayed apart from the throng until later that evening, when a more simple meal was served. He took a place near the back of the hall, at a table set aside for Lincoln's household knights, and viewed the company that was assembled on the dais.

The Templar had only seen the king a couple of times before, in the days when John had been just a young prince, but he seemed not to have changed much in appearance since then. He was about Bascot's own age, a few years past thirty, of medium height and with dark auburn hair. The young woman who had so recently become his wife sat beside him. She was very pretty, almost lushly so, Bascot noticed, with a ripe figure that belied her youth and a beguiling smile that was turned with frequency on her new husband and less often, but with only a little less radiance, on the company that surrounded them.

Nicolaa and Gerard, as hosts, flanked their royal guests. Ranged along the high table with them were various barons, William Camville and Richard de Humez among them, and a phalanx of prelates of high rank. Scattered amongst these were those ladies who had accompanied their lords on the trip to Lincoln, while Richard Camville, as son of the sheriff and castellan, had claimed the privilege of serving the king, standing behind John's chair with basin and ewer at the ready for the monarch to rinse his hands, and a piece of crisply folded linen for use as a towel.

There was a multitude of squires and pages in attendance on the company, both from Lincoln's household retinue and

those of the visiting barons. Among them Bascot saw Alain
and Renault serving one of the tables that flanked the dais
and, farther back, young Hugo and Osbert waited on a group
of ladies that included Alys and Alinor. Near them, accompanied by the castle chaplain, was Baldwin, his eyes alight with
elation as he gazed on the king.

The evening went smoothly. Nicolaa's lady troubadour
played for the king's pleasure and was rewarded by John
with a gold piece and an appreciative glance at her ample
bosom. Minstrels roamed the aisles, strumming rebec, lyre
and viol. The freshly strewn rushes on the floor gave off a
pleasant herbal tang and the castle hounds behaved themselves. On high perches behind the exalted company, falcons
peered down at the assemblage with sharp predatory eyes.
Bascot knew that the sheriff intended one of them, a fine
gerfalcon, as a gift for the king. Wine flowed freely throughout the evening, but no one over-imbibed. Torches flared at
regular intervals along the walls to illuminate the huge
room, and thick beeswax candles gave extra radiance to the
company on the dais. It was all very decorous. Only the
strained look on Nicolaa's face and the watchful glances
William Camville gave his monarch would have given a hint
that these two were on edge; both fearful of John's reaction
to the rumours of treason that had surrounded the squire's
death.

The next day saw the reception of King William of Scotland, come from his quarters in the guest lodge of the abbey
at Torksey. The two kings met on a knoll just outside the
walls of Lincoln and there John received homage from
William for the lands the Scottish king held in England. It
was a formal ceremony, William going down on one knee
and placing his hands between John's in acknowledgement
of his acceptance of the other as lord. An old wrangle, this
warring for rights of sovereignty over the disputed lands,
one going back many years. The assembled company gave a
great sigh of relief when the deed was done. John's satisfaction was evident, his supremacy recognised in front of a
plenitude of witnesses. He presided with extreme good humour over the feast that followed in the castle hall. The only

marring of the day's bonhomie was the arrival of a messenger from London with the news that Bishop Hugh had breathed his last. The emissary also told them that the body of the bishop was being brought back to Lincoln, and would, in accordance with Hugh's wishes, be interred in the grounds of the cathedral. After a brief respectful silence followed by a short prayer, John announced his intention of staying for the obsequies; whereupon William of Scotland proclaimed that he also would remain and join with the English king in paying their final respects to the saintly bishop.

Bascot stayed apart as much as he could from the mass of people that crowded the bailey and hall, his thoughts still on Tostig and the murders the forester had committed. His own part in the discovery of the man's guilt still bothered him, mainly because of Joanna's words blaming his persistence in the investigation for the deaths of the charcoal burner and his sons. His satisfaction at discovering the perpetrator of the crime was tainted by the burden of responsibility that had accompanied it. He began to think again of rejoining the Templar Order. But, if he did, could he bear leaving Gianni to the care of others?

Late that night, as he was sitting in Ernulf's quarters, ruminating once again on what he should do for the future of both himself and his servant, the serjeant came in from a last check on his men and the castle defences.

"The lords and ladies are all abed, thanks be to God. I'll be glad when this royal visit is over. As will Lady Nicolaa, I'll warrant." The serjeant poured himself a cup of ale and pulled off his boots before sitting down beside Bascot.

"You are up late, my friend," Ernulf said to him. "Is the bed I gave you too hard to induce a restful night?" He cast an eye at Gianni, curled up fast asleep on a straw pallet in the corner.

"No," Bascot replied. "I am thankful for it. I have slept on far worse."

"Aye, I've no doubt you have. Still, sleep is not always dependent on a soft couch, is it?"

Bascot shook his head and made no reply. Ernulf, seeing his mood, changed the subject. "I've just been talking to an old comrade that rode in here today from Torksey. Strange doings been going on there, it seems."

Bascot roused himself to be sociable. "How so?"

"Two bodies found floating near the banks of the Trent, tied to one another at the wrists. Vagrants, by the look of them. Or brigands. Unkempt hair and beards, a few scraps of ragged clothing left on their bodies. Both had wounds, one an arrow-hole in his leg, the other's back and face a mass of bruises and gashes."

Bascot looked up, startled. "Did your friend say what they looked like?"

"The one with the arrow wound was yellow bearded and thickset. He'd been throttled, his larynx mangled. My friend said he had some twists of dead ivy wrapped around his arms."

"And the other?" Bascot asked, almost expecting the answer. Gianni had described Green Jack to him and the Templar had told Ernulf.

The serjeant's expression was knowing. "Sounded just like Fulcher, the brigand that Roget's men beat almost to a pulp. Had a knife wound in his chest. Probably bled to death."

"You said they were tied together?" Bascot's mouth suddenly tasted sour.

"Aye," Ernulf confirmed. "Tight as lice in a beggar's armpit. The bindings were river weed."

The serjeant poured another cup of ale and handed it to Bascot. "Looks like Fulcher kept the promise you told me about. Made sure Green Jack kept him company on his journey to hell."

IT WAS EARLY THE NEXT MORNING THAT OSBERT CAME to the barracks and asked to speak to Bascot. "Lady Nicolaa sends a message from the king. You are to attend him in his chamber—that is, the one that is usually Lady Nicolaa and Sir Gerard's bedchamber—at the top of the keep."

Bascot straightened his tunic and pulled on his boots. "Did she say what it is that the king wants of me?" he asked as he splashed cold water from a ewer on his face.

Osbert shook his head. "But I don't think it's anything bad," he replied cheerfully. "She didn't look unhappy at sending for you."

Bascot followed Osbert across the bail. Servants and animals were just beginning to stir, shaking themselves awake in readiness for the onerous demands of another day tending to the needs of a castle overflowing with guests. The page trailed through the hall in front of Bascot, then up a flight of stairs to a room Bascot had never been in before, a well-appointed chamber with a large bed set in a wall space and draped with covers and hangings of finely worked tapestry. Alongside the bed was a huge carved-oak clothes press and an ironbound chest secured with triple locks. Under a narrow recessed window was a small table. On its surface was a flagon of wine and cups, a holder with thick lighted candles, and a sheaf of parchment and writing implements. It was at this table that the king was seated, sunk deep in the depths of a furred bedgown, his feet comforted by soft shoes of lambskin. In one corner a brazier of charcoal burned. There was no sign of the queen.

"Sit down, Templar," John said once Osbert had announced Bascot and left the room, motioning towards a stool. "And pour yourself a cup of wine. It is good Rhenish, my favourite. Nicolaa knows my tastes."

Bascot went down on one knee and bowed his head in obeisance before accepting the king's offer. John's saturnine gaze regarded him obliquely for a few moments before he spoke.

"I have been told by Lady Nicolaa of the part you played in discovering the man responsible for the death of Hubert de Tournay," John began. "It seems that without your assistance the forester would never have been found guilty of the crime."

Bascot hesitated to make any response to this statement. He did not know how much of the story Nicolaa had told the king. Was John aware that the boy had been the source of a rumour about a plot to undermine his crown? Had he been told that Nicolaa's own husband and her brother-by-marriage, Richard de Humez, had been suspected of complicity?

"I am pleased to learn that Lady Nicolaa holds my help in

such high regard," he finally said noncommittally. "But, in truth, Your Grace, many others contributed to the discovery of Tostig's guilt. My own part was negligible, for I did not have any knowledge of the squire before his death."

John had been watching him carefully as he answered. Now he leaned back his head and laughed.

"There speaks a diplomatic answer," John remarked with a chuckle. "Say nothing of import and cast no aspersions." The king shook his head, amused. "You have no need to be careful, de Marins. Nicolaa has told me all, of the machinations the boy hinted at, as well as the possible culpability of some of my barons. That is why I value Nicolaa so much. She is loyal and she is honest. Speaks when there is need and stays quiet when there is not. I could wish more of my nobles were made of such stuff, especially the de Tournay family."

His tone became heavier. "Godfroi came to me decrying the rumour that was being bruited abroad about his family. His protestations were vociferous. So much so that it made me not of a mind to believe him. I will ensure a sharp eye is kept on him and his brother in future." Bascot felt a small stab of pity for Godfroi. Whether he was guilty of treason or not, the murder of his half brother had affected the de Tournay family in more ways than one.

John rose, his mood seeming to have plunged into darkness as he picked up his wine cup and walked to the window. It was deeply silled on the inside, and all that could be seen through the narrow slit of its opening was a patch of dull grey sky. He stood looking out of the embrasure for some moments and when he spoke again, it was on a completely different topic.

"You were given as an oblate to the church when you were young, were you not, de Marins?"

"Yes, Sire, I was."

"I, too, was entrusted to the care of monks during the years of my childhood. To the tender mercies of the abbot at Fontevrault. I have no doubt that the rest of my family hoped I would stay there for all of my days, permanently immured in an anchorite's cell." The king's voice was bitter as he, no doubt, recalled the perpetual squabbling that had plagued his family, and also of how he had betrayed both father and brothers in their never-ending struggle for supremacy.

Then he gave a short bark of laughter and lightened his tone, saying musingly, "How different both our lives might have been, eh, de Marins, had we been left to the guidance of the good brothers? I might never have been a king, or you a Templar. Perhaps it would have been better so."

Bascot made no reply. There was none he could make. John walked back to his chair and sat down, pulling, as he did so, a piece of parchment from the pile that lay on the table. "I have been persuaded by Lady Nicolaa to give you a reward for your service. The fief that your father held before his death is still vacant of possession, having since that time been in the charge of the crown. I have promised Lady Nicolaa that I will restore it to you."

Taking the chance of offending the king, Bascot interrupted him. "My lord, much as I would be honoured by such a boon, I cannot hold land. I would be forsworn of my vow of poverty."

Again John smiled. "I can see why Nicolaa appreciates your service. Most men only remember their promises to God when they lie on their deathbeds. But let us deal with that obstacle later. First, hear me out."

He held up the parchment in his hand. "This is confirmation of your fief, de Marins. It only needs your acceptance. However, there is a condition attached if you should decide to take it."

John's dark eyes sparkled as he enjoyed the obvious discomfiture of the Templar. It amused him to see that other men besides himself might be prey to the horns of a dilemma. "The fief is a small one, as you know. It can be ably managed by a castellan of your choosing, but meanwhile you would enjoy the revenues and ultimately have an inheritance to leave any son you may have or"—here the king paused and held Bascot's eye with his own—"to any male you have chosen for your heir."

John paused to give weight to his last words, then he continued. "The condition is that you remain in the service of

Lady Nicolaa, as a senior knight in her retinue, with liberty to visit your fief when necessary. You will be recompensed for such service out of her own coffers, and well above the usual rate for a household knight. Not only will you have a fief, its revenues and a good salary, but a legacy to pass on as you choose."

The king laid the paper down on the table. Bascot could see the royal seal dangling from it, thoughts of the benefits to Gianni leaping to his mind, as, he was sure, the king knew they would. John watched him with amusement.

"Well, de Marins," he said finally. "Is it worth a vow or not?"

AFTER DUSK THAT NIGHT BASCOT WALKED ACROSS THE bail to the old keep where he and Gianni had their quarters when the castle was not filled to capacity with guests. Slowly he climbed the stairs, up three floors and past his usual chamber, then through the archway that led to the ramparts and onto the guard walk that circled the inner side of the wall. It was bitterly cold. The rain had stopped and the wind had stilled. Above was a clear winter sky, stars shining in pinpricks of hard light, looking as though they had been punched into the blackness with the point of a lance. Already, ice was forming on the battlements.

Bascot leaned into one of the parapet's embrasures, pushing his shoulder against the stone merlon at his side. Not far from him, one of Ernulf's men-at-arms was pacing his duty round. He saw Bascot, saluted, then turned about and retraced his steps. Something in the stance of the Templar told the guard that Bascot had not come up onto the ramparts to pass a few moments in idle chatter. He wanted to be alone.

Below the castle, spreading south, Lincoln lay like a reflection of the sky, darkness pervading with the occasional glimmer of light from a torch or candle. Bascot threw back the hood of his tunic, felt the icy air swarm onto his neck and ears with the snap of a wolf bite. Reaching up, he undid the thong of his eyepatch and let the leather shield fall loose. Only in solitude did he remove the cover from the pit of

ruined flesh that had once been his right eye. Now he welcomed the freedom from constraint.

King John's words echoed in his mind. Was his father's
fief worth breaking the vows he had taken when he joined
the Templars? Poverty, chastity and obedience. He had made
those vows not only to the Order, but to God. Even though
not now an active member of the Templars he had, for the
most part, kept to his promise of poverty, breaking it only
for the expenditure of small gifts for Gianni. As for chastity,
his thoughts had succumbed to temptation, but his body had
not. Obedience was the hard one, for he had not obeyed his
senior Templar officers, not since the day he had returned to
England and found that his family had all perished during
those long years he had been a captive of the Saracens. It
had been the compassion of the Order that had kept him in
their ranks, not his own honour. What was the wording of the
oath? "To obey his Templar Master, or those to whom the
Master has given authority, as though the command had
come from Christ Himself."

He looked down on Lincoln town, then up into the night
sky. Crystals of ice were beginning to form on his hair and
beard and his ears burned with the cold. Silently he prayed
for guidance. What was God's purpose for him? He begged
for aid from heaven, some sign that would tell him what to
do. But there was no answer.

Author's Note

The setting for *Death of a Squire* is an authentic one. Nicolaa de la Haye was hereditary castellan of Lincoln castle during this period and her husband, Gerard Camville, was sheriff. Late in the year of 1200, King John travelled to Lincoln to receive the homage of King William for lands the Scottish monarch held in England, and both kings lengthened their stay in order to attend the funeral of Bishop Hugh, a man who was destined to be revered as a saint.

For details of medieval Lincoln and the Order of the Knights Templar, I am much indebted to the following: *Medieval Lincoln* by J. W. F. Hill (C.U.P) and *Dungeon, Fire and Sword* by John J. Robinson (M. Evans & Company). And for information on forests to: *Historic Forests of England* by Ralph Whitlock (A. S. Barnes & Company, Inc.).

Maureen Ash was born in London, England, and has had a life-long interest in British medieval history. Visits to castle ruins and old churches have provided the inspiration for her novels. She enjoys Celtic music, browsing in bookstores and Belgian chocolate. Maureen now lives on Vancouver Island in British Columbia, Canada.